Bill Copeland has published several short stories and poetry, and has won several awards from the National Writers Association for this and other novels. He has been writing for ten years and this is his first published novel. He is an historian and avid student of the Holocaust and this novel reflects hours of research filling the manuscript with details and historical background to accurately portray life in the concentration camp.

Ashes to the Vistula, award winner, National Writers Association Novel Contest, for 2003& 2006.

www.billcopeland.net

ISBN 1-905988-16-8   978-1-905988-16-7

Cover by Kelly Leonie Walsh
Cover Photograph courtesy of Julien Robitaille

Published by Libros International

www.librosinternational.com

Acknowledgements

I wish to acknowledge the patience and sacrifices of my wife and daughter, Kathy and Lily, and thank my father-in-law, Bill Wellborn, for his unfailing support. I must recognize the efforts of others as well: Suzanne Allen who goaded me into writing; Carol Griffith for her editing skills, Greg Sango for his enthusiasm; Charles Freedman for his praise; David Luttrell for keeping me on my toes; and Roy Lee for his positiveness. All of them offered me much encouragement and to them I dedicate this book.

Ashes to the Vistula

Bill Copeland

Libros International

AUTHOR'S NOTE

In writing this story, I've attempted to make the names easily pronounced for the English reader. For this I apologize to readers of the Polish language and hope you understand.

For instance, Oßwieçim in Polish is presented here as Oswiecim. However, to avoid confusion, the German name, Auschwitz, is primarily employed as the most recognizable. Another use of a name other than the Polish is Wisla, which is better known in the West as Vistula. Jakub's hometown of K·ty is more easily pronounced as Katy.

Character names were selected using the same principle, the ease of pronunciation and the reduced tendency to stumble over the more complex Polish names. The exception to this is the historical characters. Military rank is used both in German for realism, and English for clarity, for instance *hauptmann* for captain.

A character list and terminology page are included at the end of the story.

CHAPTER ONE

"Filip Stitchko? Yes, he's here."

I look up from my desk when I hear my name and see a constable standing in the doorway, filling it completely. Shivers run down my back and I fear something is wrong.

"Filip, you're wanted in the office. Gather your things and accompany this gentleman."

I hesitate briefly and glance outside where the rain is still falling, the third day with few breaks. I get my rubber boots and raincoat and fill my bag with books, still puzzling about the large man waiting for me.

"I'm ready." I nod and feel the tightness in my stomach as it slowly rises to my chest. I step in front of him as he motions towards the front of the school. He is very tall and I feel very small next to him.

We enter the office and he instructs me to sit, as he bends to one knee, but is still looking down. His eyes are round and he looks at the floor and swallows hard.

His voice is soft. "All the rain, son, has swollen the creeks and streams, forcing the Wisla River from its banks. This morning the flood washed over the fields and through many homes. Your home was one of those taken from its foundation."

I look at him and feel tightness in my chest. I want to say something, but my throat is constricted and I can't do anything except shake my head.

He places his hand on my shoulder and clears his throat. "Your family... er." He hesitates. "We've found the bodies of your father and sister." He lowers his head and speaks slowly. "We're still searching for your mother and baby brother. We can pray they have survived."

I walk with the constable to the home for orphans run by the local Catholic Church, and am shown to a hall with ten beds. I move to the end of the hall and sit on a straight-back, wooden chair that is wobbly and place my coat and bag on the bed. I just sit there and look at the floor. I haven't spoken since the constable called my name, and can't make a sound now.

I don't understand these feelings and don't have any experiences to compare them to. I've been alone before, but this is different, as it is crushing me, because I can't go home. Home, Mama and Papa, Ewa and Dominik, gone. But maybe, I hope, Mama and Dominik will come and get me. Maybe I won't have to be alone like this.

"Now, now, we mustn't put things on the bed." A tall nun comes towards me, her hands inside the sleeves of her habit, and her eyes narrow. "You are new, so I won't punish you this time. But don't put your coat and things on the bed." She hangs my coat on a hook behind me and points to the bed. "Place your bag on the floor."

I look up at her and nod.

"Stand up, boy. Don't you have any manners?"

I stand quickly upsetting the chair, which I set aright and turn to face the nun.

"Well, can't you speak? Are you dumb?"

I try to say something, but there's a lump in my throat and I can't get anything out. I feel the tears in my eyes and rub them with the back of my hands.

"Well, you must be a mute. At least it will be a bit quieter around here." She pulls a small pad and pencil from inside her habit. "You can write, can't you?"

I nod and accept the pad and pencil.

"Write your name."

I look at her and speak against the tension in my throat, and hear a raspy sound. "Filip Stitchko."

"So you're not dumb after all." She jerks the items from my hand. "You had best learn to obey your elders quickly, boy, or you'll have a rough time here." Her lips are tight and she looks at me with squinted eyes. "Mind what I say, boy." She turns and walks out, leaving me alone.

I again sit down on that wobbly chair. I just stare at the floor and pray for my mother and brother, hoping they are still alive. I pray that I won't have to stay here and feel these awful feelings.

It isn't long before some other boys come in. They look in my direction then go to the other end of the room, glancing occasionally at me. They make me feel more alone than I felt without them nearby. None of them speak to me or sit with me at the evening meal. Everyone, the boys and nuns, look me over, but no one bothers to talk with me, not even the tall nun who knows my name.

It is still raining when they tell us to go to sleep. I close my eyes and feel the tears roll down my cheeks and a bubble build in my chest, which comes out with a burst of air and I begin crying. I cover my face to stifle the sobs, but it is of little use.

"Oh, listen to the baby." The call comes from the other end of the hall. "Cry, little baby, cry for your Mama and Papa."

I pull the pillow tighter against my face and bite my lower lip stifling the sobs.

"Cover your face, little baby, cry for your sister and brother. Boo hoo, hoo."

I take in a deep breath and stop the crying, but I hold the pillow over my face to block out the world.

I listen to the rain and hear the creak of the floorboards, but not soon enough to stop the attack. They hold the pillow tightly over my face, as hands hold my legs from kicking and the boys begin hitting me in the stomach, one, two, six, a dozen or more, and still they hold the pillow tightly and I am gasping for breath.

"You tell anyone about this, baby boy, then we'll give you more and a lot worse."

He releases the pillow and I take a deep breath. I put my hands on my stomach and pull my knees to my chest. I listen to the laughter from the other end of the room. I recognize these feelings and, for the first time in my life, I feel hatred and anger towards people. And I'm afraid.

How quickly my life has changed. With a loving family only this morning, now an orphan subject of the scorn of nuns and the target of bullies.

I am left alone the following day. I mostly sit and stare out at the drizzle, hoping the rain is over and expecting to see the sun at any moment. I don't see it and darkness comes and the fear is renewed. I am left alone during the night, but I stay awake afraid they are coming again.

"Filip Stichko?" It's another nun, shorter and older with a sour expression and dark eyes. "This valise is filled with clothes. Gifts from the generous people of this parish. Put on something clean and be ready in three minutes."

"Yes, ma'am. Am I going somewhere?"

She turns back to me and nods. "They're burying your people today. You should be there."

The funeral is brief, as a priest speaks solemnly and softly, praying as two coffins are lowered into the dark, dank earth, the ground still wet with the waters from the Wisla. Granite markers for my parents, and two smaller ones for my sister and brother, stand waiting to mark the graves, sentinels marking a point in my life, noting a change in its course taking me to I know not where.

I'm numb as I stand beside the graves and I realize I'm alone, even with the gravediggers waiting to fill the holes and the nuns waiting, and I dread what is to come and wipe the tears from my cheeks.

"Come, boy, we can't just stand here. We have things to do and you have places to go."

I walk behind the others wondering where I have to go, still numb with the reality of my life. As we approach the orphanage I see an old man, a priest, standing beside the steps with my brown suitcase next to him. The tall nun stops and speaks with him and points in my direction. As I near them she motions for me to come towards her.

"Filip Stitchko, this is Father Jan. You will go with him. He has generously found a foster home for you with good Christians." She smiles at the priest and walks into the orphanage.

"Come, boy, we have to catch a bus. It is a long ride to Katy."

We walk at a brisk pace and he turns occasionally to see if I'm following, nods and continues to plod on. He is quiet and intent on walking to where we can catch a bus.

I don't talk either, surprised to be leaving the orphanage and wondering about my new parents, wondering about a town I've never heard of. I follow the old priest and move the valise from one hand to the other whenever the pain in my arm or shoulder demands it.

We walk into the city, over the river, and into the depths of Krakow, not stopping and keeping a steady pace. We reach a building with a large dirt lot, churned into mud by the rains, with buses lining the streets where passengers board. I wait outside while the priest goes inside. He returns holding two tickets and points to a bus at the end of a long line of vehicles.

We board it and take seats halfway back, he on one side of the aisle and me on the other with my valise. There are two other passengers, both of whom are in front of us and they don't bother looking in our direction.

The driver, whose face is long and sunken with deep lines beneath his eyes, follows us. He calls out the stops along the way ending with "Brest".

The vehicle is old and starts with a jerk and a grinding of gears, tossing me about and forcing me to hold onto the seat in front of me. If I knew what was to come, then I would be more excited, but now I'm just scared.

Father Jan sits and nods and speaks to me occasionally, but he seems to be at a loss for something to say.

"Katy is a small town, my boy, not like Krakow or even Brest. My church is small, but it is large enough. I no longer desire a large church with an unruly congregation." He clears his throat and glances in my direction. "I once wanted to be in Warsaw, or even Rome, but I shepherd a small farming community in Central Poland. Perhaps it's God's will."

He falls silent and looks out the window. He seems ancient and steadfast. "There are good people in Katy, good Christians willing to take in a twelve-year-old boy." He turns towards me and gives me a crooked smile.

Neither of us speak as I sit across the aisle from him on the rickety, squeaky bus which jostles us along the dirt road leaving a long trail of dust to float slowly to earth, as the fumes from burnt oil waft from the engine through the open windows.

"Eastern Poland, my son, is a vast plain that sweeps eastward across the Bug River into a land that is as ancient as Poland, once the lands of Byelorussians and Ukrainians. It stretches many kilometers across the forests and plains to Russia. It's a fertile land that feeds Eastern Europe, producing wheat season after season." He gestures with his hands, clasping them and then waving them about, clasping them again, looking about and searching for something to say.

He tires of talking as the hum of the bus lulls him into a nodding sleep, one of many I will witness in my growing years. All I know is that Katy is in the middle of the country and as far from my home near Krakow as from my parents in heaven.

Those thoughts swim through my mind as I suppress tears and the choking aloneness I feel in the depths of my chest, trying to envision what my life will be like, what it is to become an orphan. I am thankful the old priest dozes and can't witness my pain, as I close my eyes to stop the tears and squeeze them tightly. I ask God to stop my heart's racing, stop the fear running through me, and I remember the beating I got at the orphanage because I cried. I vow to never let anyone see my pain again, as I wipe the tears from my cheeks and sleep, a deep, dreamless sleep that blocks the reality of what has become of me.

I awake with the driver's announcement of "Katy". The gloomy village is hidden in darkness as the bus creeps into the town square, stopping before a lone store, the entrance lit by a small lamp, more of a beacon in the night than an effort to give light. I awake, grateful for the darkness to hide the redness of my eyes and my tear-streaked cheeks, which I quickly rub to remove the evidence of my fear and pain.

Father Jan motions without speaking, his face deeply lined, his shoulders bent forward, as he steps from the bus with only a nod at the driver where the circles under his eyes are darker. I sit on the steps beneath the lamp as the vehicle grinds its gears and lurches away trailing the fumes and smoke of its old engine. The gloom of my feelings is matched by the town, empty and abandoned for want of people, of activity, of sunlight.

"They were to meet us." He shakes his head and speaks more to the night and himself than to me.

Silence again falls between us, as I don't know what to say or even if there is a need to respond.

"Never you mind, boy, we'll sleep in my house for the night and see to them in the morning." He strides towards the modest church set off the square, not even glancing at me or waiting for me to follow.

I pick up my valise, my only possessions within, and shuffle after the priest, not even trying to match my pace with his. I feel the tears just beneath the surface, the choking in the back of my throat as I clear the phlegm with a nervous cough. But I fight the urge to cry and remember my vow to never let anyone know my pain or witness my fear.

I bed down on the floor atop an old musty quilt, surrounded by a monk-like house, more of a room than building, sparse in its furnishing, evidence of Father Jan's poverty.

His snoring fills the night, deep resonant noises from the back of his throat, and I imagine it is a lion skulking in the darkness. I fall asleep finally, with the roar of floodwaters overflowing the banks of the Wisla and sweeping my family into the swirling waters, as my face is covered and my body pummeled, leaving me in black darkness.

CHAPTER TWO

I am roused by the gentle rap on the door and the interruption of the priest's breathing, followed by coughing and clearing of his throat. He rises slowly as a second set of sounds echo a little louder than the first, and I sit up expecting to see the brightness of day as the door opens.

It is dark still, but the man holds a lantern before him, giving evidence of his worn pants and tattered shirt, and deep lines accenting his leathery skin. His eyes almost sparkle and he seems ready to laugh, speaking softly and showing a mouth of missing and rotting teeth.

"I've come for the boy, Father." His smile is meek as he looks around the old priest and nods towards me. "I wouldn't have come now, but you know Maria. Work on the farm comes early and she said I had best fetch the child."

Father Jan nods and turns towards me. "Filip Stitchko, Mr. Melichek." He returns to his bed and the fatigue shows in his eyes and is etched on his face as he stares at the floor. "Joseph and his sister, Maria, will take care of you. You go with him and be a good boy." He yawns and still doesn't look at me.

I quickly dress and get my small bag as Melichek stands in the doorway smiling. He nods as I present myself, ready for what lay ahead, not feeling as tired as I thought I should.

"You, Joseph!" Father Jan's voice is loud, his words quick. "I expect the boy to be in school. You tell that sister of yours that I'll visit her myself if she keeps him out."

Melichek nods and says nothing, as he pulls the door closed

and holds the lantern to light the path. I follow beside him having no difficulty keeping pace as he drags along staring straight ahead. He is quiet and doesn't ask any questions until we are out of town and the horizon lightens with the coming day.

"It's good to have you with us, boy. I need the company of another male in the house." He speaks without looking at me and still holds the lantern in front of us, its light less effective the more we walk.

"My name is Filip, and I'm not a boy." I don't know why I told him that, but the need just seemed to build within me. And I didn't feel like a boy anymore.

"No, I guess you aren't." He looks at me briefly and smiles, and lowers the lamp to his side. "Well, Filip, my name is Joseph."

We continue on for several more steps before he again speaks. "You may call me Joseph whenever we're alone, but call me Mr. Joseph or Mr. Melichek whenever we're around Maria. And never call her 'Maria', it's Mrs. Chapulski."

He chuckles as he turns to me, his eyes sparkling. "Mr. Chapulski took our cows to market four years ago and kept going. I expect he had had enough of his wife. I've had enough of her, too, but the farm's half mine and she's my sister. But I envy Mr. Chapulski." He turns back to the road and increases his pace. "I'm afraid you'll see for yourself soon enough, my boy... er, Filip."

A bond begins between me and Joseph, a conspiracy to defy his sister and to counterbalance her will and domination. She is younger than Joseph, with gray strands set in dark brown hair, but her face is smoother than her brother's and I can see a beauty beneath the sour scowl with which she greets us.

"You've taken your time." She nearly snarls at Joseph. "He's smaller than I imagined, not likely to have a strong back or the will to work." She turns and walks into the kitchen. "Come on, you'll be wanting some feed before you begin."

"Father Jan said he's to be in school, Maria." Joseph faces his sister, one hand on his hip and his chin high, as he tightens his lips to a thin line.

She faces him and stares at him harshly, glancing at me occasionally, before turning back to her preparations. "School. What a waste of time. And just now when I get some help, that priest goes back on his word and insists the boy go to school." She sets a plate in front of me and turns back to Joseph. "No, I'll not have it."

"He says to tell you he'll come here himself if you don't let the boy go to school." Joseph speaks loudly, his head thrust forward, but quickly pulls it back and places his hands in his lap, as he accepts a plate from Maria.

She shakes her head. "I don't need that priest out here, asking to be fed and taking our money. No, I don't need anymore beggars on my doorstep."

She wipes her hands on her skirt and looks at me shaking her head. "Okay, boy, you can go to school, but not today. Tomorrow maybe, or the day after, but not today."

"His name is Filip."

She glares at Joseph, her lips tight, and then turns her gaze upon me. "Okay, Filip, you can go to school tomorrow."

It is an uneasy day as I work at various jobs, mostly with Joseph, but accompanying Maria on a few of her chores, as she talks about the harshness of farm life, of how the burden falls on her to do the work, and of how Joseph likes vodka too much. "That priest, too, likes his vodka and makes his own whenever he can get enough potatoes, a rarity now that Mr. Chapulski is gone. It was he that showed the priest how to make the potato concoction, and he was a worthless man. It is glad I am to be rid of him.

"It's a hard existence on the farm, boy. My husband drank often and came upon me forcefully, always drunk and sloppy, unable to function as a man and too much of a coward to face me. He was mean too, free with a slap or punch whenever Joseph wasn't around, showing meanness only a bully can show." She continues to work and looks at me to see if I'm listening. "Joseph, too, is much like my husband when filled with vodka."

But true to her word, I'm allowed to go to school on the second day, wearing my only pair of clean britches and a donated shirt that was worn and threadbare. I nearly run the four kilometers to school, so excited to be away from the farm and meet some kids my own age.

As I near the village I see five boys in a circle, pushing a skinny kid from one to another. I feel the soreness of my stomach and know I must do something. As I run towards them, I see the boy in the middle is crying and the laughter of the others angers me.

I step between two of the boys and push the skinny kid out of the circle, whispering for him to run. I face the tallest of the five and narrow my eyes, my fear replaced by anger and desire for revenge against those who attacked me.

"I want to play." I step closer and look him in the eyes. "You want to push me around?"

The boy reaches with both hands and pushes against my shoulders, but I throw a punch against his stomach, doubling him. I start to hit him again when the others grab my arms, turn me, and throw me to the ground. All five of the kids surround me and I know I'm about to get a worse beating than the orphanage.

Before they can begin, a man moves into the circle and kneels beside me. "Go on, boys. Go to school or I'll talk to your parents."

The boy I struck glares at me, and then motions for the others to join him, as they run towards the town.

"Thank you, mister."

"You're welcome. That was my son you protected. He came and told me. Thank you." He smiles and helps me to my feet. "I'm Moses Galinski. My son is Jakub."

I tell him my name and thank him again. Looking around for the bullies, I run towards the school fearing I'll run into them, if not this morning, then someday.

I arrive early and smile at Father Jan who returns it with a nod of his head and a sparkle in his gray eyes. "I see the woman still doesn't like my visits. Well, at least, she listens and obeys." He continues to nod and pats me on the shoulder. "Go in, Filip, and find a place to sit."

The room is empty and I take a seat against the far wall in the middle of the row, out of the way, but certain someone will sit in front and back of me so I won't be isolated and alone. And I feel alone and scared.

It seems a very long time before I hear the rustlings of others entering the building and room, two girls who look at me and quickly look away, taking seats against the opposite wall. Others come and also look at me; some staring, and others just seem to avoid looking in my direction.

The skinny kid comes in. He sees me, smiles brightly, and moves to where I am, taking the desk in front of me. "I'm Jakub."

He reminds me of kids I had seen in a hospital in Krakow, those my father said were too simple to live among normal people, and he is skinny.

Another boy follows and takes the seat behind me. "I'm Aron Galinski and this is my brother, Jakub." He offers his hand. "Thank you for helping him."

"You're welcome. I'm Filip Stitchko." I don't know what else to say, realizing there isn't anything else.

Jakub breaks the awkward silence. "Fi... Fil... Filip. I'll be your friend."

Aron smiles and puts his hand on my shoulder. "Sure, Jakub, we'll both be his friends."

The five boys who were picking on Jakub come in and take seats at the back of the room. They stare at us.

"Excuse me." Aron nods and walks to where the boys are sitting and looks at each of them. He addresses the boy I hit. "Mat, if you or any of these sheep ever touch my brother or my friend again, then I'm going to come after you. You don't want that. You know I'll hurt you." He returns and sits behind me. "Together, Filip, I think the three of us could take them."

For the first time I don't feel scared or so alone anymore.

School is good and the boys leave us alone. Jakub proves to have the endless curiosity of a child, and asks questions none of us can answer.

But Father Jan is uncomfortable with Jakub, avoiding his questions and scolding him for not being still or for not paying attention. I, too, am a little uncomfortable around him, unaccustomed to boys like him. I don't understand him, don't know what to say or do.

Aron smiles and talks slowly. "He's a good kid." His smile is slight, but there is a softness about his features whenever he looks at his brother, the same gentleness I remembered from the constable who came to the school when my parents died. "He's not like the rest of us."

"You can say that about him, Aron, he's not like anyone I know." I try to smile.

Aron shakes his head, but doesn't return my smile or share my frivolous tone. "It's not like that. He's just not as quick to grasp things like us, but there's not a mean thing about him."

I want to say something to let Aron know I understand, but I don't understand and Jakub makes me uncomfortable. Yet, we three are constant pals.

I love the fields and woods around Katy, pristine and isolated from the town and farms, but even the farms are wonderful places to run and hide as we play our games and chase each other through green fields of wheat and soy, only to end in a coppice to hide and catch our breaths. Jakub is always with us and Aron always waits for him to catch up, but I run ahead and hide from them, enjoying their efforts and shouts for me to come out.

Aron slides in beside me and looks out from behind the tree for his brother, but Jakub isn't in view. We wait and grow impatient. Finally, worrying, Aron starts back through the ripe field of oats, and I follow, irritated at having to stop our game to find the troublesome brother. We find him kneeling in a field, cradling a large, beautiful bird in his lap. It's alive, but injured.

He looks up at our approach. "Aron, help me." He looks at me, his eyes filling with tears, pleading for me to help him. "Filip, please, help me."

Aron and I kneel in front of him and look at the bird. Aron strokes it softly on the neck, but the bird remains still. "I don't know, little brother, but let's take it home. Papa will know what to do."

Jakub cradles that bird as carefully as he would an infant, and walks faster than he would normally. I can't believe he is so upset over a wounded bird, but Aron respects his feelings so I don't say anything.

"It's a capercaillie." Mr. Galinski places the bird on the kitchen table and examines it carefully. "It's from the grouse family and is prized for its beautiful feathers." He hesitates before continuing, looking at Jakub. "It's hunted for its meat as well, and that's why he's hurt."

"Help it, Papa. Don't let it die." Jakub's plea is that of a small child and I realize he is just a child.

"I can't control life or death, Son, but I know the bird is suffering and we can't let animals suffer."

Tears roll down Jakub's cheeks and Aron's eyes are misty as well. Mr. Galinski places his hand on his son's shoulder. "Jakub, we can't let the bird suffer."

He sniffs back his tears and seems to understand. "We can't let it suffer, Papa."

The man nods and speaks softly. "I'll take it outside." He picks up the bird and starts for the rear yard.

Jakub follows closely behind him only to have Aron grab his arm and stop him. "No, Jakub. You don't want to see this."

He shakes his head and turns to face his brother, his eyes narrow. "See what, Aron?"

"Papa is going to kill the bird. It's the only way to end the suffering." Aron puts his arm around his brother and looks at him.

Jakub remains calm and just looks at the rear door. He nods and seems to grasp what is happening. "Killing will end suffering." He turns and looks at Aron. "There's no suffering for dead birds."

I glance away as Aron looks at me then speaks softly. "That's right, little brother. Papa will kill the bird gently and end its suffering."

"And we'll bury it." Jakub looks at Aron, his eyes wide. "We'll give it a funeral. Just like Mama's."

Aron releases his brother and turns to me. "Mama died of fever three years ago. Jakub was six, but still remembers it."

I nod and want to change the direction of the talk. "Maybe your father will clean the bird, too. I've had grouse before and it makes a good meal."

"No!" Jakub turns to me, his eyes wide. "We will not eat the pretty bird."

"It's okay, Jakub. We won't eat the bird. Filip was just making a little joke." Aron looks at me, squinting his eyes, his face constricted. "Weren't you, Filip?"

I am irritated, but don't want to anger Aron. "Sure, Jakub, I'm just kidding."

Jakub straightens and looks from me to Aron. "We'll have a funeral for the pretty bird."

There is another funeral a year or so after we buried the bird, for Mr. Galinski contracts fever and dies. Father Jan makes all the arrangements and Joseph and Maria agree to take Aron and Jakub into their home. I am delighted to have them with me, sharing the same bed and sharing the chores of the farm. But our time together is brief.

We sit on the porch listening as Father Jan faces Maria. "The boy is disruptive to the class and isn't able to keep up with children even younger than him. No, I'm afraid he has learned all he'll ever learn."

Maria stands with her hands on her hips glaring at the cleric.

"Then what am I to do with him, Priest?" Maria spits her words at him.

"Watch your tone, woman. You'll obey and do what you're told." Father Jan releases a long breath and faces her. "Aron and Filip will go to school and you'll watch the boy until they come home in the afternoon."

"I have a farm to run. I have chores that keep me busy. Joseph has chores to keep him busy. We have no time to be watching over an idiot."

Aron and I look at each other, then at Jakub who is looking at his foot that is swinging back and forth.

At the anger in Maria's voice, Father Jan's eyes widen and he turns his eyes from hers. "Alright, Maria, I understand your problems." His voice is softer. "As Aron is the oldest, he'll continue in school. I'll excuse Filip from further schooling and he can watch over Jakub."

I can't believe what I hear. I'm to watch over Jakub while Aron continues in school. Little do I understand what this means for me.

CHAPTER THREE

"Damn it, boy, you got to watch him more carefully." Joseph shakes his head and purses his lips. "He's too simple to take care of himself, so you had better do a better job or I'll take the strap to you."

Jakub had wandered several kilometers from the farm and had meandered amidst the hives of a local beekeeper. He wasn't harmed, but he is disturbed with Joseph's anger and my irritation.

"You can't just ramble anywhere you want. You must stay close to me, Jakub." I turn away to continue my chores, but he follows, brushing against my sleeve, standing very close. I pick up the pitchfork and start towards the barn, only to have Jakub follow and stand next to me, closer than before.

I turn to face him, surprised by the grin and glint in his eyes. "What're you doing?"

"I stay close to Filip." He continues smiling. "I don't want Filip to be angry."

"I'm not angry. Just stay close, okay?"

His grin becomes even wider and there is a sparkle in his eyes, as he leans against me. "Okay. I stay close."

I realize he is joking and put my hand to his chest, easing him away. "Okay, but not that close. Here, help me with the hay."

Several days later, our chores finished, we walk about the farms and countryside, just anywhere to be away from Joseph and Maria. Even Jakub is quiet for a change, exploring everything that catches his interest, bending or squatting to poke and examine it more closely.

I don't realize where we are until Jakub is already among the hives. I become irritated and fearful at the same time, and start in his direction to pull him away before he gets stung. As I approach the first hive, I feel an insect beneath my shirt, going down my back. I pull my shirt from my pants and dance about trying to shake the bee loose. I slap at it and receive a sharp sting for my efforts. I continue to slap until I notice Jakub is standing beside me.

"What's wrong, Filip?"

I pull the shirt away from my body and the insect falls to the ground as I rub the tiny bump with my finger. "I got stung. These bees are dangerous. You were told to stay away from those hives."

Jakub is squatting beside the insect. "Bees aren't dangerous. Bees are my friends. They won't hurt me."

"Well, it stung me. And they'll sting you, too."

He picks it up and holds it gently in the palm of his hand, rises, and shows it to me. "Bee is dead." He looks at me and his eyes are misty and he is biting his lower lip.

I watch as he returns to the hives, kneels on the loose soil, digs a small hole, and places the insect inside, covering it with dirt. As he works, bees hover around his head and hands, and several alight on his face and fingers, but it doesn't bother him. He rises and smiles at me. "Bee not suffer anymore."

I'm not certain that afternoon who learns from whom, but I allow Jakub to explore further and farther than I would have before, more confident in his ability to stay out of trouble.

Yet, trouble finds us. Jakub and I are exploring near the village when Mat and his cohorts surround us, grabbing my arms and throwing me to the ground, as two of them hold me. Two of the others grab Jakub, whose eyes are wide and he bites his lower lip.

Mat sets a large sack of flour in front of him and taunts Jakub. "You're not white enough, boy." He opens the bag with a knife and takes a double handful of flour and throws it into Jakub's face.

Jakub coughs and jerks his head from side to side, but Mat continues to throw flour, getting some on his friends, who let go of Jakub and laugh. All of them laugh as I struggle against those holding me.

But Jakub backs away and looks at his hands that are coated white with only small lines showing through. He walks towards Mat, who holds the knife in front of him, and I pull against the two holding me. Mat backs away from the sack and motions for Jakub to come towards him, but Jakub crouches to the flour and begins coating his body white from his shoes to his hair, smiling broadly and enjoying his new appearance.

All of the boys laugh and Jakub laughs with them. I pull my arms free and watch as Jakub dances around to the amusement of Mat and his friends. They don't watch me as I rise and pick up a stick. I push the first boy aside and swing my weapon at Mat, striking his wrist, forcing him to drop the knife. He grabs his arm and a bone is pushing against his skin.

"You broke my arm!"

Two of the boys grab me from behind, but Jakub picks up the stick and strikes them hard enough to make them let go. He stands next to me and glares at the boys, just as Mr. Oliwitz, the village constable, arrives.

"Well, I've found the stolen flour and the thief." He looks at Mat.

Mat nods towards Jakub and me. "He broke my arm."

Oliwitz looks at Jakub then me. "You break his arm, boy?"

"My name is Filip. He had a knife."

"He's a damn liar. He had the knife. Just ask any of my friends. They'll tell you."

"I'll bet they'll swear you didn't steal the flour, either."

"I didn't steal it."

"Mr. Spiegelman says you did."

"You'd take the word of Jew over that of a Christian?"

Oliwitz shakes his head. "You've never been strong on religion, Mat, and I would take the word of Marek Spiegelman over you and these boys any day."

The constable picks up the knife and looks at the sack of flour, stands and looks at Mat and smiles. "Since it is strongly suspected that you stole this sack of flour, and as there is an opening that has been made with a sharp knife, and after looking at Jakub here all covered in flour, then I'm going to conclude that the knife is yours."

He turns to the others. "Any of you want to say differently?" He waits until they look away. "Good. Now one of you pick up the flour and the rest of you go home. I'll be having a word with your parents, so you'd best tell them yourselves." He motions towards the village and looks at Mat and his friend. "You two go on over to Dr. Levi's office."

Oliwitz watches as they leave, with Mat holding his arm tightly against his body and as his friend totes the sack of flour that is spilling onto his shoes and pants. He turns to us. "Okay, you two, you'd better get home and get Jakub cleaned up before Maria sees him." He smiles. "And, Filip, you need to be careful. Mat and those four may try to get a little revenge."

Jakub smiles and puts his arm around my shoulders. "I'll watch over him, Mr. Oliwitz. I'll take care of Filip."

And I feel like he is taking his statements seriously, because he insists on staying near me, warning me that Mat and the others might catch me alone and he wouldn't be there to help. "If I'm there, Filip, then we can beat them."

Even Aron jokes about it. "Five against two? I guess you two don't need me after all." His smile turns to a more serious look. "Were you afraid?"

I looked down and shook my head. "No. Not me." I looked at Jakub. "Were you afraid, Jakub?"

He bites his lower lip, and then grins. "No. I thought it was funny."

Jakub and I stay together and share interesting times, but it's more like answering a child's endless questions. The highlight of our day comes with Aron's return from school. We both clamor for his attention, and Aron is always patient, seemingly understanding both of our needs, and talking with both of us.

Aron is a good student and rarely has studies at home. After supper, he pretends to be a teacher, with Jakub and me as his students. It is just for fun he tells us, but I think he is trying to give to us what he is getting at school. But Jakub is slow and Aron can never teach us all he is learning.

We learn slowly through the year, Aron in school and Jakub and I on the farm. I am removing manure from the stalls when Aron, bristling with sweat and waving his arms in the air, bursts into the barn with news.

"Filip, you and Jakub are going to school. There's a new teacher in town and he's opening a school at Spiegelman's store. He said it's called a yeshiva. He'll teach the Jewish children their Bible, but he's promised to work with Jakub."

Jakub runs in and notes his brother's smile. "Aron is home." He reaches out and punches him on the shoulder. "Aron is happy?"

"Very happy, Jakub. You're going back to school."

Jakub's smile fades suddenly into a frown. "I don't want to go to school."

We both look at him and start to ask why.

"I want to stay with Filip." His eyes narrow and he puts his fist in his mouth and starts to cry. "Filip is my friend. I want to stay with Filip."

Without looking at me, Aron steps forward and puts his hand on his brother's shoulder. "I'll talk with Rabbi Zacharz. Maybe he'll let Filip come too."

"I don't want to go to a Jewish school." I turn away and walk a few steps from them. I'm afraid to tell Aron my feelings about the Jews. I am aware of them in the village and of their church outside of town, but we don't associate with them except when necessary, and then only with the Spiegelmans at their store and Dr. Levi whenever we need a physician. "I want to go to school with you."

"I want to go to school with Aron, too." Jakub is smiling, no longer upset at being separated from me.

Aron shakes his head and turns to me. "Filip, the Rabbi is a good teacher, Dr. Levi and Marek Spiegelman both suggested Jakub attend the school."

"Jakub, Aron. Not me." I step between the two brothers, my back to Jakub. "I should go back to school at Father Jan's."

Aron continues looking at me and lowers his voice. "Jakub won't go to the yeshiva without you, Filip. It's the only way I can get Jakub schooling."

"What about me? I want to go to school with you, not some, yesh... not some Jew school."

Aron straightens with my attack.

"I want to go to school with Aron, too." Jakub has stopped smiling and looks from his brother to me, his head pulled into his shoulders, as it always is when he thinks anyone is angry with him.

Aron steps to the side facing both of us. "I want Jakub to get some schooling. Father Jan won't do it. Rabbi Zacharz will." He places his hand on my shoulder and is more a brother than friend. "You need schooling, too. Go to the yeshiva with Jakub. Be a brother to us both."

He smiles and punches me lightly on the shoulder. "I promise, they won't try to make a Jew of you."

Jakub also punches my shoulder. "Yeah, brother."

Jakub and I meet Rabbi Jakim Zacharz the following day. We are his first students, as the Jewish kids aren't scheduled to begin for several days. He spends a long time with us both, quickly ascertaining where I am in my studies, and giving me a book to read.

I watch him with Jakub, surprised at the patience he exhibits, repeating questions and calming Jakub whenever he can't answer. The difference between he and Father Jan, who was nearly as old, shows in his eyes and his voice, which is strong.

"Now, Jakub, I want to see if you know your numbers." He has some cards on the desk that he holds up for Jakub to see. "Can you tell me what you get when you add one and two together?"

He looks first at me then the rabbi. "Uh, three."

"Very good, Jakub." The teacher glances at me. "Don't help him, Filip."

I hadn't and chafe at his warning, but return to the book.

"Now, Jakub, answer this one." The rabbi turns again to see if I am watching, then turns to Jakub. "What do you get when you add two and one together?"

Jakub's eyes widen and he smiles. "Me, Aron, and Filip. We're brothers."

The rabbi turns to me, a puzzled expression on his face, but I just smile and return to the book. "No, Jakub, I want you to add two and one together."

Jakub continues smiling. "I did. Me and Aron. Two. Filip. One. Three brothers."

Rabbi Zacharz laughs at Jakub's joke and I laugh with them. "That's good." He turns to me and wipes a tear from his eye. "Back to your book." He is smiling this time and I like the man.

"Now, I want to see how you do with your colors."

I look up to see Jakub straighten, pleased with himself and seemingly having a good time, and I wink.

"Jakub," he holds up a bright red card, "what color is this?"

Jakub winks at me and grins. "A rooster." He laughs at his joke and slaps the desk.

I can't contain myself and laugh with him.

The rabbi smiles and looks at me. "So, this is the comedy hour?"

He rises and motions for me to follow. "I think it would be better if you read in here."

Separating us allows him to complete his assessment and he is prepared to talk with Aron when school is out.

"He's a good boy, Aron." He motions for Aron and me to sit and asks Jakub to join him on the bench. "He likes to laugh a lot, don't you, Jakub?"

Jakub lifts himself from the bench with outstretched arms and nods.

"He's capable of learning simple things, like counting and some simple arithmetic, adding and taking away. I think multiplying and dividing may be too much to ask." The rabbi puts his arm around Jakub and smiles. "And he'll learn to recognize words, like signs or labels, but I don't think he'll learn to read much beyond that of, say, a first year student."

"Will he ever be able to live on his own, Rabbi?" Aron's eyes narrow and he tilts his head slightly, biting his lower lip.

"By himself?"

"Yes, sir."

"I don't want to live by myself. I want to stay with you and Filip." Jakub's face contorts with lines and tears form in his eyes.

Rabbi Zacharz pats Jakub's knee. "I think Jakub will be able to do well on his own most of the time, but I don't think he'll ever be able to live completely alone. Do you understand?"

Aron nods. I know his fear and fear it will fall upon me to care for Jakub the rest of my life, but I don't know what to say.

We continue in school, but are separated. Rabbi Zacharz works with me and assigns one of his students, Zus Malbin, to work one-on-one with Jakub. Jakub likes the young man immensely, but laughs at his hair and the ringlets dangling beside his face, and at the funny hat he wears. But Zus and Rabbi Zacharz tolerate Jakub's laughter with good humor and are unaware of my own feelings about the young teacher.

Zus is only a year older than Aron, only two years my senior and a teacher, and I am still a student. I resent him and the schooling he has received and envy his authority over us. He is of an age to be a playmate, but of a status to be better than us. I thought, perhaps, it is because he is Jewish, thus I have more reason to dislike Jews.

So it continues with Aron in one school and me and Jakub at the yeshiva, and all three of us on the farm, listening to the bickering of Joseph and Maria. Their unhappiness affects the three of us as well.

Father Jan, his shoulders bent and his gait a slow shuffle, and Aron walk up the store's steps and ask to speak with me. Both wear frowns. On the porch, Aron gives me the news. "Maria has run off with Mrs. Wodjik's husband."

I shrug my shoulders, not fully understanding the consequence of her action.

Father Jan's face sags with deep, dark circles under his eyes and his shoulders droop. He looks at me and purses his lips. "Joseph doesn't want to be responsible for you three boys. He is asking that only you stay on the farm and that we find homes for Aron and Jakub."

"A home for them? Leave me with Joseph?" I can't believe it. "I will be the only one on the farm, and Joseph will be drunk most of the time, with no Maria to come between us."

"I agree with Filip." Aron steps closer to the old priest. "I'm sixteen and old enough to be on my own. I want to take over my father's farm and run it. The three of us will be able to do this and still go to school."

His confidence is stronger than mine, but I am glad he is arguing to keep us together.

"You have no tools. No animals. No seeds. How will you make the farm work?"

"I don't know, but I want the three of us to stay together."

The priest ponders for a moment. "Joseph has animals and seeds. He'll need more than just Filip to work the farm. I'll get him to let the three of you stay together."

Joseph reluctantly agrees, not so much for our sake, but because the priest threatens him with damnation and frequent visits.

It is a good time for us, working on the farm in the early mornings, then going to school, and returning to the farm in the afternoons. And there is safety in numbers, too, as Joseph, when drinking too much vodka, can't abuse any one of us. But we listen to his ravings about the unfairness of it all, of how Maria had run off and left all of the responsibility on him. After a short time, our feelings towards Maria soften and we better understand the burden she shouldered.

The farm does well and we work hard, mostly without Joseph, as he tends to drink more and stay gone for longer and longer periods. But we don't object as we are together and free to do whatever we wish.

Then one morning, as I am carrying the milk to the house, Father Jan and Dr. Levi appear on our doorstep, just as the sun shows itself above the fields. "Good morning, Filip. Are Aron and Jakub about?"

Jakub comes out first, smiling and rubbing sleep from his eyes. "Good morning." He greets each of us in turn as I set the bucket of milk on the porch.

"It's a little early for a visit." Aron is frowning. "I take it there is bad news."

He gestures to the chairs and picks up the milk, handing it to Jakub. "Put this in the kitchen, little brother."

Jakub leaves, looking over his shoulder and spilling some of the milk, which is quickly lapped up by our three cats.

"Joseph is dead." Father Jan looks off into the distance, signaling Dr. Levi to continue.

He clears his throat. "We're uncertain how he died, but believe he fell from his horse last night."

"Drunk, I suppose." Aron's voice is sharp, louder than normal.

Jakub rejoins us and stands to the side listening.

"Do we have the horse?" Aron's voice is calmer, more matter-of-fact.

Father Jan stirs and looks at Aron. "Yes, and no."

Aron doesn't respond, but tilts his head and looks at the priest frowning.

"The horse, boys, and the cows and chickens, and all the animals, will be sold to pay for the farm's debts and for the funeral." He nods his head slowly. "But the farm is yours to work until such time as Maria or another relative claims it."

"We need animals. How're we going to plow the fields?" Aron's voice rises and he speaks quickly.

"You'll manage." The priest stares at Aron and doesn't attempt any other comment.

"I'm sorry, boys, but Joseph ran up a lot of debts and these must be paid." Dr. Levi holds his hands towards us and nods his head.

"But we can stay together?" Jakub steps forward, his eyes wide and his hands crammed in his pockets.

Dr. Levi nods. "Yes, Jakub, the three of you can stay together and you can all stay in school."

"How?" Aron's eyes are narrow and he leans towards the physician. "How can we go to school and run this farm? And if we don't keep the farm going, you'll make us separate and go with other families."

"No, Aron. You and Filip are now old enough to take care of Jakub. No one will try to separate you."

"But no one will help us either." I feel the pressure knowing I would be saddled with Jakub.

Dr. Levi and the priest look at me like an outsider, before turning back to Aron. "You're the oldest, Aron, and the responsibility falls on your shoulders." He smiles. "At least for another year."

I look from the physician to Aron and back again. "What happens in a year?"

Aron turns to face me, but Dr. Levi interrupts him. "Aron has been accepted at a military academy in Warsaw. He'll study to become a soldier, an officer. He'll make our village proud." Even the priest smiles.

"And what'll become of me and Jakub?" I sense I will again be asked to watch over him.

"We'll see in a year or two, Filip." Father Jan's face is expressionless, his eyes dull. "We'll find something for you."

"I want to go with Aron and study for the army, too."

"Me, too." Jakub steps forward, smiling and waving his arms. "I'll go with Aron and Filip."

Dr. Levi looks at Jakub and then Aron. "We'll decide later. Now, you have to find a way to stay together. He stands next to the priest. "And you, Aron, must continue your studies. Work hard and you'll do well in Warsaw."

We watch them leave, walking slowly, the pace dictated by the priest, and they are out of sight before I turn to Aron. "When were you going to tell us this?"

Aron sits on the steps and motions for us to sit with him. He puts his arm around Jakub and clasps me on the arm. "Jakub is my brother and you're my best friend, almost as close to me as Jakub. Also, my brother."

"Okay, brother, when were you going to tell us?"

"When I thought you would be less angry."

"Then now isn't a good time. Because I'm angrier than a swarm of bees."

"Bees are my friends." Jakub is smiling. "Filip is my friend, too."

CHAPTER FOUR

The year passes quickly, too quickly as I fight back the tears and embrace Aron. He, too, is misty-eyed as he bids us farewell, marking a time in our lives when everything is changing. Jakub cries openly, then bites his lip as Aron boards the bus.

We stand there a long time, long after the bus disappears over the hill, even after the dust from its wake settles back onto the road, leaving everything as it is, everything except the three of us. For Aron it is an adventurous unknown, for Jakub and me the unknown isn't as adventurous as it is dreaded.

"Come on, Jakub." I want to be cheerful, but it just isn't in me. "We have work to do."

He follows after me, his hands thrust deep into his pockets, and his shoulders bent forward, feeling the strain I feel. "Yeah. More work. Aron's work, too."

We shuffle down the dirt trail towards the house, our chins dragging the ground, unprepared for what lays ahead.

"Aron's work, too." He repeats it several times and I keep looking back at him, as he just shakes his head and says it again.

"Yeah, Jakub, Aron's work, too."

"Aron's work, too. Filip has to do Aron's work, too. Poor Filip."

I stop and stare at him. "Why me? Why not Jakub?"

He smiles broadly and shuffles on past me. "Aron oldest. He do more. Now Filip oldest. He do Aron's work, too."

I turn to follow and run to catch up. "I'm now the oldest and I tell you what to do. You now have to do my work and your work." He stops and looks at me as I run by him, forcing him to chase me.

We settle into a routine easier than we had imagined, and Jakub surprises me taking on more than ever. But the schoolwork suffers, at least during the spring, late summer, and into the fall, when the farm demands more of our attention.

It is during this time, just after the last crop is picked, canned, and stored that Aron comes home. With him is a friend from school and the boy's sister. She is almost my age, eighteen, and pretty in a way, not like girls whose pictures I had seen in a magazine, but simpler, without the fancy hair and makeup. Klara's hair is brown with red hints whenever the sun shines through it, and her eyes are light brown, which sometimes seem darker, more mysterious. She is heavier than me, solidly built, with a woman's bosom and thick body, the appearance of one accustomed to hard work, yet her hands are smooth and soft, the nails even and polished.

"Filip Stitchko, this is Jan Walusky and his sister, Klara." His grip is strong, but his hand smooth.

I turn and offer her my hand, and she smiles and nods slightly, leaving me with my hand outstretched, not knowing what to do with it.

Aron continues. "This is my brother, Jakub."

While he tells us about Jan and Klara, I am so drawn to this woman that I don't listen. She is the first woman I remember since my mother, except Maria, and she doesn't count as a woman. But Klara is pretty in my eyes and stirs feelings in me only a woman can stir in a man.

They return to Katy and we visit with Aron, hearing about his schooling and looking at his uniform. I say little during the night, thinking of Klara and wishing she was here with us, with me. My fantasies grow as I lay on my bed imagining being with her, kissing her, and chasing her through fields of wheat.

With morning I am up before the roosters, hoping to finish my chores early, hoping there will be time for me to see and talk to Klara. It isn't long after dawn that I see her walking towards the farm, her arms swinging freely, her steps sure and quick. She waves when she sees me and comes running towards the house. I intercept her before she reaches the porch, surprised to find her neat and clean despite the walk from town.

"Good morning, Klara. You're up early."

"My brother wants Aron to join him for breakfast." She smiles at me, and leans against the post.

Before I can ask him, Aron is standing in the doorway. "Breakfast in town?" He looks at me and tilts his head, holding one hand towards me.

"Jan says to bring Filip and Jakub if they want to come." Again she smiles at me.

Jakub comes out and hears the invitation. "Yes. Say yes, Filip."

I look at Jakub and Aron, then at Klara, holding my eyes on hers a little longer than the others. "I can handle things here, Aron. You and Jakub go on." I again turn to Klara and smile.

"Let me change my clothes and I'll walk back with you." Aron smiles at Klara as Jakub watches us both.

He looks from Klara to me, and back again. "Maybe Klara will have breakfast with you, Filip."

I never thought of kissing him before, but I want to now. I suppress the excitement I feel and speak as calmly as I can. "Sure, I would like to look at someone other than you at breakfast." I smile at her, but feel the panic in my stomach. "Will you stay and have breakfast with me, Klara?"

She raises herself from the post and brushes the back of her skirt. "Well, I generally have my brother or parents with me, but I guess it'll be okay."

Aron is dubious, but agrees and admonishes me. "Okay, Filip, but she's the sister of one of my best friends. Don't do anything that would get you into trouble, okay?"

I have no idea what will or what won't get me into trouble, but I know what I want to do with Klara. She helps with the meal and talks freely of her home in Lublin, and of her family, friends, and the boys she likes. She helps me wash the dishes, throwing the basin of water into the yard as I dry and put the plates and glasses on the shelves.

Afterwards, I ignore my chores and show Klara the farm. "It isn't ours, not really, but as long as Maria or one of her relatives doesn't claim it, then we can stay here and work it."

"That seems so unfair." Her lips are full, her eyes sparkle.

"We do everything by hand, but we're saving for a horse to pull a wagon and help us plow the field." I want to touch her.

Klara smiles, reaches for my hand, and holds it. "You work hard, don't you, Filip?"

I am elated. "Yeah, I guess I do."

She smiles and leans towards me. As her lips meet mine, I nearly explode and reach for her, but she laughs and runs from me, looking back and inviting me to chase her.

I am faster, but don't want to catch her until she is near the house. To my surprise she runs towards it and stops at the door, breathing hard and holding her hand to me. I take her hand and she pulls me to her, and kissing me vigorously and squeezing me tightly.

She looks down at my pants and smiles. "You do work hard. I'll take care of you." With another kiss, she takes me into the house and pulls me to the bed. She removes her blouse and reveals her bosom, like large honeydew melons, and pulls me to them.

This is the best morning of my life. I've discovered what it's like to be with a woman. She is filled with energy and knows more than a young woman her age should know, but I think I'm in love and want something between us, something akin to a relationship.

"Oh, Filip, you're so sweet. I don't think I've ever been with anyone as gentle as you." She kisses me again, tenderly, affectionately, but without the passion of her earlier kisses. "I've got to finish school before I can have a boyfriend." She looks away and holds it for a moment, before turning back to me. "I don't think I could live on a farm, though," she hesitates, "or in a small town."

I watch as she walks back to town, her arms swinging and her steps as quick as they were when she came. I don't know what I feel, but it's like the feeling I had at Joseph's funeral, sad to see her go, but glad too. I realize as she disappears over the hill that she isn't someone I could look at everyday, and I seriously doubt I would have the stamina to keep up with her in bed and be expected to work a farm.

There is no need to worry about the farm, as Maria returns without Mr. Wodjik, briefly visits her brother's grave, and signs papers selling the farm. She leaves without a word to either me or Jakub, as Father Jan informs us we are without a home.

We take what we can and move closer to town into the house of Aron and Jakub's parents. It is dark and musty, the home for birds and insects, but it is all we have, the only thing we can do to stay together. We work as hard as we can, cleaning and scrubbing, patching and repairing, and getting the house where we can live in it. But it isn't a farm anymore, as the lands were sold off to pay taxes, and we have no seeds anyway. We are also informed there are more taxes outstanding on the property and house, and that these would have to be paid as soon as possible.

There is little I can do. I can't leave Jakub by himself and can't find work for the two of us. Aron is still in school and can't help, but I know he would come if I asked him. Yet, his education and the army are important to him, and I choose to solve the problem myself.

It is Father Jan and Rabbi Zacharz who find the solution.

"So, Filip, you're being a good boy?" The rabbi pats my shoulder.

"He has never been any trouble." The priest nods and stands slightly behind the Jewish teacher.

Jakub joins us on the porch, his eyes wide.

"Sit, boys." The rabbi motions with his hands. "I have some things to say."

I don't know what to expect, but they both are smiling and I sense it isn't more bad news.

"You know, Filip, Mr. Oliwitz is old." Father Jan's eyes seem to look past me.

"And he's tired." The rabbi nods his affirmation. "We want you, Filip, to go to Brest and study to be a polizei." Rabbi Zacharz lets his words sink in before continuing. "The village has agreed. You'll come back and be our village's constable. Perhaps, one day you'll be mayor."

I've never thought of being a policeman, but it is more of an opportunity than any I have before me. "I would like that, but what of Jakub?"

"I want to go with Filip." Jakub's eyes narrow and he bites his lower lip.

The rabbi looks at him and smiles. "The school is for only a month. You can stay with someone until he comes home."

"Who, Rabbi?" I am as concerned as Jakub.

"Zus Malbin has agreed. But only while you're gone, Filip."

The Jewish teacher, I think to myself, remembering my dislike of him. "Malbin?" I don't know what to say, don't really know why I don't like the man. "If Jakub says okay, then it's okay."

Jakub tilts his head and looks at me, his eyes intense, before relaxing and smiling. "If Filip says okay, then it's okay."

The two men look at each other before turning their attention to me.

"It's okay. Jakub can stay with Zus until I come home." I turn to Jakub. "Just until I come home, okay?"

He smiles slightly and looks down. "Okay." He quickly looks at me and smiles broadly. "Then I help Filip. I'll be a policeman, too."

I leave the following month, carrying my extra clothing in the same worn-out, brown suitcase I brought with me to Katy seven years earlier. The bus seems the same too, battered and dented, belching black smoke as it raises clouds of dust behind us. But I'm alone and feel more alone than when I sat on that rickety chair in the orphanage. I don't look back, too afraid I'll see Jakub, too afraid his tears will bring my own.

The month is passing quickly when I receive a note from Aron, reassuring me everything is fine. He is on leave and taking care of Jakub.

"But the house is gone," he writes, "taken to pay taxes. You'll be given an office with a small apartment as part of your pay. I'm searching for something for me and Jakub. We hope to be settled before you return."

I wonder what he can find for Jakub. Aron will be going back to the army and Jakub will be left alone. At least he won't be my responsibility, yet I worry what will happen to him.

CHAPTER FIVE

Aron is recalled to Warsaw before completing arrangements for Jakub, asking me to keep him a little while longer. I agree and am pleased to see him, conflicted in my feelings, but accept him in my new home.

Aron said it was a small apartment, but it is spartan in its space and furnishings, nearly as small as Father Jan's home, as plain and bare as my position, I reason. But it is part of my salary, and better than anything we have at the time.

We settle into a routine borne of necessity, as I take to my duties as the police magistrate and share what time I have remaining in a day with Jakub. There is little for him to do and most of my time is spent keeping track of him, and finding something to occupy his time. I have a small salary, but it is sufficient for our needs, supplemented occasionally with money from Aron. But it still isn't the best situation for either of us, and I write Aron that I don't have time to watch Jakub and do my job. He promises to come home and make some arrangements.

It is summer and there are whisperings of dangerous times ahead. I sit on the porch watching Jakub playing with some children and listen to Marek, Zus, Father Jan and Dr. Levi discuss the news that has everyone excited.

"Russia and Germany at peace. What does this mean?"

Marek Spiegelman wipes his hands on his apron. "It means, Samuel, that Poland is a buffer between them."

"Poland is in no danger. We do not threaten anyone." Father Jan rarely sits with these men, but tonight is a rare occasion. "No, we have nothing to fear from Hitler or Stalin."

"That is why Poland is in trouble. We aren't strong enough to stop either of these powers from marching us into dust."

"Zus, you're young. You don't remember the last war. Poland was created to keep these enemies apart. Why would these nations want Poland? We're the reason they have peace. We stand between them." Marek glances into the store.

"We stand in their way." Zus pulls on a ringlet and leans forward. "This chancellor of Germany, this Hitler, he wants more land for Germany, he wants… er, he wants 'lebensraum', a German word meaning 'living space'."

"Where does he want this space?"

"In Russia, Father Jan. Germany's living space is in the East, in Russia."

"But what of Poland, Zus?" Dr. Levi rests his arms on his knees.

"Yes, what of Poland? This Hitler doesn't say, but he has declared that all Jews are enemies of the world and will be eliminated."

"Jews? Enemies of the world?" Dr. Levi straightens. "How can this be?"

"I don't know." Zus sits back in the chair.

Merek glances into the store. "Marta doesn't like for me to talk like this." He unties the apron and pulls it over his head. "I think Poland is in the best position to negotiate a peace with Herr Hitler."

"In his book, Hitler says that Germany will solve the problem of the Jewish menace once and for all."

"Menace?" Marek shakes his head. "We're a menace?" He looks at the priest. "Are Jews a menace, Father Jan?"

The priest hesitates then looks a Spiegelman. "No, no. Be calm. This German just talks to rally the rabble around him. Poland is in no danger. This talk of living space is just talk. Haven't Germany and Russia agreed to be friends?"

Zus turns to me. "Filip, what do you think?"

I am surprised that he would ask me and more surprised to find Marek and the others turning towards me. "I don't know much other than what I've heard tonight, but if Germany and Russia have decided to be friends, then I think Poland could be in danger."

"Exactly."

I'm uncomfortable speaking as an expert and not sure I like agreeing with Malbin. "We'll know soon enough. Aron will be home tomorrow."

Jakub and I are excited with the dawn and anticipate Aron's arrival. The old bus stops in front of the store, as dust settles around it and puffs of black smoke permeate the area with its acrid smell. He steps from the bus and is greeted by Malbin.

"Zus. It's good to see you." He offers his hand. "How's Jakub doing with his schooling?"

"Well, Aron." Malbin nods and motions to a chair on the porch, sitting on the edge of the bench. "He's slow and can't be expected to learn many things, but his life can still be useful."

"Has he learned to read?"

"No. Just simple things." Zus strokes his beard and pulls on a ringlet. "But he can do simple math, addition and some subtraction."

Aron leans forward and looks at the Jewish teacher. "Is there anything else?"

"Yes, there are many things. He's always cheerful and will do whatever is asked of him." The teacher clasps his hands together. "He gets into trouble when he tries to find something to do on his own or when he tries to do too much. He needs supervision, and I think he'll do well in an activity that requires repetition."

Malbin nods. "Jakub has a good heart, a good attitude. You've done well with him, Aron."

Aron removes his hat and wipes his forehead. "Filip has done as well as I."

"Yes, Filip has done well, but it isn't the same as when the three of you worked the farm. No, Filip now has duties to perform, and he can't give Jakub the supervision he needs."

Aron is silent for several moments. "So, he really has no skills."

"I wouldn't say that. He has learned to drive a truck, a large one." Zus looks around the town, but turns back to Aron. "It is a dump truck with four or five gears. Filip taught him."

"A dump truck? Filip hasn't mentioned that to me. If he can learn to drive a truck, then there must be other things he can learn to do."

"Of course. But we must be careful and not ask too much of him. Simple things, Aron, and he'll be happy." Malbin nods and looks at Dr. Levi who is walking towards them.

"Welcome home." He shakes hands with Aron and smiles at Zus. "Good morning."

They return the greetings and explain their conversation, as the physician nods and holds his hands in front of him. "Good."

Dr. Levi faces Aron. "Your father was my friend; he was my good friend." Levi places his hand on Aron's shoulder. "The day Jakub was born, I put the tiny bundle in his arms and watched as he drew him to his chest." Levi looks away for a moment, a tear forming in his eye. "He honored me when he allowed me to name Jakub. It was my father's name, a good strong name."

"Yes, Dr. Levi, it's a good name, much like the one you gave me."

"Ah, I'd forgotten. Yes, Aron, the priest, the peacemaker. Better that I should have named you Joshua." He smiles brightly and waves his hand from the top of Aron's head to his feet. "But you shall be Poland's general and stop these bloody dictators from again enslaving us."

"Thank you. But I'm not a general, yet." He smiles.

"An oversight, Aron. You're still young, but you'll be a general someday."

Malbin rests his hand on Aron's back.

"Maybe, my friends, but I still have to think of Jakub."

"I, too, have thought of that ever since you wrote." Dr. Levi turns and sits on the bench, motioning for Zus and Aron to sit. "Aron, I don't like this hospital of which you wrote. Jakub would be unhappy there, and I fear he would die."

He stops and faces him. "Filip, too, has said no. He says they will find a farmer who needs laborers and hire themselves out."

"No, I'll not allow that either. Filip is a good friend and almost like a brother, but he must have his life too."

Aron leans forward and Dr. Levi speaks softly. "I'm alone now." He looks at the floor and then meets Aron's eyes. "I have room in my house and I would welcome Jakub to share it with me. And when you're here, you can stay as well." He hesitates and clears his throat.

Aron stops and releases a breath slowly. "And Filip would still be near."

"Yes, Filip will be near and can see him whenever he wants."

"And still be our magistrate." Zus nods and pulls on his ringlet.

"I will be most appreciative, Dr. Levi. I will contribute to his upkeep, of course."

"As you like. But," the physician pauses and faces Aron, "mine is a religious household where certain dietary taboos are practiced. I'll want Jakub to learn these things and practice them while he lives with me."

"You mean you want Jakub to become Jewish?"

"No, Aron, only learn what it means for me to be Jewish. When he is with you, he can behave as you behave."

"I'm not a religious man, Dr. Levi. It's all the same to me."

"Good." The physician points his finger at Aron. "But a soldier should have religion, Aron. You'll need God before this is over."

"God I have. It's religion that's missing." Aron holds his hand out. "Believe me, my friends," he turns and looks at Malbin, before turning back to the physician, "I pray whenever I look across the border and see the buildup of German forces." He nods. "They're coming. Like Satan from Hell, Hitler and his murderers are coming."

He pauses and smiles. "But I think we'll be ready. Just six more months and we'll have an army that'll stop them."

"Then it is true. Poland will be squeezed between the Germans and Russians."

"Yes, we're told we must be ready."

"Surely Hitler and Stalin won't work together? Do you think they'll now shake hands on a pact of friendship?"

"They already have. And we're told they'll come soon." Aron speaks softly and his words have finality about them.

"Aron Galinski!" Marta Spiegelman exits the store and embraces him. "Already you're a captain. So many promotions."

She is joined by Marek. "It's good to see you so well, Aron."

Aron accepts the embrace from Marta and holds his hand for Marek. "Thank you both." He turns to face Mrs. Spiegelman. "Only those promotions that I've earned."

"And several he has earned and not received, I'll wager." Dr. Levi holds his hand on Aron's shoulder.

Mr. Spiegelman looks at the physician. "So, Samuel, have you told him?"

"Yes, Marek, we have told him." He motions towards Malbin.

"That's good." He turns to face Aron. "And Marta and I will help." He glances at his wife and smiles. "And if Jakub needs another place to stay, he can stay with us."

Mrs. Spiegelman places her hand on her husband's arm and reaches for Aron. "And we'll find work for him here. We'll train him to help out around the store, to help customers, and we'll pay him, too."

Mr. Spiegelman nods his agreement and smiles, holding out his hands in surrender. "It's the least we can do, Aron. Your parents were good people and helped us many times. You've been a good friend, as well. It's the least good neighbors can do."

Aron embraces Marta and again offers his hand to Marek. "This lifts a great burden from me. Now I can go about my duties without worrying about Jakub. This is such a relief. Filip, too, will be grateful."

He steps back and looks at each of them. "Your generosity overwhelms me. I promise this is something I'll one day repay."

"There is nothing to repay, Aron. We do this because we want to do this. It's our way of saying how important you and Jakub are to us."

I see Aron from my office and join them at the store. He sees me and walks towards me, embracing me as warmly as when he left for Warsaw. Zus and Dr. Levi, too, step from the platform leaving the Spiegelmans alone.

"How are you, Filip?" Dr. Levi is smiling warmly as Zus offers his hand.

I take the teacher's hand and nod. "I'm fine. I'm even better now that my friend has come home."

"Where's Jakub?" Aron's face is taut.

"He's fine. He wants to surprise you. He'll be along shortly." I, too, want to surprise Aron.

We all hear the sounds of grinding gears and hunched our heads into our shoulders, but the roar of the engine soon replaces it and the truck bursts into the square. Jakub sits tall behind the wheel and waves at his brother, as he steps on the brake and forgets to depress the clutch, forcing the vehicle to jerk several times before stopping. He starts to jump from the cab when I stop him.

"Set the brake, Jakub. You must remember to set the brake." My voice is higher than normal, my words quick and short.

"Okay, Filip. I remember." He pulls the lever setting the brakes, alights from the cab, and embraces his brother. "Aron, I miss you."

Aron clasps the young man behind the head. "And I miss you, too, little brother. What's this? You, driving a truck?"

Jakub beams with pride. "I can drive, Aron. I show you."

"I've seen, Jakub. I'm very proud of you."

Jakub smiles shyly and lowers his head. "Now I find work. I make my own money. I won't worry Filip anymore."

"Of course. You'll be a man, Jakub, a man who pays his own way." Aron looks at me, a slight smile upon his lips, then each of the others.

"And he will, I promise you, Aron." Malbin lets go of the ringlet and looks earnestly at everyone. "There are jobs for truck drivers. We'll find a good job for you, Jakub."

"Yes, there'll be a job for you, Jakub, even if it's only working in the store."

A competition has arisen between me and the Spiegelmans, my influence in teaching Jakub to drive, or theirs by offering him a job in the store. I want to argue and wish I hadn't complained to Aron. But I remain silent, realizing we are working for Jakub.

"It never hurts to have more than one skill, eh, Zus?" I turn to face Aron. "He can drive a truck or work in the store. It'll be good training for you, Jakub."

"But I want to drive the truck."

"And you will, my boy. But if you want, I can teach you things in the store." Marek Spiegelman looks at me and smiles, an almost imperceptible acknowledgement one opponent gives another, and I get a feeling he thinks I will fail to teach Jakub well enough to get a job.

I, too, have my doubts, lacking confidence in myself as much as in Jakub, but I swear I will be more patient and work with him every day. I don't look at the Spiegelmans again, but I want them to know I understand the challenge. "I'm confident you'll learn this, Jakub, and I know I'll be able to find many jobs for a skilled truck driver."

Aron looks at me. "And where did you manage to find a truck?"

"The driver had had more than enough to drink. He ran off the road and knocked down a sign. I confiscated the truck for thirty days, or until he repairs the damage done." I'm aware everyone is watching me, perhaps judging my actions as wrong. "I decided to take the opportunity to teach Jakub to drive."

Jakub beams and Aron returns a tight-lipped smile before turning to me and looking sternly. "I'm pleased you're doing this, Filip, and I know you'll be patient with him. But, if there are no jobs, I'll expect him to work with the Spiegelmans learning what they have to teach him."

The rebuke stings as much as the self-satisfied expression on Marek Spiegelman's face. "Of course, Aron, I'll encourage Jakub to learn all he can."

Mrs. Spiegelman's eyes dart between me and her husband, at the near confrontation as she steps in front of Marek. "Whenever Jakub isn't learning to drive, then he's welcome in our house and our business. We'll teach him whatever he wants to learn." She turns to me and smiles. "You, too, Filip, are welcome in our home. Your presence will reassure our friend."

Jakub steps into the middle of our ring and looks at me. "I want to drive the truck." He turns to look at Aron. "I want you to see I can drive."

Aron agrees to his brother's request and Jakub climbs behind the wheel. I climb up beside him and speak more softly than he is accustomed to hearing, but I want them to see I have patience. Jakub only grinds the gears a couple of times, forgetting to double-clutch between shifts, but Aron is pleased and Jakub is elated.

Aron's visit is too brief as the demands of his post pull him back to Warsaw. He is to be reassigned to the border on the Odra River, but is confident the Germans are just trying to scare us, to get our government to give up territory and force severe diplomatic concessions upon us. But he knows the government won't cave in and that war looms on the horizon. He reiterates that there is to be no trouble for at least a year, and Poland only needs six months to prepare and build up its military.

It's August 15, 1939.

CHAPTER SIX

We don't get the six months. The storm comes on September 1, from the sky and earth, as stukas strafe the manned positions and drive back the army. German tanks roll across the plains and smash into the lines, routing the Polish forces. But Poland fights back and it isn't as easy as Czechoslovakia.

By the middle of September, the Germans are at Warsaw and Aron comes home, wounded and under orders to report to Brest.

"Aron, please sit." Marek Spiegelman motions to a chair for him, just as Dr. Levi and Zus arrive. I watch Jakub as he feeds the Spiegelman's chickens listening as best as I can. "Tell us. What news is there?"

"We were overrun." Aron stretches his wounded arm. "The English and French kept us from building our military, urging us not to give Hitler provocation to make war."

"But they've now declared war on Germany. They're our allies." Zus's eyes were wide as he reached for his beard. "Surely they'll attack Germany soon."

Aron turns his head to look at the young teacher. "They won't attack soon enough. Poland will be under Hitler's boot before they can even mobilize. We shouldn't have listened to them."

"Is there no chance, Aron?" Dr. Levi bites his lower lip, his hands in front of him. "Is not our army able to hold them back?"

"Our men are courageous, but they are too few. Our guns are accurate and reliable. With more of them we could have stopped them as soon as they crossed our borders."

He releases a deep breath and continues. "Our light tank with its diesel engine is better than theirs, but it isn't a match for their heavy tanks. And their stukas are like birds from hell, screaming as they dive upon our lines, and we have nothing to stop them."

He leans back in the chair and turns towards the physician. "No, Dr. Levi, there's no chance. It's just a matter of time before they overwhelm us."

"And you, Aron, what are you to do?" Mr. Spiegelman crouches beside the chair.

"I'm going to Brest. There I'll assume command of a new battalion, one equipped with our new guns." He smiles brightly. "With them, maybe we can cause enough damage to force them to negotiate a peace." He looks towards the ceiling and shakes his head. "If we can get the guns delivered in time."

"I'll go to Brest with you." I volunteer just as the silence becomes strained. "Poland will need all of her men for this war."

I look at Zus only to have him look away. Maybe that's why Joseph and Maria didn't like Jews, they don't seem willing to fight.

"Yes, my friend, Poland will need soldiers." Aron's smile is wide and he nods.

"Then you and I'll go together. Just like when we were children." I can feel the excitement building in me.

"Yes, Filip, like when we were boys, only now it's real."

His mood deepens and I can feel the weight resting upon his shoulders. "It is real, Aron. Before we killed imaginary Germans and Russians. Now we can kill the real ones."

"The real ones aren't as easily killed."

"But they can be killed. And we, you and I, will kill as many as we can." I become worried with his seriousness, so unwilling to shake off the severity of the situation.

He remains silent a long time before smiling at me. "Yes. I think I'll like having you with me, Filip. I'll have you assigned to my unit, somewhere close to make me feel stronger."

The spark that is so much a part of his personality is returning. "I would like that. Maybe you can get me a commission and a pretty woman to hold my hand."

"It's not your hand you're thinking of, my friend."

They all laugh at Aron's joke, and I, too, chuckle, but am not as comfortable with humor at my expense. Nor am I as quick with retorts as Aron. "Perhaps, my friend, but first we'll kill Germans."

Dr. Levi is kneeling beside Aron changing the bandage. He looks up and is quick to relieve my embarrassment. "Yes, Filip is right. Push the Germans back into Germany first, then there'll be enough women for all of you."

Jakub interrupts and wanders among us. "Does it hurt, Aron?" He points to Aron's arm.

"Yes, little brother, it hurts." Aron's eyes are misty and he smiles slightly when he looks at Jakub.

"I'm sorry it hurts. How'd it happen?"

He looks at all of us and takes it as a signal we all want to hear. "They started early, just three or four hours past midnight. I was asleep near my guns."

Aron stares out of the door and holds his gaze for a long time. "I was commanding a four-gun placement and my crew were all seasoned men. At the first sign of German activity, we were all at our posts, straining to make out some targets.

"They had lobbed smoke shells between them and us." He sits back and begins demonstrating with his hands. "I finally saw a rough, dark shape coming through the darkness and smoke. I couldn't make it out, but I could see a white cross moving from right to left in front of me." His voice rises. "I signaled gun one to open fire. They did and the tank disappeared in a fury of fire and smoke.

"We could then make out other vehicles coming towards us, all with those white crosses. They made great targets, as all my guns scored direct hits. Yet the tanks continued to come, forcing us to ration our ammunition.

"I sent a runner for more shells and called out the targets one at a time, allowing the guns to pace their shots." He rubs his hands together. "There were too many of them. We continued our fire with incredible accuracy, destroying at least twenty or twenty-five tanks and other armored vehicles.

"They came at us very fast, followed by infantry." He pulls his left arm to his chest and fingers the fresh bandage. "We fired our rifles and pistols, but I ordered them to fall back. They fought bravely, but we were cut down as fast as the Germans could fire. I, too, started to run, but turned to face a burly man not more than three meters behind, running with his rifle and bayonet aimed at my midsection. I fired and hit him in the chest, but his momentum carried him forward, knocking me to the ground, his body atop mine. I was struggling to get up when another soldier came and thrust his bayonet into my arm."

He turns to look at Dr. Levi. "It was still dark, too dark to recognize complete forms lying on the ground." He turns and looks at Mr. Spiegelman, Malbin, and me. "I don't think the soldier could see very well, thrusting to where he thought my chest would be, and hearing my scream, he guessed he got me.

"As soon as the army passed, I rolled the dead man off me and made my way back to our command post." He shakes his head. "Everyone was dead.

"I found a gap in the advancing German line and sneaked through it. I was able to commandeer a horse from a local farmer and made my way to Warsaw." Aron again shakes his head. "Everyone was dazed. Nobody had expected an attack on this scale and we weren't prepared."

Aron rises and walks to the window, staring out for a few moments. "They promoted me on the spot and congratulated me for getting back. I was then told to make my way to Brest and assume command of a battalion of anti-tank weapons and wait for further orders."

"You're leaving?" Jakub's eyes are wide and his voice is shaky.

"Yes, Jakub. I have to go to Brest. I may be away for a long time." Aron puts his hand on his brother's shoulder. "Filip, too, will be gone."

"Filip, too? How long?"

"I don't know. There are some bad times ahead. You'll stay with Dr. Levi and Mr. and Mrs. Spiegelman. They'll take care of you."

"I want to go with you. If Filip goes, I go, too."

"No, little brother. This is something we have to do."

Aron looks at the physician and Marek Spiegelman. "I know this will be difficult. We may be gone a long time, but I'll make it up to you for watching over Jakub."

"Aron, there's no need for you to worry." Dr. Levi steps next to Jakub and puts his arm around his shoulders. "He's like my own son. We do well together, don't we, Jakub?"

"Yes, Dr. Samuel. I like being with you."

Marek joins the two of them and places his arm around the boy as well. "Jakub will be fine, Aron. Already he learns my business. He'll soon run the store by himself, you'll see." He smiles broadly at Jakub and returns his gaze to the older brother. "You worry about how to stop the Germans."

Aron rises and faces the men. "You two are a blessing, as are you, Zus, and Marta, too. My mind can wrestle with this new command more freely with your assurances."

He grabs Jakub behind the head and pulls him into his arms, embracing him. "And you, brother, will take care of our friends, won't you?"

Jakub's eyes shine as he steps back. "Yes, Aron, I'll take care of them. I'll work and take care of everyone."

We leave the next morning, hitching a ride in a passing lorry bound for Brest. Jakub remains on the porch watching us until the truck moves over a hill. I look at Aron as he wipes his cheeks and lower my head so he can't see my tears. We sit in the rear and smoke and watch the countryside pass by, both lost in our thoughts and fearing what lay ahead.

It is different. We are different, no longer boys, for he has been away for a long time, time that seems to separate us, making it more difficult to just talk. He sits in the dirty uniform and studies the fields and people trudging eastward. I wear my cleanest britches and shirt, regretting my decision to leave my uniform in Katy, causing me to look like an inexperienced peasant when next to my friend, marking the differences that much more.

I know his mind is occupied with his coming duties, saddled with fears, and burdened with concern for Jakub, and I know I am afraid.

"What can I expect, Aron?" He seems relieved with the interruption of his thoughts. "I mean, what do you think is going to happen?"

"I don't know. I'm not sure I'm ready for the command of a battalion, but it's there, isn't it?" He eases up against the side of the truck and rests his back against it. "I hope I can get you assigned to my unit. There shouldn't be any trouble, at least not now with us in a war."

He is silent for a long time and I don't know what more to ask him, but he senses my nervousness. "Scared?"

I look at him and remember a time as boys when he asked me the same question. I had denied it then and am about to deny it again, but we aren't boys anymore, and this isn't like playing in the fields. "Yeah, I think so." It sounds strange admitting it.

"I'd be worried if you weren't." He looks at the rear and tosses his cigarette, then turns towards me. "I'm scared, too."

His eyes show it and I look away before turning back to him. "How do you manage to go on?"

"What choice do I have? I was trained for this. I never thought I would have to use my training, but I know what I must do."

"What was it like when they attacked? Were you scared then?"

"At first. Then my training took over. I picked the targets and directed the guns to fire. They did the rest."

"I don't know, Aron. My training has been different. I hope I can do it." My stomach is uneasy and I hold my hands for fear they will tremble.

"You'll know soon enough, Filip. I think you can do it, otherwise, friend or not, I wouldn't ask for you in my unit."

"I'm not sure I could do this in any other unit, but with you nearby, I think I could find the courage to kill Hitler himself."

"Thank you, my friend. And I'm certain your presence will give me more courage as well."

I now realize how much Aron's approval means to me. "Thank you."

He turns to stare out the back of the lorry again, his mouth tight and his brow wrinkled.

"There's more, isn't there? More worries?"

He smiles at me and nods. "Yes. I'm worried about Jakub. I know he's all right with Dr. Levi, but what if something should happen to Dr. Samuel, or the Spiegelmans, or Malbin, or, worse yet, what if I don't make it? What will happen to Jakub?" There is a tear in his eye that he slowly wipes. "And now you're with me. If anything happens to the others, you won't be there either and he'll be alone." He continues to look out the back of the truck, staring as if he can see all the way to Katy. "He's so afraid when he's alone, so much like a little boy."

CHAPTER SEVEN

Just outside Brest, traffic from other towns converges on the narrow road taking us into the center of the city. The journey takes all day, as much of the traffic is military, serviceman and officers, making their way to Brest, escaping the oncoming horde of Huns bent on obtaining their living space, which should be in hell.

The army headquarters is still open when Aron and I report, but they are too busy to deal with us, sending us to a nearby hotel for billeting. I share Aron's quarters, sharing his anxiety as well. He is talkative much of the time, showing off his new epaulettes denoting his rank of major, sewing them to his dirty uniform, brushing it as best he can. He talks as he works, cleaning his shoes and shining them, spitting and brushing repeatedly, smearing butter over the fine leather leaving a hint of a shine.

We rise early the next morning, taking bread, cheese, sausages, and tea from a local shop, purchasing packs of cigarettes, and enjoying the morning as traffic stirs. Aron isn't in such a rush this last morning, content to sip coffee and watch. Brest, however, is in a stir, bustling about, almost at a frantic pace, too agitated for normal.

The shop's owner comes to our table and requests he be allowed to sit. Aron nods and watches the man closely. He begins with the release of breath. "You haven't heard?"

Aron looks at me then the man. "There is news from Warsaw?"

"No, my friend, it's from the east. Russia has crossed our borders."

I bolt upright. "Russia is going to help us?"

Aron and the man look at each other, before Aron speaks. "No, my friend, Russia is working with Germany. We're finished."

"Sooner than you think, Major." The shop owner rests his arms on the table. "They have already rounded up soldiers east of here, and they're coming here. They'll shut down the city completely."

"Or destroy it." Aron draws on his cigarette. "Now, I wonder what's in store for us."

The man looks at Aron and waves his hand. "In that uniform, you'll be taken prisoner immediately. I would lose it if I were you."

Aron nods. "A prisoner of the Russians here or a prisoner of the Germans at home." He releases a deep breath. "I'll keep the uniform and take my chances with the Russians."

At army headquarters, he is again advised to lose the uniform, but no further instructions are forthcoming. We learn the Russians will be in Brest by the afternoon, so we return to the shop we have just left.

Surprisingly, it is still open and the owner is still sitting at the table. "Ah, my friends, you've come to wait with me?"

Aron holds out his hands. "And why not?" He reaches into his pockets and pulls out all of the zlotys he has and lays them on the table. "Let's have a feast."

The man smiles, picks up the money, and gives it back to Aron. "No, my friend, it'll be my treat." He shakes his head and the rings under his eyes seem deeper. "I fear, for a while, only rubles will be worth anything here."

"Or marks." Aron adds. "Sit down, Filip, and let's enjoy ourselves while we wait."

The owner sets cheeses, breads, sausages, hard-boiled eggs, beer and vodka before us, with some delicate pastries covered with honey and sugar. He joins us and pours the vodka. "For me, people need to eat, so I think I'll be all right. But for you, my friends, I fear it will be some time before you'll be able to join me again for a toast to Poland." He raises his glass and waits for us to do the same. "To our beloved Poland. May she always live in our hearts."

We indulge ourselves on the fare set before us and drink lots of vodka waiting for the Russians, who arrive mid-afternoon. Despite the vodka, we're still sober and enjoying the repast. The soldiers enter behind a large tank which stops and points towards the center of the square. They surround us, weapons aimed in our direction.

I should be terrified, but I'm not. It is probably due to Aron's bravery as he watches the Russian soldiers, sitting still, his feet propped up on another chair. His smile is infectious and the soldiers relax, holding their weapons by their sides.

At the approach of an officer, Aron rises and snaps his feet together, clicking his heels German-style. "Major Aron Galinski, Sir. I'm at your disposal."

"Captain Ivan Donachevsky, Major." He salutes Aron sharply and his Polish is better than my Russian.

Aron returns the salute. "May I offer you and your men a drink, Captain?"

"Thank you, no."

Aron smiles as he speaks Russian to the officer. He lifts a vodka towards the captain and downs it. "Za vashe zdorovie." He sets the glass on the table and looks at us. "To your good health, too, my friends."

A second man approaches, his uniform simpler than the officer's, free of any signs of rank. "Captain, what is this?"

The officer motions towards our table where we remain standing. "A Polish officer, Commissar."

"Then shoot him."

Aron steps forward. "There'll be no need for that, Commissar. I'm Major Aron Galinski, and I'm at your disposal."

The political officer is taken aback at Aron speaking to him in Russian. "I'm Victor Punin, political officer for this unit." He looks embarrassed for a moment before noticing the shop owner and me.

He glares at the Russian officer. "And who are they?"

Aron quickly speaks up. "This man is the owner of this shop. He has graciously allowed me a bite to eat in anticipation of your arrival. This other chap is from a small town outside Brest."

I am curious as to why he didn't introduce us as friends, but say nothing thinking he knows what he is doing.

The commissar looks at the shop owner and speaks in Polish. "Get me a glass of water."

"Yes, sir." As the man goes into the darkness of his shop, the political officer turns to the captain and motions to Aron and me. "Take these two into custody. Put them with the others."

They shove us past the tank and soldiers quickly, before we can thank our host, but figure it would be wise for him to distance himself from us as quickly as possible.

There are forty or fifty other men and officers sitting in an alleyway, both ends guarded threateningly by machine guns and dour soldiers. We join them, sitting amongst several officers and resting our backs against the wall.

Aron turns to me and speaks softly. "I think I can get you out of here, but you must promise me something."

"I'd rather we go together." I am suddenly fearful I will be asked to do something requiring more courage than I can muster.

"No. I won't be able to escape. They're just waiting for one of us to make a run for it, and there isn't a way out." He looks at the openings and nods towards them. "But I think I can get them to release you."

"I'm listening." I listen carefully, but can feel my legs going weak and uneasiness in the pit of my stomach.

"You must promise me first." His gaze is more intense than I've ever seen it.

"Promise what?"

"When they release you…"

"If they release me."

Aron looks at me more intently, his lips tight. "If, and when they release you, you must get back to Katy and take care of Jakub."

I am relieved and wonder how I am going to get back home. "Sure, I'd do that anyway."

"I know you would, but, Filip, we're in for a difficult time. I want you to keep Jakub near you at all times. Never let him be alone for long. Stay near him and keep him out of danger." He holds his gaze on me and grips my arm.

"Okay. Okay, Aron, I promise. I'll watch over Jakub like he is my shadow."

Aron smiles briefly. "That's good, Filip. I want him to be your shadow, always where you are." His eyes relax and he loosens his grip. "Promise me that, Filip. Promise he'll be like your shadow."

"I promise, Aron, but how are you going to get me released?" The fear is returning. "And how am I going to get to Katy?"

"Getting to Katy will be the hard part, but you're resourceful. You'll find a way." He looks again towards the openings. "As to getting you released, just follow my lead and let me do the talking." He studies the openings briefly then turns to me. "Take my money." He rummages through his pockets, handing me a small knife and chain, keeping only his identification. "Give these to Jakub. And tell him I love him."

"I will." I accept the items and put them in my pockets.

We wait for an hour or more, wait until the political officer returns and begins walking through the alley. Aron stands and brushes off his uniform. He salutes the commissar as he approaches.

Punin stops and looks at him. "What do you want?" The man addresses him in Polish.

Aron glances at me and turns back to the officer. He speaks in a low voice. "This man isn't like us."

The Russian glances in my direction.

Aron relaxes his stance. "This man isn't associated with any of us. He's a peasant. He hasn't served with our armed forces. We find he has nothing in common with us, if you understand what I mean."

The officer shakes his head. "No, what are you trying to say?"

"Plainly speaking, sir, we prefer to be kept apart from his kind. We're gentlemen and he isn't."

The Russian looks at me, then Aron. "Ah, I understand. You don't want the peasant to be held with you fine gentlemen?" His Polish isn't as good as the first officer we met, but I understand it well enough.

He strikes Aron across the face, forcing him to stumble slightly. "I'll grant you your wish, Major."

He motions for me to rise and speaks in Polish. "You're a worker?"

I don't know what to say and just nod.

"That's good. We need good workers." He pulls me past Aron and pushes me towards the opening.

He turns again to Aron. "You'll stay here, Major, but the peasant I'm sending home." He walks me to the end of the alley and hands me a piece of paper. "My name is Victor Punin. You show this to anyone who stops you and they'll let you go about your business. Work hard, Pole."

I look back as Aron sits down and catch his eye. There is more pain in his expression than I have ever seen, but he smiles and nods just slightly, just enough for me to acknowledge his farewell. I start to wave but am pushed past the machine gun.

I am told to go about my business, to go wherever I call home, and I walk toward the edge of the city, to the river and across it into German-occupied Poland.

I have Punin's note, my police identification, and remember Aron's story of commandeering a horse to take him into Warsaw. He used his rank as well to get us transportation to Brest, so I imagine I can show my identification to obtain some sort of transport to Katy. I try it several times without result, lacking the courage to force my will upon someone who needs whatever there is for me to take. Finally, a farmer shakes his head and disappears into his barn. I fear he will return with a shotgun or pitchfork, but he offers me a bicycle, telling me it was his son's before he went off to fight the Germans.

I thank him and am ashamed as I pedal away from the farm, grateful this part of Poland is so flat, so easily traversed on a bicycle. It is a pleasant jaunt, even with the burning in my thighs, which I soon learn to control with equal amounts of rest and walking. Even with minor discomfort I reach home before night, relieved to see the Germans have not yet reached this part of Poland.

The day is waning as I pedal into Katy and Marta Spiegelman is lighting the lantern, the beacon of my first night in the village. Jakub and Dr. Levi are sitting together when they spot me, and it is with some humor they approach and marvel at my means of transportation. They are joined by Marek as I sit on the steps of the store, gratefully accepting the glass of water from Marta.

It is Dr. Levi who broaches the subject of Aron. I tell them what happened in Brest, telling them Aron had resigned to be captured by Russians rather than Germans. I explain the bits I understood, of Aron telling them I was unworthy to be held with Polish soldiers and officers, all to obtain my release.

I tell Jakub how smart Aron looks in his uniform with the new epaulettes and of how he sends his love. I withhold the part of drinking and eating, of the promise he exacted from me, of the look of resignation in his eyes, and the look of fear I had never seen before.

I look at Jakub as he looks at me, his eyes free of questions, free of fear. I envy him at this moment and remember again my promise to Aron to watch over Jakub as I would my shadow. It is the bravest moment of my life, as I realize I will never break my promise to Aron.

CHAPTER EIGHT

It is a restless night, as I dream of Aron and picture his eyes the last time I saw them. I keep telling myself that we will again have a day of drinking and eating such as the one we shared in Brest, but the fear in his eyes haunts me and disturbs my sleep. Jakub remains with Dr. Levi even as I remember my promise to Aron to keep him with me, but it doesn't seem to be a problem since he is accustomed to the physician and isn't alone.

I awaken to the sound of vehicles stopping in the village, followed by shouts in German. I dress quickly and rush to the window, careful not to be seen, and peek out to see soldiers rushing about the square, kicking in the doors of Spiegelman's store, while several rush in. They break down the door of Dr. Levi's as well, and two men with rifles burst through the opening. I think of Jakub immediately and remember my promise to Aron, fearful I have failed already.

A neighbor walks pass my office, going to the square, dressed in his working clothes, his hands in his pockets, seemingly as carefree as on a stroll in a wheat field. I watch him as he joins others of the village, mingling about and listening to the harsh shouts of the soldiers and their officers.

I muster my courage and join them, assuring myself that my identification is in my pocket. I walk slowly suppressing my desire to flee, realizing I have no place to go. Others from the village join us and mingle with the same curiosity as the rest of us. The soldiers stand in a line blocking any movement we might make to move closer, their rifles pointed in our direction.

Shortly the Spiegelmans stumble out the front of their store, each carrying a small suitcase. Marek's right eye is swollen and a thin trail of blood flows from a wound above his eye. He staggers down the steps and is shoved by the soldier behind him, who grabs Marta by the arm and pulls her to the truck. Both she and Marek climb up and their cases are thrown to them.

Marta catches my eye for a moment and her face is tight, her eyes wide, as she tightly grips the side of the truck. She holds my eyes for a long time and mouths words to me. I strain to make out what she is saying and realize she is asking me to take care of Jakub. I nod slowly and she turns away, and I think of how wonderful of her to be thinking of Jakub at this time.

"Einsatzgruppen."

"What?" I look at the man next to me.

"Einsatzgruppen. Schutzstaffel. They are the SS, the storm troopers and secret police of the Germans." He glances at me then continues to watch the square. "I fear for all of us. They may shoot us today."

"I don't think so." I glance at him and watch as the soldiers loot the store and smash the window. "They're taking the Spiegelmans somewhere. Why else would they need suitcases?"

At that moment Dr. Levi is dragged through the front door of his house and down the steps. He holds onto his physician's bag tightly. Jakub, too, is taken, pushed from the house by a tall soldier, his face contorted and his eyes wide. He is carrying a small duffel against his chest and he looks around him, for what, I don't know, perhaps just some understanding of why the treatment is so harsh.

Two husky soldiers lift Dr. Levi and throw him onto the floor of the truck, as the Spiegelmans squat to help him. Jakub, too, is lifted onto the truck, still holding his bag, his hands trembling and biting his lower lip. He continues looking about and spots me. My heart beats rapidly and I know my life is going to change.

"Filip, help me!" His blue eyes are wide and his plea fills the square.

I motion to the nearest soldier and pull my identification from my pocket. "I'm Filip Stitchko, constable for this town." My voice sounds calmer than it is, but I need bravado for what I am about to do. "I need to speak with someone in authority."

The man takes my identification and studies it, pretending, I guess, that he can make out the Polish language. He points towards a thickly built man directing the soldiers, the rank of a non-commissioned officer visible on the sleeve of his uniform. I recall my training in recognizing military rank as I near the man.

"Oberscharfuhrer, I need to speak with you." Again I feel panicky, but puff myself up the way I think Aron would.

"Who are you?" The staff sergeant glares at me, his hand on his pistol.

I introduce myself and explain my role in the village. "I need to know where you're taking these citizens."

"Citizens?" He laughs, then stops quickly. "These are Jews, and all Jews are to be rounded up and taken to Warsaw. Those are my orders."

"That boy isn't Jewish." I point to Jakub. "See his blond hair and blue eyes?"

"He was found in the house of a Jew."

"Yes. Dr. Levi offered him a room until the roof on his house could be repaired." I hold my hands in a supplicant manner. "He isn't Jewish, Sergeant. I swear. He's nothing more than a poor Polish farmer."

The NCO looks at Jakub and hesitates a moment. He looks from me to Jakub then motions for him to get off the truck. He is given a little shove by Marta Spiegelman who nods at me slightly and smiles.

As Jakub alights, the sergeant turns and looks at me menacingly. "Are there any other Jews in this village?"

I hesitate for a moment and start to tell him there are none.

"You lie to me, policeman, and I find another Jew, or even if I learn another Jew was here, then I'll return and burn the whole village and kill everyone in it. But first, I'll hang you in the middle of the square." He glares at me and pulls his cap over his eyes, making the skull insignia more prominent.

Still I hesitate and look around; the eyes of everyone are wide as the threat is heard by them as well. I speak quietly, hesitantly. "There's the school teacher. He isn't here."

"The school teacher? What's his name?" He puts his face close to mine and I can feel his breath.

"Zus Malbin." My bravado is gone and the fear has returned.

"Malbin, Zus. Come forward now." He walks away from me. "Zus Malbin, come out now or I'll kill everyone here."

I turn Jakub away from the soldiers and walk towards a small crowd, too frightened to look at Dr. Levi or the Spiegelmans to see the judgment and disbelief in their eyes. I have betrayed them as surely as I betrayed Malbin.

"Stop, policeman!" The sergeant comes running towards me, his pistol drawn. He points the pistol at Jakub's head. "Malbin, come out now or I'll kill this man first."

"I'm here."

We turn to see Zus emerge from the crowd nearest the store. His face is clean-shaven and he has cut the ringlets from his hair. He walks towards us and the NCO turns the pistol towards him. They walk past us and Malbin never turns his eyes to look into mine, and for that I am grateful.

"Is that Zus?" Jakub doesn't recognize the teacher at all, and I admit he looks very different with the shave and haircut.

"Yes, Jakub. Now stay with me and don't ask me any questions until later."

"Yes, Filip."

We mingle with the crowd and watch as the truck carrying the Jews of Katy disappears in a cloud of dust. All of the soldiers mount the trucks and are preparing to depart when the sergeant walks towards me.

"You, policeman. Come here."

I motion to Jakub to stay where he is and I join the German. "Yes, Sergeant."

"My name is Heinz Hirt, Oberscharfuhrer SS. I want you to watch for any Jews in this area. If you find them, arrest them and hold them for us. They're like mice. Once we see them, they scatter and run in every direction." His lower lip juts out and he stands with his hands on his hips. "You do this and I'll know who is a friend to Germany." He snaps his arm in the air. "Heil, Hitler."

I lift my hand and nod. I watch him climb into the truck's cab, as the engine roars and disappears behind the dust in its wake.

"We do need rain." A woman from the edge of the village comments as she saunters off.

"Where're they taking Dr. Samuel?" Jakub's eyes are misty as he looks at me, wringing his hands and biting his lower lip.

"To Warsaw." The impact of my promise weighs heavily upon me at that moment, as Jakub looks in the direction of the trucks and his eyes fill with tears.

"Come on, my friend. We'll stay in Dr. Levi's house while he's gone. We can watch over his things and protect the property." I don't know what else to say.

"Good. We'll keep it clean just like Dr. Samuel. We'll follow the rules of the house, too. We'll have it just like he likes it, won't we, Filip?" He wipes his tears and smiles.

"Sure, Jakub. We'll keep the house for him until he returns."

CHAPTER NINE

Jakub and I close Spiegelman's store, nailing planks over the broken window and repairing the door as best as we can. Already many things are missing, looted I suppose, by the Germans and townspeople, those always looking to get something for nothing. Yet, how are Jakub and I going to manage without the store? We, too, will be taking the things we need, but I promise to keep a tally of all we remove, not knowing how we can repay them.

The Germans continue to come through Katy looking for Jews and causing mischief. I don't see the NCO again and am grateful as I remember our last encounter, and speculate the sergeant is a man of violence who needs little pretense to exercise his authority over others.

A pall descends over our village, over all of Poland. Warsaw surrendered on October first, but the Polesie Defense group fought both German and Russian forces and held out until October 5th. The area east of Warsaw has been annexed into Germany, and the land east of the Bug River and Brest is now Russia. The center of Poland, including Warsaw, Krakow, and Katy are now considered part of the General Government. It is here the Germans intend to send all Jews.

Our village goes about its business, but all of us, except Jakub, keep watch fearing another truck loaded with German soldiers will suddenly appear in the village square. We talk about mundane things, avoiding the subjects most on our minds, not looking at the Spiegelman's store, a boarded up building that looks as sad as some of us feel. And the nights seem darker, as the lantern, our beacon, now hangs idle.

With all the changes, Jakub is happy. He feels important cleaning Dr. Levi's home and insuring the store is still boarded up and secure from looters. He busies himself repeatedly in these tasks, performing the same chores five or six times a day. I allow him to do this knowing I should find other things for him, but he's happy and I don't want to do anything that will disrupt his mood.

But he comes in today as I work at my desk, his head hung low. "Filip?"

I meet his eyes, but he looks away. "Yes."

He hesitates for a long time; so long I become irritated with him.

"Filip, I've done everything I should do." He looks around the tiny office, avoiding eye contact with me. "Can I do something else?"

"I'm going riding around the area this afternoon, just checking out everything. You want to come with me?"

He looks at me and his eyes widen. "Yes. That would be fun."

I hitch a mule from one of the Jewish farms to an old buggy of Dr. Levi's, and set off with Jakub beside me. He is smiling and looking about as eager for an adventure as when the three of us used to jump in stacks of hay.

I show him how I hold the reins, pulling both leather strips over my hand into my palm, holding them with my fingers, and pulling on them to keep the reins tight enough for the animal to respond to any motion. He watches several times before he is willing to try it.

Slowly he takes the left strap and pulls it over his hand, closing his fingers on it. He accepts the right strap and attempts to pull it over his hand, but drops the first, which falls into the dust and is dragged along.

I take back the reins and get the mule to stop. I notice where we are and, as I pick up the leather strap, I glance at the charred building across from us.

Jakub, too, is looking at the ruins and turns back to me. "That's Dr. Samuel's syn... syna... er, church."

I set the brake on the wagon and tie both straps around the handle. "Stay here, Jakub. I want to get a closer look."

I walk to where the front door used to be and kick some of the boards. I don't remember any smoke recently and don't know when the building burned. I step over some unburned timbers and push several aside with the toe of my boot. Everything is cold and it is evident the fire had been some days before and it had burned hot. I continue to look around and pick up the slight scent of coal oil, concluding the fire was deliberately set. I sort through the rubble looking for something recognizable, something to tell me what happened here.

Then I spot it: two thin pieces of metal with a clasp at the top and hinged where they join. I unsnap it and pry the two pieces apart, like opening a bag as if there was one attached to it. I look at it closely and remember Dr. Levi clutching his medical bag tightly. I feel sick to my stomach at the thought. I turn and retch, dry and forceful, sickening.

I realize that Katy's Jews weren't taken to Warsaw, but only as far as their synagogue. I think of them, of the appreciative look in Marta Spiegelman's eyes when Jakub was released to me. I remember the terrified look on Marek's face as he stumbled down the steps, and the shock in Dr. Levi's features. And I remember the resigned look of Zus Malbin as he was escorted past me, not even trying to look at me.

I turn to find Jakub standing at the front of the building, a look of concern on his face. "Are you sick, Filip?"

"No, Jakub, just something that smelled bad and caused me to vomit." I walk towards him and drop the metal frame of the bag, fearful he will recognize it too.

He starts back towards the buggy and I follow slowly, picking my way around the ashes and partially burned timbers and boards. I stumble on a large piece of wood, a cross beam, perhaps, rolling it slightly. Beneath it lies the exposed, blackened hand of a child, its fist clenched tightly, holding the cloth and straw of what once was a doll.

I feel it deep in my stomach and glance to see Jakub watching me. I struggle and suppress the urge to vomit, but my face and body break into a sweat and I feel terribly nauseous and sick, not just in my body, but in my mind and soul.

This is something beyond my imagination, beyond anything I can explain, and I am committed more than ever to my promise to Aron, for I think he knew the evil of which these Germans were capable. Now I know it too, and know all Poles, all Jews, all men and women of every description are in mortal danger.

We continue past the synagogue and witness other changes in our land, burned buildings, barns, sheds, and homes, entire farms destroyed. Jakub can only look and wonder, but I recognize them as the homes of Jews, farmers who had lived here long before I came. We don't explore the ruins of these buildings, fearful I will learn more than I want to know, and fearful it will be too much for Jakub.

It is Sunday and an old urge has arisen in me. "Jakub, let's you and me go to church this morning."

He looks at me with a funny expression. "The church is gone, Filip."

I think for a minute and realize he is talking of the burned synagogue. "No, Jakub, not Dr. Levi's church. The Catholic church on the other side of the village."

"Father Jan's church?" His eyes brighten.

"Yes, Father Jan's church."

I help him with clean clothes and brush his shoes, remembering Aron using butter to polish his in Brest. I, too, wear clean clothes, the best I have as we walk the short distance to church. Our neighbors speak, surprised to see us, but welcome us to the congregation.

Aron hadn't been a believer and hadn't taught Jakub what to do in the church, and I struggle to remember all that I was taught before I came to Katy. I instruct Jakub quietly and nudge him towards a bench near the door. The mass begins with the singing of a hymn and Jakub's face lights up brighter than anytime I can remember.

We struggle with the ritual, following the example of those around us, but don't participate in the sacrament, as I remember from my childhood the need of confession before communion. We sit back and watch as Father Jan, seemingly ancient, as old as anyone I have ever known, steps onto the platform, placing the pages of his sermon in front of him.

"Today, my friends, I wish to read from the gospel of Luke, chapter twenty, verses twenty-one through twenty-five." He clears his throat and puts on his thin glasses, pulling the pieces over his ears.

"They asked him, 'Teacher, we know that you speak and teach rightly, and show no partiality, but truly teach the way of God. Is it lawful for us to give tribute to Caesar, or not?' But he perceived their craftiness, and said to them, 'Show me a coin. Whose likeness and inscription has it?' They said 'Caesar's.' He said to them, 'Then render unto Caesar the things that are Caesar's, and to God the things that are God's.'

"Now you and I are faced with a similar situation." He lifts his head and looks at the uplifted faces. "We must render unto Caesar the things that are Caesar's."

He removes his glasses and fidgets, before gripping the podium and continuing. "Caesar is now Adolf Hitler, and Germany is now Rome. Therefore, we must render unto Germany the things that are Germany's."

He sips from his glass of water. "I'm not talking about coins or money; I'm not talking about property or land; I'm talking about laws."

He again puts on his glasses, more slowly than the first time, more deliberately. "I have received this from the General

Government in Krakow, from Hans Frank, governor general." The priest holds the paper with the German seal for all to see.

He then holds it in front of him. "All Jews are Communists and all Communists are to be killed." He lays the paper down and removes the glasses. "Render unto Caesar the things that are Caesar's."

The priest looks nervous and his speech is more strained than normal.

"I want to remind you," he pauses and looks at the congregation closely, more intently, "Communists are atheists and are not deserving of our tears or our efforts to save them. They have burned the churches of the faithful and prohibited worship in their own lands."

The priest's face reddens and he grips the podium more tightly. "I want to remind you, brothers and sisters, that an evil has resided amongst us and is now being cleansed by fire. The communists are being cauterized from our society and are being confined to the hellfire they so richly deserve."

He sips water and clears his throat. "Don't cry tears for those taken from our midst. They cried no tears when they murdered our Savior and Lord, Jesus Christ." He nods and smiles briefly. "Yes, I'm talking about the Jews. They are gone from our village and will never return."

He releases the podium and stands erect. "It is the law. Render unto Caesar the things that are Caesar's. Whether we like it or not, it is the law."

As he returns to the altar and the organist returns to her instrument, I motion to Jakub to follow me.

He waits until we are outside before he pulls on my sleeve. "They were going to sing, Filip. I wanted to stay and sing with them."

"You don't even know the words, Jakub."

He looks down and rubs his foot across the loose gravel, much the way I had seen Aron do. "I know, but I can hum. And I like the singing. It's pretty."

"Yes, it's pretty, but I don't like what Father Jan said about the Jews."

"Oh, it's alright, Filip. Dr. Levi said that is the way it is. People like Father Jan don't like people like Dr. Levi or Zus or Marek or Marta, but they still come when they need a doctor." He looks at me with his head tilted slightly. "And they come to school even though they don't like Jews."

I smile at him surprised he remembers that. "I've changed since then, Jakub."

He punches me lightly on the shoulder and shakes his head. "It's too bad Father Jan doesn't change."

CHAPTER TEN

It is a mild winter with little activity. We occasionally see Germans in trucks and trucks filled with men, workers, I think, taken by the Germans to the east. It is near spring when the tanks and other heavy equipment rolls through Katy and the other villages, all going towards Brest, and it is rumored the Germans are building fortifications all along the border with Russia. They are moving their tanks and artillery into the earthworks, which are being built by the forced labor of Poles.

We are lucky and escape the labor roundups, but that ends in March. As magistrate, it is my responsibility to find as many men as I can to work on the fortifications. As constable, I am exempt from going and can protect Jakub at the same time.

Suddenly, Katy seems deserted. Market day comes and goes with only a few vendors coming into the village, and these are women. Few men remain and those receive harsh looks from the women of the village. Jakub and I also receive those looks as we seem to be idle anyway, and we are.

Jakub continues to perform the repetitious chores of cleaning Dr. Levi's house and checking the store, all tasks which are unnecessary, at least, unnecessary to those who witness them, but they are necessary to him. I, too, am idle, what with no men to cause trouble there is little for a policeman to do.

Spring comes and Jakub wanders into the forests or walks to the nearby farms, reporting to me all the things he sees. He is saddened by the absence of the beehives, as the farmer has been gone for a long time. But he still finds things that fascinate him. I marvel at his ability to find something wonderful in the simplest things and smile at his excitement.

May brings a letter from Aron, addressed to Jakub in care of Dr. Levi. It is dated May 10, 1940, from a prison in Smolensk. I let Jakub hold it and look at the lettering as he places both hands on the table, the pages between them. He stares intently at his brother's words. Slowly he hands me the letter, his hand trembling, his eyes misty.

Jakub, my brother,

I hope you are well. It is spring now and I can smell the aroma of freshly tilled earth and can picture the rows of young wheat stretching as far as I can see.

I am well. The Russians are holding us in a prison and there is a lot of debate of what to do with us. There is a rumor we will be taken by train to Siberia where we will be forced to work. I am strong, so I know I will be able to survive that. There is also a rumor that all volunteers will be freed to fight against the Germans, as there are rumors of disagreements between Germany and Russia.

It was that way with us, as well. First the arguments, then the invasion. I will probably volunteer. After all, I'm a soldier and that is what I was trained to do. I would rather fight for Poland, but, if not Poland, then I'll fight with the Russians.

I hope all is well with you and Dr. Levi. I rest easy knowing he is watching over you, he and the Spiegelmans, and Zus, and especially Filip. Tell Filip that the memory of our time in Brest sustains me at night and will sustain me for many years to come. I've been lucky to have a friend such as he. Tell him that for me, Jakub.

Jakub, I want you to obey Dr. Samuel, Marek and Marta, Zus and Filip. They will all watch over you and see that you are all right. And remember, little brother, I love you and will see you again some day.

Aron closed the letter with a postscript advising Jakub to not drink vodka with me. I smile and hand Jakub the letter. His eyes are filled with tears that roll down his cheeks. I hand him a towel and blink several times suppressing my own tears.

He pulls out the chair and sits, resting the letter on the table. "Show me my name."

I can't resist the look on his face, not sadness, but curiosity, yet more, perhaps a determination to read. I point to all the places his name is written, not saying a word and not growing irritated with him.

He runs his finger over his name as if imprinting it there. "Show me Aron's name."

I do and feel more patience with him than I have ever experienced.

"Show me your name." He looks at me with wide eyes and turns to the page, staring at the writing.

We do this several times a day for more than a week, and the pages are becoming tattered and the names are slowly disappearing. I copy the names onto another piece of paper, fold Aron's letter and put it in the envelope in which it was delivered, and start to put it away but Jakub asks to keep it.

I see him about the village stopping people, particularly children and showing them the letter, bragging about his older brother and pointing at the names of the people in it. He is proud of his brother and the letter, but it only makes him want more. I check every day, but there are no more.

He becomes sad for an hour or more, then pulls out the letter and pretends to read it as if for the first time. His desire to read all of the letter doesn't fade and he asks me each night to show him all the words and show him how to write them. That leads us to his letters, one of the things he retained from his time with Zus.

He continues to walk the lanes and visit the burned-out farms, but stays away from the burned synagogue. "I'm glad you don't go near Dr. Samuel's church, but I'm surprised as well."

"It's not a good place, Filip. It feels funny, like the cemetery, only worse."

I wonder if there really are such things as ghosts, if Dr. Levi, the Spiegelmans, Malbin, or that little girl remain at that site warning Jakub and others away.

The Germans come again towards the end of May, led by Oberscharfuhrer SS Heinz Hirt. A chill goes through me as I recall his threat when he took Dr. Levi and the others, but he has seen me and motions to me. As I approach the truck, I see Jakub standing against the railing looking at me, tears streaking his face. There are others, too, men I recognize from surrounding villages and farms.

I speak first. "Greetings, Oberscharfuhrer. What brings you to Katy?"

"These men, Constable. Lazy men idling about. Germany has need of men to do work." He looks at the truck and sneers.

"That man is not an idler, Sergeant. He's a farmer and without farmers, the people here will have nothing to eat." I walk towards the truck and point at several of the men, ending with Jakub. "Those, too, are farmers. You must leave us some men, Sergeant."

He is quiet for a few moments. "That one, the young one in the middle." He walks to the truck and points at Jakub. "You think I don't recognize him, don't you? I remember him. The one found in the home of a Jew, but you said he wasn't Jewish."

"He isn't, Sergeant, I swear."

"I think he is. Oh, don't talk about the blond hair, that probably came from a passing German soldier from the last war." He smiles at me. "He's probably a soldier's bastard with some Jew bitch."

"It's been twenty-two years since the great war, Sergeant. Jakub is too young to have been born of a German soldier."

Hirt turns full on me and hits me hard, striking me on the left cheek just below the eye. I spin and fall on my face. "Get up, you goddamn Polack! You think I can't add? You think you can correct me?"

Two soldiers stand above me, their rifles pointing at my chest. At the sergeant's order, they grab me by the arms and jerk me to my feet, while one of them spins me to face the NCO.

"I'm sorry, Oberscharfuhrer, I did not mean to correct you." My cheek burns and I can feel my left eye closing.

"Goddamn Polack." He grabs me by my shirtfront and pulls me to the back of the truck. "Get up, Constable. You can go along with the Jew-boy."

I climb aboard the truck slowly, only to have Jakub hold out his hand to me. "I will help you, Filip."

"Yeah, that's right, boy, help Filip." The German glares at us for a few moments then motions for his soldiers to climb up with us. He then proceeds to climb into the cab of the truck and bellows more orders for the driver.

The truck jerks off causing us to reach for the railing to keep from falling. I feel my cheek for the first time and realize it has swollen a great deal, putting pressure on my eye and forcing it closed. I look at Jakub who is watching me, his expression stern.

"I'll be okay." I smile as best as I can. "Where did they pick you up?"

"At Dr. Samuel's church. I was just watching it." He turns away and watches the fields go past. Then, almost in a whisper, he speaks. "Are you angry with me?"

I put my arm around him. "No, Jakub, I'm not angry, just curious about where we're going."

I realize I'm not afraid. I don't know what I feel at the moment, but I have never been struck in the face before and I'm in shock. As the truck bounces and speeds over the dusty road, my cheek aches with every bump, and my feelings turn to anger, anger towards the staff sergeant. I swear I will one day repay him for that punch.

Our direction takes us southeast to Lublin, where we board

another truck and join a convoy going further south. Oberscharfuhrer Heinz Hirt doesn't come with us, much to my regret, as my anger is still hot and needs to be spent upon him.

The pace is slower and much dustier, as we are twelfth in a long line of trucks, most of which are filled with men. It takes the rest of the day for us to reach our destination, and the sun is low in the sky when the convoy stops at a prison in Tarnow. We are all tired from fighting with the motion of the truck and want to sit down, but the German guards force us to remain standing. It is dark before we are allowed to climb down from the truck, and our sentries have been reinforced by many soldiers, all of them wearing the SS on their uniforms. We march past the trucks and into the prison, more than a thousand Polish men going to an unknown fate.

Jakub turns and looks at me. "Filip, what's going to happen?"

A man with a long stick leaps out of the darkness and strikes Jakub across the back. "No talking!"

The form disappears into the darkness and Jakub again turns to me. I shake my head and hold my hand to my lips. He nods, but I can make out the tears in his eyes. I think he understands that we are in for a difficult time.

CHAPTER ELEVEN

I discover my crueler side at Tarnow. The prison is terribly overcrowded, with criminals in all the cells and we prisoners filling the hallways, leaving only a small aisle down the middle. Space against the wall becomes the most desired, allowing us to sit with our backs against it, pull up our legs and sleep without falling onto the person next to us. Those in the middle are the most uncomfortable, nodding and catching themselves before they fall, or falling and taking a blow to the head for doing so. Those with corner spaces are the most comfortable, but only the strongest and most brutal of us hold the corners.

Sanitation is a large problem, with several buckets at either end of the hall where all of the prisoners have to relieve themselves. Space in this area is even less desirable due to the stench and filth.

Jakub and I swap spaces often, first me against the wall, then he. He sleeps slumped over and occasionally leans against the person next to him, causing harsh words and a rude shove. But that soon ends whenever I speak with them and make them realize I won't tolerate harsh behavior towards him.

As I lightly doze, listening to the rumbling from my empty stomach, Jakub sees an empty space against a cell door. He runs to it and sits in the space, smiling broadly. He waves to me and I return the gesture with a nod, and lower my head.

But as he gets comfortable, large hands come through the bars and wrap around his throat, stifling his cries and choking him. He isn't strong enough to struggle against the brawny man, larger than any man in the prison, but his kicking and flailing is enough to alert and awaken me fully.

I am no match for this man. I quickly run to the end of the hallway and pick up a bucket of filth. It is more than half filled and the vilest stuff I have ever handled. As I approach the cell, the man stands, attempting to pull Jakub to his feet, and sees me. I don't hesitate. I throw the sewage into the man's face, filling his eyes, ears, and mouth with the vile mixture. It flies into his hair and down his shirt, covering him and his cell.

But he releases Jakub. I pull Jakub to his feet and push him behind me, as we watch the convict wipe the crud from his face and scream words as vile as the stuff he is spitting from his mouth.

Jakub and I return to our space to find it is wider than when we left it, room for both of us to sit against the wall. I clean him as best as I can, and tell him he can lean on me if he wants to sleep.

The red marks on his neck are still prominent and his eyes are round and sad, but it is the look of a small boy who is sick and is sipping chicken soup from his mother. "Thank you, Filip." His voice is hoarse and raspy. "I'm sorry."

I wish I had some chicken soup for him. "It's all right. You sleep now."

They supply water for us mornings and nights, tepid and cloudy, and finally feed us on the third day. It is soup, much the temperature and appearance of the water, only flavored with turnips. It is bland with only a hint of taste, and I have never wanted salt more in my life. Jakub bears it well, better than some of the others in our hallway, not complaining, but looking at me with that hungry puppy expression. I smile and drink my soup without complaining, and he copies me.

A week passes and Jakub is more himself again, finding enjoyment in little things, even in the discomfort of the prison. Once we are settled together against the wall, he adjusts better than any of us, finding pleasure in the roaches and mice that scurry about. Most of us are repulsed, but he is fascinated and studies them whenever they come near. He puts out his hand and they climb into his palm, unafraid, the same as when the bees hovered about him. We watch with awe at his feat, surprised and disgusted at his ability to calm the vermin of the prison.

His skills don't work with all the vermin. Jakub, after relieving himself, is walking back to where I sleep and is attacked by a muscular individual accustomed to obtaining whatever he wants with the force of his strength. He pulls Jakub into his corner and is trying to force him to his knees. I know his intention before I have fully risen, and run to the corner as quickly as I can. The men part like a biblical sea clearing a path for me, and, as I reach the man, I kick with all my strength to his groin.

He roars with the attack and the pain, grabs between his legs and bends over, his head pushing Jakub against the wall. I again thrust with my foot, with more force than the last, striking his hands. The crack of the bones in his fingers is loud enough for everyone to hear as he again emits a loud bellow.

I pull Jakub from in front of the man, pushing him behind me. The rapist still clutches his groin and moans with pain, slightly bent over, but away from the wall. I grab his hair and pull his head up, realizing he is at least a head taller than me. I slam his face against the wall, shattering his nose, pull him back and slam it forward again, smearing the wall with his blood.

I slam his face several more times and can feel his body sagging, as his legs are about to buckle. I pull him away from the corner and shove him towards the opposite wall, a distance of seven or eight meters. There I throw him to the floor, where he lands in front of the waste buckets.

I reach down and tear his shirt from him, return to the corner and wipe the blood from the wall. I throw the shirt in his direction, and a couple of the inmates pass it to him, where it lands in a bucket.

Jakub looks at me, his eyes wide and he tucks his head into his shoulders. He doesn't speak, but starts to return to our space. I stop him and point to the corner.

"Now, my friend, you'll have a good place to sleep."

He looks at me, tilting his head, then looks at the corner space and the prone body behind me, before turning back to me. He shakes his head and lifts his hand towards his attacker, but doesn't speak.

"No one will bother you again, Jakub. Now you're safe."

His eyes brighten as he understands and pats me on the chest. "Thank you, Filip."

For the remainder of the time at Tarnow, both Jakub and I are allowed plenty of room. Some men look away when I look at them, but others hold my gaze and nod. The man who assaulted Jakub is taken from the prison, I thought to the hospital, but later learn he was shot. I don't feel any compassion for him. I'm not bothered as I think I should be and wonder if I am changing and becoming more like the bullies. But it doesn't matter. I am keeping my promise to Aron and Jakub is always with me.

Jakub continues charming the mice and roaches, but his talent is interrupted by the Germans as they come for us early in the morning. I learn it is June fourteenth as we are greeted with a battalion or more of well-armed soldiers. They are fully equipped with machine guns mounted on vehicles and motorcycles with sidecars also equipped with machine guns. They march us out in two lines and we walk a kilometer or more to a train siding.

They cram seventy-five to eighty men into railroad wagons, rickety old cattle carriers, which smell of manure and hay. Jakub and I are in the fourth car and there is standing room only, but the other men part and offer us spots by the open slats that make up the side. I nod my thanks to them, but Jakub doesn't seem to notice as he peers at the countryside. For him it is another adventure.

The sun is breaking the horizon when the train moves off, with German guards sitting atop the cars to prevent anyone escaping. It is strange that they consider us so dangerous as to lock us into rail cars and still post sentries.

We all wonder where we are being taken, but there are no answers other than west. Some of the men, including me, are relieved we aren't moving eastward and won't be building the earthworks around Brest, yet we know wherever we are going isn't good, and we begin to hope it isn't as bad as Tarnow.

We become excited with the approach to Krakow, a city few of us have ever seen, as I recall my home ten years earlier. We are struck by its beauty and cleanliness, even with Germans crawling over the city. The locomotive slows as it passes through the station and we can hear an announcement coming over a loudspeaker.

The German guards cheer. I don't understand the German and wish Aron was here to tell us what is being said, but one of the passengers interrupts my thoughts with a tremor in his voice. "Paris has fallen."

Our interpreter wipes tears from his eyes and speaks with a firmer voice. "The Germans have taken Paris. The French are no longer in the war."

Several of the men cross themselves and begin praying. Jakub looks at me, but the news is lost on him and I don't feel like explaining. "It's okay."

He smiles and turns back to look at the city.

Our visit in Krakow is brief as the train continues moving west. I lean against the slats next to Jakub and think what the fall of Paris will mean to us. It isn't good, I know, not the loss of an ally who could force the Germans to free Poland, and not the loss of supposedly the greatest army in Europe, for they had done nothing to help us since the war began, and I doubt their presence will be missed now.

The farmer next to me mutters softly and crosses himself. I think he is praying, but he turns to the man next to him and whispers. That man also blesses himself and calls on the Blessed Virgin to deliver him.

I change places with Jakub and nudge the man with my elbow. "What are you talking about?"

He looks at me, his eyes wide and I think it is fear of me. "Don't be afraid. I mean you no harm."

He shakes his head. "I don't fear you. I fear the Germans. They're taking us to Oswiecim."

"I don't know this place."

"Understand, it's just a rumor, but I heard it in Lublin, that the Germans are building a large camp, a labor camp at the town of Oswiecim. I heard it will be a place where they'll work us to death."

I think of what this means to me and Jakub. At least we are together and I'll be able to watch over him, but still, I don't like the uncertainty of it or the lack of control it puts on me.

"Jakub?" He turns to face me. I speak softly wanting him to listen carefully as I explain our situation. "Whatever you do, make sure you stay next to me. We mustn't get separated, you understand?"

"Yes, Filip, I'll stay next to you." He moves a little closer so our bodies are touching.

I am surprised when our bodies touch and I turn to him. He is smiling and I remember the joke he played on me many years before. "I think you understand."

He continues smiling and nods. "I stay wherever Filip is."

The train again slows as we pass over the Wisla River, reminding me of the flood that had left me alone. It is now named the Vistula, and the train crawls into the station at Oswiecim, and it, too, has been given a German name, Auschwitz. The train slows and moves onto a siding taking us to the station with a platform and single building. It stops smoothly with a squeak of its wheels and a burst of steam escaping its boiler.

We wait for several minutes until the sentries get down from their perches and take positions with their rifles and machine guns. The doors are unlatched and pushed open.

"Out! Out all of you. Line up facing the commandant." The German soldier's uniform is new, the colors still crisp, and it fits his build tightly, accentuating his muscles. He carries a long stick and holds it in front of him in both hands, his feet set apart, and barks his orders. "Out now. Line up. Los! Hurry. Move, you dogs."

A foreboding comes upon me as I look around at the massive show of German might and the impressive entourage facing us on the platform. As we wait our turn to jump off the car, I turn to Jakub and speak softly. "Don't say anything to anyone, Jakub. Be quiet and only speak if you're asked a question, and don't talk too much." We are nearing the opening. "Understand?"

He doesn't speak, but taps me on the shoulder. As I look at him, he is smiling broadly and nods his head, his eyes twinkling. I hope he won't try to joke with these Germans.

We alight the cars and stand five deep, and Jakub and I are in the third row next to each other. Shortly a tall German with the rank of untersturmfuhrer SS, a second lieutenant, steps to the microphone. He speaks in German with an interpreter repeating the address.

"You Poles are the first to come to Auschwitz. Here you work. Arbeit macht frei. Work makes you free. Say this everyday and you'll be happy and your work will be excellent.

"From here, you'll be taken to the showers and then you'll be disinfected. We want no diseases here and we expect you to be clean. After you're clean and disinfected, you'll be given soup and new clothes to wear."

He is interrupted by one of the other men on the platform, who whispers to him. He nods and removes his hand from the microphone.

"You'll not receive your uniforms until some time later. For now, keep your clothes and bathe in them.

"After you have eaten, you'll then be selected to perform jobs that meet your qualifications. Afterwards, you'll be allowed to go to barracks and rest until tomorrow.

"Your workday begins at four-thirty. You'll be given breakfast and coffee and you'll give us a full day's work."

He steps away from the microphone and nods to the guard nearest us. The German runs to the far left and motions for the men to turn left and move off, leading a column of five abreast towards the showers.

We enter the building and are pointed in the direction of a large room, where we are pushed towards the opposite end and another set of doors. Along the ceiling are showerheads dripping water from the last group, and I select one and pull Jakub with me. There is a bar of soap on the floor and I reach for it, only to have it snatched from my grasp. I straighten and meet the eyes of an elderly man whose eyes suddenly widen as he hands the soap to me. I take it, embarrassed with my effrontery, yet pleased with the power fear gives me.

The doors slams shut and water pours from the showerheads. I quickly rub the soap into my hair, face, and over my clothes. I bathe Jakub as well, and receive some surprising looks from the nearest bathers, but I don't care and continue rubbing the soap on his clothes.

I hand the soap to the old man who nods his thanks. As Jakub and I stand under the streaming water, I speak softly. "If anyone asks what kind of work you do, tell them you're a carpenter's helper. Can you remember that?"

"But I drive a truck."

"I know, Jakub, but there are no trucks here." I rub the water through his hair washing out the soap. "You're a carpenter's helper. You must remember."

He whispers to himself several times and nods. "Carpenter's..."

"Helper."

"Carpenter's helper. I'll remember, Filip."

I only hope he will.

The water stops and the doors near us open with a slam and a loud voice. "Out! Come this way. Make room for the others."

We are again herded into another large building with a wooden stall. We move into it and a German guard sprays us thoroughly with a white powder, delousing, I reason, as I tell Jakub to hold his breath. I should have warned the others as well, for several breathe in the dust and cough violently.

Jakub is again having fun, enjoying the experience of being covered with the white dust, just like the time the bullies were picking on him, throwing flour in his face. Jakub laughed then, too, thinking it was a lot of fun.

Our barracks are solid buildings of brick with wide bunk beds that can sleep three or four across and three levels high. Jakub wants to sleep on the top bunk and I join him, not all that comfortable, but he is happy and it isn't much of a problem for me.

They call us to formation immediately and give us a watery soup with a hint of turnips for flavoring. I drink mine quickly and watch as Jakub drinks his slowly. There is no indication from his eyes or face that he is enjoying the soup or hating it.

We again queue up in two rows and march to where the German officer who addressed us stands alongside another man of lesser rank. It is slow and Jakub stands in one line and I the other, he heading towards the younger noncom and me to the officer.

I stand several men back of Jakub and watch as the young sergeant asks Jakub what he did.

"Er… carpenter's…"

"You're a carpenter?"

Jakub doesn't say anything and he isn't smiling. He looks about and his lower lip begins to tremble.

The German turns to the officer. "Lieutenant Grabner? Could you help me, Sir?"

The officer stops and steps towards the younger man. "What is it?"

"I think this man is stupid."

Grabner's eyes widen and he smiles. "He's Polish, isn't he?" He laughs and starts to return to my row.

"I think, Lieutenant, he is mentally defective."

"Hm. Maybe." Grabner takes a step closer to Jakub, more intent on questioning him.

I step out of line and take a step closer to the German. "He is a laborer, sir."

Grabner looks at me with a cold stare. "And what kind of laborer is he?"

"Odd jobs, carpenter's helper, and farm worker. He's a good worker, Lieutenant. He can drive a truck, too."

Jakub speaks softly to the young noncom. "I'm a truck driver."

The German officer turns and looks at Jakub, then whirls and slaps me with the back of his hand, forcing me to catch myself. "Don't you dare address an SS officer unless you're told to do so. Understand?"

"Yes, Untersturmfuhrer. I'm sorry, Untersturmfuhrer." My heart is filled with anger and I make a mental note that there is another I will have to kill before all of this is over.

Grabner releases a breath and nods towards me. "And what's your profession?"

I hesitate, but tell him the truth. "I'm a constable in a small village, sir."

"A policeman, eh?" He turns and smiles at the noncom. "We need policemen. I'm going to make you a kapo, Pole." He pulls Jakub from the line and puts him next to me. "And I'm going to put this man in your kommando for construction. There is much work to do."

Grabner sneers at me. "And if this man fails to pull his load, then I'll shoot the both of you." He shoves us towards our barracks and laughs loudly, loud enough for all of us to hear and shouts, "Arbeit macht frei."

CHAPTER TWELVE

We rise early the next morning with whistles and the ringing of bells. We gather in the yard beside the barracks, row upon row of us dressed in our wrinkled clothes, some with chafed skin from the baths the day before, as the harsh soap wasn't rinsed away thoroughly. Jakub and I feel pretty good, as I move him into a rank, and I walk along the line to report to another kapo who walks back and forth in front of the prisoners.

I stop short of the man and wait for him to turn in my direction and, as he does so, he stops and stares at me a long time. "There'd better be a good reason for you to be standing here, Polack." He frowns and stands with his hands on his hips.

"I was told to report to you. Untersturmfuhrer Grabner made me a kapo and told me I was to work in the construction kommando." It is bold, but I don't feel there is a lot to lose.

He studies me for a few moments and glares at me, his voice not as loud as before. "And what crimes have you committed that would make you a kapo?"

I guess, at his question and appearance, that he is accustomed to working with criminals, and, perhaps, is a criminal himself. I know it's best to hide my former occupation as constable. "I've committed no crimes. I was defending a friend."

He continues to glare at me. "And that makes you tough enough for this work?"

"After I smashed his face and threw him in the sewage, the SS dragged him away and shot him." I don't smile or change my expression.

He smiles slightly and nods slowly. "Okay, Kapo. I'm Boris, arbeitkapo for these barracks." He shows me his baton. "I catch you going easy on these men, then I'll smash your face and throw you in the sewage. You understand?"

"Yes, Kapo Boris. You'll have no reason to doubt me." I turn without being dismissed and walk back to where my barrack mates stand.

I receive an armband denoting my rank and a baton, smooth and evenly painted, obviously unused. We receive numbers as well, and, as a kapo, I receive one of the first, number forty-four. Jakub is given number eighty-nine, which I commit to memory so I can get him to practice it.

We get coffee that is barely colored and tastes of grain more than coffee, and soup again, watery with a bare taste of turnips. Then we march to a marshy field and are given tools. I watch as Jakub holds a shovel and looks around, confused as to what to expect.

A rough looking kapo approaches Jakub and pokes him in the ribs with his baton, scaring him. I run quickly to where the man is about to strike him again, but stop him with my own stick, slapping him across the forehead, dislodging his hat. "You tend to your group and I'll tend to mine."

The man backs away and seems a bit cowed by my temerity. I kick him in the rear and send him off with a warning. "You come here again and I'll thrash you so you'll know your place."

I turn to Jakub. "You must work. Look at the others and do what they're doing. Look busy, my friend."

I push him towards the marsh causing him to stumble. "I'm sorry, Jakub, but I must be hard on you. Otherwise, we'll both be shot."

Jakub smiles and nods. "I'll do what you say." He walks towards one of the workers and mumbles softly. "Filip is not mean. He protects me."

He learns to watch and do as the others do and we have no further trouble from the other kapos. When necessary, I strike a worker who isn't working as hard as others, but only when other kapos, Kapo Boris, or the SS are watching me. Boris even congratulates me for handling the other kapo, teaching the man to do his own job.

There are several construction gangs in the stammlager, or Auschwitz as it came to be called. The construction company was called Bauleitung, or the Auschwitz Construction Company, and we are the slave labor for all the projects. We build barracks, mostly, large buildings with six rooms filled with bunk beds like our own billet.

I learn the thirty kapos before us are mostly criminals who come from KL Sachsenhausen, a concentration camp in Germany, transferred to Auschwitz to serve as inmate police for the SS. They are a bad lot and sadistic in their treatment of the prisoners, showing no regard for age and physical condition. One afternoon I watch as three of the kapos pummel an old man to death for losing a shoe. One of the kapos later produces the shoe from behind a woodpile, laughing at his joke. I learn that any man without shoes is shot by the SS or killed by the kapos, and his body thrown in a large pit.

I am one of them, but vow not to be like them. Yet it affords me extra rations and bread, which allows Jakub to have more as well. Often, Jakub endears himself to one of our fellow prisoners by giving away his extra bread. They take it greedily, but he doesn't mind, always asserting they work harder than he and need it more. I reason it is his own innocence and gullibility that leads him to show such generosity.

We have been at the stamlager for nearly three weeks when we are mustered one morning for roll call. There is a prisoner absent from a labor gang further down the lane, but we all have to remain standing as another count is taken. We kapos walk back and forth in front of our gangs and count and recount the number of prisoners. There are ninety-four men in my labor gang and they are all there the first and last time I count.

The SS is furious, storming back and forth and slapping several of the kapos, finally deciding Kapo Boris is missing a man from his gang. The guards spread out and begin searching through the barracks, until Untersturmfuhrer Grabner arrives. He is fuming and curses the noncom in charge. He slaps Kapo Boris, strips the armband from his arm, and takes the baton. Grabner begins beating the arbeitkapo about the head, opening the man's scalp, and forcing him to his knees. The German kicks Boris in the stomach and spits on him, then orders him to take the place of the escaped worker, ordering all labor gangs to remain standing until the escaped man is found.

It is my unpleasant task to keep my gang on their feet, as I circle around them and in between the rows, urging them to stay awake, tapping them with the baton, goading them. But I do and only have to use the stick a couple of times to get a man's attention or to force one to his feet.

Jakub, too, is uncomfortable and doesn't understand why he can't sit down. I watch him closely and talk to him often. "Stay awake, Jakub, shuffle your feet, stamp them, but stay awake."

"I'm tired, Filip. I want to lie down." He sags and starts to lower himself.

"No, Jakub." I push the baton into his ribs with enough force to make him shrink away from me, but his eyes are alert and he is again awake. "Don't make me do this, Jakub. I don't want to hurt you, but you can't lie down. You must stand here."

I notice an SS guard walking towards our gang and quickly move away from Jakub, and find another man squatting. I hit him with the stick and rouse him from a light slumber. "Get up! No one can rest." I strike him again for the benefit of the guard.

We stay on our feet and repeat this exercise all through the day, with me rousting the tired and bewildered laborers, hoping we will be sent to barracks when darkness comes. But we remain on our feet even as the night envelops the camp.

My enthusiasm is waning with each passing hour. Former Kapo Boris is taken to the hospital along with a number of other workers who fall on their faces and receive severe beatings. We never see any of them again.

My gang makes me proud as none of them fall, or those that do are helped to their feet by those around them. Some are leaning on their neighbor, but manage to stand on their own whenever the SS come near. I goad them to be the only labor gang in Auschwitz to not give in, to stand firm and show them that Poles are as strong or stronger than Germans.

Jakub, too, responds, finally understanding it isn't me forcing them to remain on their feet, but the Germans. He smiles at me whenever I approach and looks pleased to see me. "I'm standing, Filip. I don't fall down."

He makes me proud and I return his smile. "Thank you, little brother."

Grabner returns after midnight. He looks at each of the gangs and speaks to the guards as he walks. He passes me and my labor gang, stops and motions for me to come before him.

I trot towards him and stop just out of reach. I don't speak, but stand at attention.

"You're the policeman, aren't you?" A hint of a smile shows on his face.

"Yes, Untersturmfuhrer." I try to avoid meeting his eyes for fear he will see my hatred of him.

"I'm told you have managed to keep your gang on their feet without any collapsing or going to the hospital."

"Yes, Untersturmfuhrer."

He looks them over and turns his steely gaze on me. "You're too easy on them. Maybe they're allowed more rations than the other gangs. Maybe you don't push them enough."

I realize the trap in his questions, but know I can't argue with him. "Yes, Untersturmfuhrer. I'll be harder on them. I'll see they only get what they deserve."

"Take your gang back to the barracks. Keep them there until they're called." He nods and moves off.

I had feared another slap; relieved it hadn't come. I turn to the gang and motion towards the barracks where we all collapse and sleep soundly.

But it is a short sleep. The bells ring and the SS guards roust us from our bunks at the normal time and push us outside for assembly. The count comes first and I have to keep clearing my mind and concentrate on the prisoners before me. Twice I count and get different numbers, but I count twice more and reach the figure of ninety-four both times. I report to the SS noncom and give him my count.

We receive our coffee and soup, and I find a potato in my bowl, the first real potato I have seen since Tarnow. I take a bite and relish the taste of it, but feel guilty. I turn to Jakub and give him the potato, which he takes and smiles at me. He eats the potato as slowly as he had accepted it, chewing it very carefully and swallowing the juice.

Shortly after the escape incident, all of the kapos in barracks are given separate quarters in the same building. The SS figure there is strength in numbers and guess the labor population won't seek revenge on us while we are together. That is what we are told.

I think differently. I feel they give us these quarters and extra rations to have more control over us, to harden us towards the prisoner population and to push them more ruthlessly.

And it leaves Jakub alone. I talk with his bunkmates and tell them he is protected by me and any harm to him will bring pain from me.

It is okay for several days, but an outsider, a laborer from another building sneaks into the barracks and finds Jakub moving more slowly than usual. He attacks Jakub, hitting him about the head and attempts to pull off his pants, tearing them.

But Jakub fights back, kicking at his assailant and lashing out with his hands, striking the skinny man several times. Yet it is to no avail, as the man overcomes him with a blow to the face. He is turning Jakub onto his stomach when several of laborers return to the barracks.

The man holds his hand over Jakub's mouth and threatens to kill him if he makes a noise. They remain still until the laborers leave, but the assailant is afraid and removes his hand from Jakub's mouth. He makes Jakub remove his shoes and hand them to him.

Jakub is too frightened to resist, even though he knows anyone without shoes will be taken by the SS. With the shoes, the skinny man jumps from the bunk and runs out of the room. Jakub attempts to follow him, but can't catch up.

He comes to me. "Filip."

I see the bruises about his face, the trickle of blood from his nose, the torn trousers, and the missing shoes, and I guess what happened. "Jakub?" I start to ask him if he is okay, but can see he isn't. "Who did this?"

Tears well in his eyes. "He stole my shoes." He wipes the tears with the back of his hand. "I don't want to go with the guards."

"You won't."

"But I have no shoes." He pulls up his trousers to show me.

Thankfully it is still dark and I have time to find him shoes. I walk him back into the barracks and search all the rooms, and I listen as he tells me what happened, again thankful he isn't hurt worse. Search as I can, I don't find any shoes.

As we exit the barracks, Jakub points to a tall, skinny man walking quickly towards his labor gang. I watch him as he stands to the back of the gang next to mine. I tell Jakub to return to the barracks and wait for me.

I complete the count and make my report. I get my soup with another potato and drink it quickly, putting the potato in my pocket. I align myself along the pathway and wait for the skinny prisoner to come along. As he nears me, I throw my baton into his midsection, causing him to stumble and run into me.

"You oaf!" I strike the man across the face and knock him flat, just as his kapo walks up.

"What's this?"

"This musselmann, this garbage ran into me. I'm going to teach him a lesson." I turn to the kapo and nod. "If you don't care."

"He's nothing to me. Do what you want. One less matters little to me." With that he walks a quick pace towards his labor gang.

I grab the man by his arm and lift him to his feet, and turn to my gang. "Go to work. Mind your business and work, or I'll pound you 'til you drop. Go!"

I don't watch them leave, too much in a rush to complete the business with the skinny assailant. I push and drag him into the barracks and confront him with Jakub.

Jakub nods. "He took my shoes. He hit me."

I slap the man with the baton, buckling him and forcing him to the floor. He moans.

I quickly remove his shoes and hand them to Jakub. "Put them on. Quickly."

"These are not my shoes, Filip."

I slap the man with my hand and growl in his ear. "Where are his shoes?"

The man hesitates and I strike him again. "Where are they?"

"I gave them to a friend."

"Then you'll die." I lift him from the floor and kick him out the door, where he lands sprawled in the dirt.

Jakub and I walk past him and I hand Jakub my potato. "Eat quickly. Tonight, I'll move you closer to the kapo room, but you must learn to get out of the barracks sooner, Jakub. I don't want something like this to happen again."

"I'll learn, Filip, you'll see." He eats the potato faster than he ate the first and wipes his hands on his pants. "He tore my pants, too."

I push him along walking as fast as I can, seemingly goading him with the stick. "I'll get you some pants, too."

We reach the labor gang before they arrive at the work site, relieved Jakub can join the work without being noticed. I walk among the laborers and tap them on the shoulder with the baton, thanking them for working without prodding.

One of the older men looks at me, his eyes narrow. "Is the boy all right?"

It is the first time anyone has acknowledged Jakub's existence and showed concern. I think it unusual, in a place like this, that anyone can show concern for someone other than themselves.

"Yes, he's okay. Thank you."

I realize that day that the men under me act much like the people of Katy towards Jakub, understanding he isn't as capable as them and needs help and protection. He received it from Dr. Levi and the others of the village and I hope he will receive it here as well.

It is a long day and I am hungrier than usual. I wish I had eaten the potato and wish I had one for everybody in the labor gang. I don't hit any more people this day and feel better for it.

The man that assaulted Jakub didn't join his work gang and wasn't where we left him. I later heard he was found by the SS and was taken to block eleven where he was put against the black wall and shot.

Like the rapist in Tarnow, I should feel badly about his death; after all, I knew they would kill him, but I don't feel much of anything. Again I have fulfilled my promise to Aron and taken care of Jakub. I never knew the promise would require so much of me, or require that I become someone who would be a stranger to him.

CHAPTER THIRTEEN

The months pass slowly or quickly, depending on what you are doing and whether or not you accept it. For most of the prisoners it is drudgery of rising early, drinking tasteless coffee and worse soup, being counted, and marching to work, only to be counted again; then work at the endless task of clearing the marsh and erecting more barracks, lining up for another count and marching back to their bunks, where they are counted yet again.

It is different for Jakub and me. I like my role as kapo. I like the privileges it gives me as well as the power to protect Jakub. He, too, seems to like his routine, always waiting for me as I roust the others, smiling as always, eager to spend the day in the fields working.

I find different jobs for him, simpler jobs of carrying materials to the carpenters or bricklayers, and running errands for me whenever it doesn't necessitate his having to communicate a lot or come under the scrutiny of the SS. He is happy with anything asked of him, always giving his best to whatever he does.

Towards the end of winter we see Hauptbannfuhrer SS Rudolf Hoss, the commandant of Auschwitz, accompanied by Obersturmfuhrer SS Josef Kramer, Auschwitz's second in command. They walk near my labor gang and I send Jakub to the far end with some boards, telling him to stay there until the Germans leave.

Hoss talks with Grabner, his manner very animated with his hands sweeping in a panorama of the entire stamlager. Grabner listens intently to his superior, making notes on a small pad, shuffling his feet occasionally to stay in step with the commandant. Behind them follows a small entourage of SS and Kapo Bruno Brodniewicz, inmate number one, the senior prisoner in Auschwitz. With him is Rapportfuhrer Leon Wieczorek, prisoner number thirty, who is in charge of discipline in the stamlager. Both men had come from Sachsenhausen to be the whips of the SS.

I know them both and have felt the lash of their tongues for going too easy on my charges. I take this opportunity to show them I'm not as soft as they think I am. I walk amongst the members of my gang and yell for them to put their backs into it. I push and shove several of them and strike one across the buttocks. I help raise a wall, standing between two men and pushing with one arm and screaming as loud as I can.

Hoss and his party stop and glance in my direction. Kapo Leon is sent in my direction and I imagine I will be congratulated for working my gang so hard.

He stops some distance from me. "Kapo, come here." His voice is harsh and urgent.

I trot towards him and stop just out of reach. "Yes, Kapo Leon."

"We're expecting some important visitors in two weeks. During that visit, you will not raise your voice to the prisoners, nor will you carry your stick." He stares at me. "Do you understand?"

I disregard safety for curiosity. "No, sir. I don't understand. Could you tell me why?"

"Why?" He speaks harshly in German, a sneer on his face. "Hier ist kein warum." He takes a deep breath and speaks softly so I will understand. "There is no why here." He studies me for a moment. "You only need to do as you're told."

"Yes, sir." I don't turn away, feeling he is very dangerous and will take it as insolence.

He doesn't dismiss me, either. "Tell no one what I'm about to tell you."

He puffs himself up and looks over my head to the half

completed barracks. "Reichsfuhrer Heinrich Himmler is coming to inspect the stamlager. Everything will be in perfect order for him."

"I understand. I'll make sure my gang is in perfect order."

"Good." He starts to leave, but turns back to me, looking at me briefly, before diverting his eyes. "You'll be given new clothes tonight: uniforms. You will wear a purple letter with yellow trim at all times on it." He looks at me briefly. "You'll instruct all of the haftlinge, the prisoners, that failure to wear the uniform and letter 'P', will result in their death." He again looks away and takes a breath. "If any of them fail, Kapo, they'll be shot and so will you."

We work very hard for several weeks, and even plant flowers throughout the camp. A sign is erected over the entrance with the slogan Grabner had used on our arrival, 'arbeit macht frei'. We work, but we aren't free. I doubt we will ever be free.

The commandant desires to make a good impression on Himmler demonstrating German efficiency. I receive orders to form a lagertischlerei, a carpentry workshop, near our barracks. I remember the old man, the oldest man in our gang, the one from our first day here, is a carpenter.

"You, what is your name?" Few people are ever asked their names, as our pasts belong to another world.

He hesitates. "Jan." He looks away briefly before turning to face me. "Jan, Kapo. My name is Jan Vodijik."

"Well, I have a job for you." I motion for him to join me away from the others. "You're a good carpenter."

"Thank you, Kapo. How may I help you?"

"The Germans want a workshop, a carpenter's workshop. Can you set one up for the lager?"

"Yes, if I have the right tools and the right workers."

I put my hand on his shoulder and step closer to him, forcing him to raise his head to look at me. "You may choose whomever you wish, but you must also take one of my choosing."

He smiles and holds his position. "Of course, Kapo. The boy? I'll watch over him for you."

"Thank you, Jan. You'll be my vorarbeiter and select twenty men to work under you."

"I don't want to be an underkapo. I'll just be Jan Vodijik, carpenter."

"You'll be a kapo, or I'll have to find someone else. Understand?"

"Yes, Kapo."

"You don't have to beat anyone, Jan, but someone has to be in charge."

He nods slowly and starts to leave.

"Jan?" I wait until he faces me. "I'm sorry about the soap."

He nods and smiles.

"I'm Filip, Jan, and as kapo, you get extra rations."

Jan takes Jakub and begins the work of creating the workshop and by the time of Himmler's visit, everything is prepared. The prisoners are assembled for the count, dressed in their striped uniforms with the purple "P" sewn over the heart. Our meal is more substantial as each man receives a potato in his soup and a slab of bread. The coffee, too, is black and hints of real beans, and, as weak as it is, it is wonderful.

After the morning assembly, we march to our work sites. It feels unusual to walk without my baton, but it is resting on my bunk, idle until the dignitaries leave.

I see the convoy of cars coming towards us, creating clouds of dust and announcing their arrival with the roar of engines. Himmler and Hoss sit in the lead car, a Mercedes convertible with a powerful motor, which sounds like a truck engine. The dust cloud envelops them, and as the dust settles, I can see Himmler glaring at the camp commandant. He brushes his uniform and exits the vehicle with a long stride, returning the salutes of the SS, his right hand raised casually.

He wears riding breeches and walks with a very stiff stride, studying the new barracks, occasionally commenting to Hoss, who fawns over the Reichsfuhrer. They are accompanied by

Grabner and other SS officers from Auschwitz, some of whom I recognize and others I don't, assuming they are from Berlin.

I continue to work and urge my men to do the same, occasionally checking the carpentry shop to ensure our visitors don't find anything that will lead to punishment. I stand at attention whenever they get close enough, too nervous to continue my rounds and too frightened to do anything else. They don't take notice of me and continue talking as if I am one of the entourage.

I overhear the instructions Himmler gives Hoss, Kramer, and Grabner. The Reichsfuhrer stands with his hands behind his back and nods, his face contorted. "You've done well, all of you." He shifts his right leg, taking a half step and resting his hand on his thigh. "But there's much to do."

He accepts a piece of paper from a man introduced as Adolf Eichmann and hands it to Hoss. "We want you to enlarge the camp. There'll be many prisoners of war coming here. These are your orders." He accepts a small envelope from the adjutant and holds it in his hand. "We can expect many prisoners will die from work, illness, or from wounds received in battle."

Himmler brings his gaze to each of the men. "There'll not be enough room to bury them all, thus we have found a way to be rid of them." He hands Hoss the envelope. "These are the blueprints for a crematorium. All bodies of prisoners are to be cremated and their ashes properly disposed of."

Lieutenant Kramer clears his throat and speaks quickly. "And how are we to dispose of the ashes?"

Both Himmler and Hoss glare at the man's effrontery, as Grabner just looks at his feet.

Himmler answers, his voice icy and his retort terse. "That isn't my problem. It is yours."

They climb into the large car and continue their inspection, the car driving slowly so as to not raise a cloud of dust. I relax. Turning to the labor gang I observe some of the men crouching beside the steps. I quickly make my way to where they are and find them kneeling beside an older man. His frame is thin and the uniform is cavernous on him. His shoes have been taken and a rough pair with a loose sole have been left beside him.

I force the men to go back to work, shoving the last who is reluctant to leave. "His name is Michal and he is my friend." His cheeks are wet and his hands shake. "Help him, please."

The man's emotions shake me. I turn Michal over and listen to his chest, hoping for a heartbeat, or hoping he is free, I'm not sure. It is silent and I know Michal is dead.

"Go to work." I shove the man gently. "It's too late for Michal." I look at the dead body then at the man. "He's free now."

I pull Michal's body away from the steps, surprised how easy it is, how light a body could be, and leave it for the body crew. I return to my gang and motion to them to keep working. I walk the length of the crew, surprised at how my thoughts remain with the dead man, puzzled as to why I hadn't noticed him before. The gang is large, but, still, I hadn't noticed a man starve to death. It troubles me.

It is summer and we hear our first news. Germany invaded Russia and is making massive gains against a weak and surprised Russian army. We learn this as Russian prisoners-of-war begin arriving, filling the barracks we have just completed. It is overwhelming with the number of POWs, as a horde of defeated soldiers are crowded into Auschwitz.

My construction gang goes to work on the crematorium, called Krema I, but Jakub continues in the carpenter's shop assisting the old man.

The Russian prisoners keep coming and the crematorium nears completion, and we turn to building more barracks, too far from the carpenter's shop for me to watch over Jakub. The old man assures me Jakub is a good worker and promises he will watch over him. Reluctantly I agree as Jakub seems to like the old man and sees himself as taking care of Jan, much like it was with Dr. Levi.

It goes well for a week or more, but I find Jakub nursing some bruised ribs and large welts on his back. He tells me a new kapo, a Pole, beat him because he had tried to go with the old man to the hospital. I fear for the old man and slowly learn the kapo had beaten Jan very harshly, causing bleeding from his head and nose.

I am sorry for Jakub's new friend, but more concerned about how to get Jakub reassigned to my labor gang. The following morning I see the kapo in front of Jakub's gang, barking orders while another prisoner counts the workers. It surprises me he would allow a simple laborer to make the count, where it would be easy enough to miscount and tell the kapo an incorrect number.

Then I realize he can't count, something the SS or lagerkapo would frown upon.

As the gangs queue up for their coffee and soup, I approach him and tap his chest with my baton. "I need a favor."

He sneers at me and brushes me aside. I step in front of him again. "I have something valuable to offer. Aren't you interested?"

He looks around and glares at me. "What do you have that I would want?"

I smile and again tap him on the chest. "Your life. Or, at least, your position here."

He relaxes his stance. "How so?"

"You don't know how to count. If Kapo Bruno learns of this, you'll be sent back to the labor gang. If the SS learn of it, you'll be shot." I relax my stance and just look at him.

He hesitates, pondering his options. "What do you want?" He squints his eyes and speaks softly.

"Transfer one of your men to my gang."

"Sure. Take anyone you want." He sneers at me, obviously not understanding how thorough the Germans are about keeping track of prisoners.

"Yes, my friend, but it'll be necessary for you to transfer him to my gang so no one will ask questions later."

"How am I going to do that?"

"A good question. I'll give you one of mine to work in the shop, because he's a skilled carpenter. You tell them I complained of the loss of a man and that you gave me two men."

"Two? Which two?"

"The two you beat yesterday, the old man and boy."

"The old man's in the hospital, but you can have the boy." He spits on the ground. "He isn't worth much without the old man."

Jakub joins my gang as we march out to the new site, a glint in his eyes and a smile on his lips. I can only marvel at him, as do the others around him. I thought of how strange the world has become, caring about someone like Jakub, but even the more hardened among us seems to like him and are willing to protect him.

The following morning, I again encounter the kapo. He is still allowing a prisoner to make his count, but as he spots me, he comes over and shakes his head.

"I can't give you the old man."

"And why?" I don't like this man.

"He and the other Polish men in the hospital were taken to block thirteen. There, along with a bunch of Russians, the SS killed them with some sort of gas. They were cremated right after." He shows no expression at this news.

"How do you know all this?"

"My brother. He's a Sonderkommando over there. He says that they're going to kill all the Russians." He delivers this news like a weather prediction.

I want to smash him, to break open his skull with my baton, but see Jakub and realize I'm not that free. I hope a day will come, but, until it does, I will bide my time.

We continue in a tiring monotony of effort, one borne of routine of which the SS seem so fond. Their fondness doesn't extend to our cleanliness, as we aren't provided soap or clean water, forcing us to use the same murky water day after day. But Jakub washes everyday, stripping his shirt and splashing the turbid water onto his face and torso and running his hands through his hair.

His actions confuse me, almost a ritual. "Jakub, why do you bother with this? The water is filthy and you have no soap."

He smiles and looks at me, tilting his head slightly. "Meister Jan told me to always wash."

"Jan?" I don't connect the old man at first.

Jakub shakes his head again and squints his eyes. "He's my friend. He teaches me to be a carpenter. I watch over him."

I don't tell him the old man is dead and won't be coming back and hope he won't ask. "But why bathe in such water?"

"Because, Meister Jan says we mustn't forget we're men." He smiles and watches me.

"I don't understand, Jakub. What does being men have to do with bathing in dirty water?"

Jakub releases a long breath and again shakes his head. "Because if we don't bathe, then we're just animals." He again cocks his head and looks to see if I understand. "Animals are killed, Filip. We're men."

"I see, Jakub. Yes, we're men, not animals." With that I strip off my shirt and splash water under my arms and across my body, hoping to remove the scent of sweat, replacing one odor with another. But, as I wash, I think of the old man and feel ashamed I hadn't allowed him the soap first. But I swear I will remember the name of Jan Vodijik.

CHAPTER FOURTEEN

The following month new SS units arrive with more Russian POWs and Polish slave laborers. New barracks have to be built along with more crematoria and other buildings for the SS. The site of this new construction is about three kilometers from the stamlager and is designated Auschwitz II, or Birkenau. It is to be a larger camp, much larger than the first, but it isn't a place I want to work.

With the SS units comes Heinz Hirt, newly promoted to technical sergeant. He struts even more than the last time I saw him in Katy, the time I swore I would one day kill him. He spots me as well and comes towards me, his steps deliberate, a crooked smile on his lips.

"So, Polack, you didn't die after all." He seems very smug and I know I have to be careful.

I stand straight at his approach. "Yes, Hauptscharfuhrer. Congratulations on your promotion. I believe that's a new decoration as well." I think it's best to disarm him with compliments and my awareness of his success.

He beams at me and places his hands on his hips, stiff-legged and feet apart. "Yes. I was wounded fighting partisans in Russia. But I killed many and was decorated as you see."

"I trust you're well-healed from your wounds?" I can hope he will die from them.

"I'm well, fit for duty, as you see." He looks around. "What of that boy you were protecting?"

I want to lie and pretend Jakub is dead, but I can't risk it, not with a man as sadistic as Hirt. "He's part of my kommando, Sergeant, a good worker."

He smiles his crooked smile. "Good. And your labor gang builds barracks. Is this not so?"

I wonder why his interest. "Yes, Sergeant."

"Then I'll have you transferred to my block, Kapo." There is a sparkle in his eyes, one I don't trust. "We're building a lot of barracks in Birkenau, and I plan to earn another promotion for our work there. And you, Pole, are going to get it for me."

I pretend Auschwitz or Birkenau have no meaning for me, that it matters little where I work, but I don't trust Hirt nor trust myself should I be alone with him. But Jakub is another matter and it disturbs me that he is interested in Jakub.

Our barracks are similar to the ones at the stamlager, with six rooms lined with bunks set in tiers of three, with a room for the kapos. My entire labor gang is transferred to Birkenau, thus it isn't a difficult transition for Jakub. There are new prisoners as well, Poles mostly, but also Russian civilians who had crossed the paths of the German army and brought undue attention upon themselves.

The prisoners bring stories, pieced together by those who speak Russian, and some who speak Polish. I listen from a distance as a group encircles the storyteller, eager to hear news from outside the camp.

"It is easy to know the intent of these Germans, as they wear a skull on their hats. They have police units, soldiers and policemen, called Einsatzgruppen." He pauses for a translation and I remember the name from Katy with the arrival of Hirt. I remember, too, that Dr. Levi and the others hadn't been taken to Warsaw.

"They round up anyone they don't like: Russians, Poles, and Jews and kill them on the spot. This isn't an army, but killers, murderers." He takes a breath and looks around at the men as they listen to the Polish interpreter.

"The Germans picked me up in Kiev, minding my own business and forced me into a truck. I was shoved and poked while they were screaming at me, but I couldn't understand them. I became frightened."

He clasps his hands together and waits for the silence. "Outside the city there is a lovely woods, a place of peace, a place a man can take his girl, or a woman he likes. It's called Babi Yar and it is there the trucks stopped.

"We waited in the woods and could hear the shooting and the screams, but we couldn't see anything. It lasted for hours and I thought I would go crazy. I was scared. I knew I was going to die, and I hadn't told my mother goodbye."

The Polish interpreter speaks with the man in Russian before continuing. "But an eerie silence settled on the forest and the Germans forced us to walk to the site. I said my prayers and asked God to watch over Mama."

The man wipes his face and wrings his hands. "Beside the trench was a long pile of lime and many, many shovels. They told us to get a shovel and start shoveling the lime over the bodies." He shakes his head. "I quickly got a shovel and did as I was told. At first I watched where the lime landed, seeing a young woman, her legs twisted strangely, then a man, his mouth open, silently screaming.

"I stopped watching when I saw the little girl." The Russian chokes on the words and wipes tears from his eyes. "She had been no more than two and pretty, lying atop her mama, I suppose." He shakes his head and continues. "I just threw the lime after that and paid no attention where it landed. I wasn't even afraid that I would be killed next."

Again he and the Polish interpreter exchange words, continuing at a nod from the Pole. "The worse was when I had almost covered all the bodies in my area; I heard a groan, a young person's cry. I hesitated, but I looked and saw a boy about eight or nine or ten, I don't know, but he was sitting up, crying, wiping the lime from his eyes."

The Russian is quiet for a long time. "I started to jump into the pit, but was prevented by the man next to me. Just as I was pulled back, a soldier with a rifle stepped to the edge and fired a bullet into the child's head, shattering it and spattering blood onto me and others around me."

He releases a short breath and looks at us. "Afterwards, we are put on a train, in cars used for hauling cattle, and brought here."

One of the laborers looks at the interpreter. "Who were they? Who were the ones the Germans shot?"

The Pole and Russian speak back and forth, before the interpreter translates. "He says they were Russians. Russian Jews."

"Jews? What's it matter? Good riddance."

I don't know why, but his words anger me. I move quickly into the group and, as the man stands, I smash my baton across his face shattering the nose and cheeks, and knocking out several teeth. Everyone else quickly disperses and distances themselves from me. I kick the man into consciousness, and he sits up and stares at me. I crouch and look him in the eyes. "When you die, then I'll say 'good riddance'."

My anger subsides with my duties and the growing population. With the building and opening of Birkenau in the spring, more and more prisoners come to Auschwitz, and with them come their possessions. The work gangs think the nation of Canada is a place of vast wealth, thus they call the six collection and holding barracks in the stamlager, Kanada. It contains all of the belongings of all the prisoners who have come to the camps, which is proving to be a great sum, all destined for the Third Reich.

It is known that any kapo or prisoner working at Kanada can steal, or 'organize', enough to buy food or anything else, thus insuring their chances of survival, that is, if they aren't caught. I want to be assigned to those barracks and, although risky, I'll risk it for both me and Jakub, and deal with Hirt.

Sergeant Hirt again inquires about Jakub. I can't guess his interest or his intention, but I listen and give as little information as possible, keeping the NCO at bay as best I can. He pursues the matter and I guess his intentions are baser, more evil than I had expected, and I realize Jakub is in serious danger, and it isn't the time to make my request.

Still I put off the sergeant and his inquiries become more urgent. He becomes more polite to me, under a veil of anger and animosity, and I realize he doesn't want to force Jakub to come to him. I continue to stall, waiting for a propitious moment.

The moment comes with the arrival of a new prisoner, a German, Jan Freimark. Younger than most of the laborers under my charge, he is more fragile and less conditioned for the nature of the work. He is blonde with blue eyes and his features are delicate. I know he will be a target for some of the more hardened men in the kommando, thus I make him a lauferin, a runner, within my block, carrying messages to and from the various vorarbeiters, or underkapos, of the camp, knowing I'll use him to protect Jakub and deal with Hirt.

Hirt comes early this morning and I'm polite and show the deference expected of someone of lesser status, although I feel I have a power over him. "Hauptscharfuhrer, I think you need an assistant."

He looks at me, the look in his eyes expressing relief of pent-up anxiety. "There's more to this job than anyone realizes. There's always pressure from Hoss or Kramer or Grabner, and from Berlin. You don't know."

"I can understand, Sergeant, I see the pressure and often feel it myself, especially when you're feeling it." I stand on unsteady ground dealing with an irrational man, but I feel my judgment of him is accurate.

"Yes, there're times I come down too hard on you kapos. I know we can't do this without you." He shifts his feet, obviously uncomfortable with the conversation.

I want him to go on, to thank me, to apologize for hitting me in Katy and sending me to this hellhole, but know that is asking too much. "You need a pipel, Hauptscharfuhrer, a young assistant. I know of the perfect one."

His eyes widen with my suggestion. "And where would you get such a person." He looks at me with hard eyes. "I suppose he's probably Russian, or a Pole, or some Jew."

I smile at him. "I wouldn't make such an offer, Sergeant." I back away, showing my hands, pretending fear. "He's German, and I've protected him from abuse. He runs for me. He's my lauferin."

Hirt looks about and shifts his feet, then turns his head towards me, his hands on his hips.

"I would be happy to talk with him about becoming your assistant, but…"

"But what?"

"I respectfully request a favor from the hauptscharfuhrer, one that would also serve him as well." Now I feel nervous, but I have played my hand and have to continue. "I would like to be transferred to the Kanada kommando as kapo," I swallow hard and hope this won't kill me, "and have the boy from my village as my lauferin."

He stands with his feet apart for a long time, his gaze hard and steely, and his expression harder and more ruthless. Finally, he smiles. "Maybe, Kapo. Let me see this runner of yours."

I trot to the edge of the building where I can look down the length of the barracks and see Jan. I wave when he looks my way and motion for him to come to me, and I return to Hirt. Shortly Freimark turns the corner and the sergeant actually takes a breath. His eyes widen with surprise or desire, I'm not sure which.

I turned to Jan. "Never mind, Jan. Go back and help Jakub. But watch for me, I may need you in a few minutes."

He does as instructed and I turn to Hirt. "Do you think he would be suitable as your assistant, Hauptscharfuhrer?"

He quickly composes himself. "I think I would like to have someone in the Kanada kommando, but I'll have to get Grabner to let me select you." He smiles at me and nods. "But first, I'll have to catch the other kapo stealing."

"That should be easy, Sergeant, I understand he's quite a thief. He's even grown fat."

"Well, soon he'll be fertig, finished."

Two days later we are brought together in the punishment yard, as the Kanada kapo and two of his workers are lined up against a wall. Untersturmfuhrer SS Grabner stands with Sergeant Hirt and watches as the German guards take aim and fire their volley, smashing the bodies of the kapo and his assistants.

I have become much like my German masters, amoral and without conscience concerning my fellow man. Yet, I remember my promise to Aron and console myself that I am protecting Jakub.

As I march my kommando off to the construction site, I encounter Lieutenant Grabner. "Kapo."

I send the group on and stand before the German. "Yes, sir."

"I remember you. You've done well, Pole."

His compliment surprises me. "Thank you, Untersturmfuhrer."

"As you have seen, I need a kapo I can trust." He looks around and stands at ease with a hand in his pocket. "Select two hundred of your kommando you can trust and go to the storage facility in the stamlager. See to it that all material is sorted and separated. Any theft from anyone will be punishable by death. You understand?"

"Yes, Untersturmfuhrer. I'll personally see that there is no theft."

He nods. "Good, good." He turns and leaves.

I march the kommando to the construction site and pick the men to go with me to Kanada. The remainder I leave with the arbeitkapo at the barracks site.

At Kanada, Sergeant Hirt meets me. I report to him with Freimark at my side. "Good morning, Sergeant."

He hides his smile and pleasure at our presence. "Has Lieutenant Grabner spoken with you?"

"Yes, Sergeant."

"There are six buildings. You'll sort all items and prepare shipments for Berlin. Items not sent to Berlin are to be sent over to SS headquarters. You'll receive further instructions later. Do you understand?"

"Yes, Sergeant." I keep my features expressionless and don't look at his eyes. "I've spoken with my runner, sir, and explained he'll be your assistant." I don't say anymore.

Freimark doesn't offer any expression, either, but, at Hirt's signal, the young man stands behind him.

"You and I'll talk later, Kapo." He pulls the bill of his hat lower and stands stiff-legged, hands on his hips.

I acknowledge his announcement, concerned my days are at an end. "Yes, sir."

I move my gang into the large building, overwhelmed with the suitcases, bags, and parcels that wait processing.

"We've been together a long time. This work is considerably easier than what we have done before, but it offers many opportunities to get into trouble and face the SS. I'll caution you against stealing and taking things from these buildings, but I won't watch too closely." I smile and look around the room. "Be careful. If you are caught, there is nothing I can do for you."

I break the men into groups and divide the buildings as well, as men open and empty the contents onto a large table, sort and pile items on the floor, where they are picked up and carried to a section for storage.

I quickly realize we can be overwhelmed by the job before us and ask the SS officer to allow some large boxes with wheels be made available to us. They are and our work is faster and more efficient.

We ship large crates of material to Berlin, where the SS takes possession of it. All food items, liquor, canned goods, and other perishable goods are sent to the administrative offices at the camp for storage in the basement.

As I watch the work, I become aware that the shipping department can be relocated to a separate room, one less visible to the laborers, one more controllable. It is here I plan to set up a scheme that will make Hirt rich, and offer me and Jakub the protection of his office.

Yet, I have a fear that everything can go wrong, a sneaky image in my imagination that says all is doomed. I feel the Germans will eventually tire of all of us, and slowly liquidate the camp and everyone in it, including me with my illusory protection; or that they will be defeated in the end and, before they face their enemies, they will eliminate the witnesses to their crimes which include all of their friends and aides. Either way, I will be dead and Jakub, too, will be swept away in whatever flood takes the Germans.

But, I tell myself, it is just an imaginary fear, nothing more.

CHAPTER FIFTEEN

Even with more rations and better foods, winter is still the worst time. There is seldom any heat in the main barracks and prisoners are only given a thin blanket to keep them warm. At times straw is provided for them to spread on the bunks and to use as insulators against the harsh Polish winter, but that is one of the ways lice and disease-carrying insects find their way into the camps.

Jakub still complains of the cold even with the improved working conditions in the Kanada kommando. We work the first shift for twelve hours, from the early darkness of the morning to the dimness of the afternoon, seeing little of the outside. Our barracks are close and we don't have to make a long march like some of the other labor gangs, particularly those that worked in the aussenlagers, external camps, or the nebenlagers, extension or sub camps.

I study the routines of the SS and other kapos and learn there is much theft occurring from the building, both on the part of the SS and kapos. Even the laborers are stealing such things as money and jewels, and purchasing foods, tobacco, and alcohol. It is as much an industry as the collection itself and even involves Untersturmfuhrer Maximilian Grabner.

The second lieutenant created a small business for himself and is apparently enriching his superiors with handsome gifts, while hoarding much for himself. The problem is the SS Department of Economic Administration in Berlin, which considers everything collected at KL Auschwitz is the property of the Third Reich.

As Hirt is a subordinate to Grabner, his ability to enrich himself depends solely on the generosity of the lieutenant, and in that lays my strategy. I will first organize the smaller lager, isolating the shipping room from the work area, allowing the second shift a free hand in preparing their shipments, particularly the ones bound for Grabner. The actual shipping will be done on the first shift, the shift I control, and small shipments will be siphoned off to Hirt. This will lead the second shift arbeitkapo to believe Grabner has received everything marked for him, leaving Grabner to believe the missing items have been shipped to Berlin, and, of course, few questions can be asked.

I explain my strategy to Hirt.

"I think I like you, Pole."

"My name is Filip." I still have hard feelings and want something from him, perhaps respect, but something that will make it easier to work with him.

He turns his head and stares at me. He holds the stare for several uncomfortable moments. "When we're alone, I'll call you Filip, but if there is anyone around, you're kapo."

"As it should be, Sergeant." I chastise myself for my recklessness in thinking this man would ever treat me as a human.

"And how will you get the stuff to me?"

"Our lauferins. We can use them to exchange the packages."

He is hesitant. "No." He turns and looks at me. "Your man and Jan would immediately identify us as responsible."

"I agree." I look at him for a moment, waiting for a suggestion or solution to the problem, but he is without an answer. Momentarily, I question how Germany can be so powerful with men as stupid as Hirt, realizing it is through sheer ruthlessness.

"I think I have it." I turn to look at the workers. "I'll have a vorarbeiter, one my underkapos, bring the package to whomever you select, with the instruction that either another lagerkapo or Grabner has instructed them to deliver whatever it is."

"That might work." He smiles briefly.

"And if they're caught and point the finger at me, then I'll deny it and accuse them of stealing."

It is shaky, as the SS tend to punish everyone involved, regardless of their involvement, but Hirt, in the absence of ideas of his own, accepts it.

As spring passes into summer, our little scheme works very well. Hirt is pleased with his assistant and bothers no more about Jakub, a huge relief to me. The success of our venture brings more food and luxuries, things like candy for Jakub and brandy for me. There is even an occasional bottle of vodka, but wine and sweet liqueurs are more evident.

They say it is July when the Reichsfuhrer is scheduled to visit, to see the progress of the building programs and the expansion of KL Auschwitz into three camps. Again I stand nearby when the motorcade approaches, going from one building to another, surprised with the sudden appearance of the black Mercedes with the flags on the front bumper. Gone is the trailing cloud of dust from his earlier visit, the road sprayed with water to dampen it.

I stop and stand as rigid as possible, keeping my eyes straightforward, praying they will quickly pass me by, but Hoss stops and addresses me.

"So, Kapo, what's your job here?"

I take note of his rank, higher than when I last saw him. "I'm in charge of the collecting, sorting, and shipping of all items, Sturmbannfuhrer Hoss." I don't meet his gaze and keep staring at the sky behind him.

"That's a big responsibility, isn't it? And how many men do you have under you, Kapo?" His voice is without the edge I generally expect whenever a German asks me questions.

"Three hundred, sir."

"You're able to sort all of the material that comes in with only three hundred?" I detect a change in his voice, an edge with which I am more accustomed.

I'm unsure how much I should say. "I'm responsible for only six buildings, Sturmbannfuhrer. This is lager one."

He pauses and continues to look at me. "I know this is Kanada I. I'm asking you whether or not you're able to maintain the work with only three hundred workers."

I stiffen and can feel his anger building. "I'm sorry, Sturmbannfuhrer. Yes, we're able to maintain the pace with two shifts." I feel it rising in my head and know I shouldn't say more, but I can't stop myself. "That is, sir, when there isn't an overflow from the number two camp, or whenever they can't handle our overflow."

The commandant straightens and glances at the Reichsfuhrer who is glaring at him and me. "Does that happen often?"

"Occasionally, sir, three, four times a month." I know I should stop, but I can't stop myself. I glance beyond the entourage and see Grabner, sweat beading on his forehead, staring at Hirt who looks terrified. "But we manage, Sturmbannfuhrer."

"Good. Good." He starts to leave, but thinks of something else. "For Reichsfuhrer Himmler, Kapo, tell us how often a shipment leaves this lager, and to where is it sent?"

"A shipment is prepared every morning," suddenly I don't know if I should address Hoss or Himmler, "sirs, and is sent to the Schutzstaffel Economic Department of Administration in Berlin."

Himmler looks at Hoss. "That's good, Hoss. Let's move along. I want to see the major warehouses." His voice is suited for his appearance, high-pitched with a whining component to it. It is hard to imagine he is second in command to Hitler, commander of the Schutzstaffel, SS, for he has none of the appearance of the soldiers who wear the SS on their collars.

Grabner stares at me as he passes, and Hirt waits until Himmler and his entourage has moved farther down the row of warehouses. "You're a fool, Polack. Any one of those men can have you shot with a single word. I could have you shot, but ..."

"But what, Sergeant." I still feel provocative.

He smiles and takes a step back. "Go to work, Kapo."

Shortly after Himmler's visit, two hundred women come to work in lager Kanada I, and I am promoted to lagerkapo for the camp, first and second shift. This allows me an office where I can sleep and have privacy for the first time since leaving Katy. It also gives me kapos to work under me, but interferes with my organizing, the term used for stealing from the lager.

Nevertheless, Hirt is enriching himself with my efforts and has given the protection I need for me and Jakub, that is until the end of summer.

Freimark comes to tell me. "Jakub was idling in the area of your barracks and was confronted by an SS officer. Jakub couldn't answer the officer's questions and..." he pauses, his eyes fill with tears and his hands shake, "Filip, they've taken him to selekcja. He'll face the doctors and be selected to work or die." Jan is disturbed and cries more openly than other men. "I'm afraid for him. I think they'll send him to the little red house."

The red house had been an old farmhouse and they use it as a gas chamber. "Let's find Hirt. I'll think of something along the way." I leave Arbeitkapo Borowski to oversee the warehouses and maintain the work, knowing he is a man I can trust.

We find the sergeant near the ramp, watching as another trainload of prisoners form two lines for the selection process. At our approach he turns to face me. "You shouldn't have come, Kapo. It's too late. It'll be the red house for him."

I am desperate. "No, Sergeant, we mustn't allow that. You must get him out of the line."

"And take his place?" His eyes are wide.

"You must, Heinz." Jan looks at the sergeant, even as the German glares at him for showing familiarity. "Please, you and Jakub are the only friends I have in the world."

Hirt lowers his head and leans towards Jan. "I would like to help, but how?"

Freimark speaks first. "You always complain that they kill your best workers, or take them from you, then accuse you of not working us hard enough."

"This is the time to protect a worker, Hauptscharfuhrer." I feel it is time to threaten him, to have him understand his position. "He's important to our whole operation. Without him, our efforts in the lager are to no end."

Hirt glares at me and doesn't speak for a long time. Finally he releases a breath and turns towards the long lines. "How? How do I get them to release him to me?"

"Argue his importance to the camp and the work efforts. Tell them anything, but get him out of that line." I feel the same emotions as Hirt.

Hirt stands and brushes off his uniform. He rubs his sleeve against the Iron Cross pinned to his left pocket and starts off, his head lowered and a determination in his quick step.

As Hirt walks across the yard, I turn to Freimark and speak softly. "Thank you for coming to tell me, Jan. Thanks for watching over Jakub."

"He's my friend." He continues to watch as the sergeant continues across the field.

"I'm sorry, Jan, sorry for giving you to Hirt. I didn't know any other way to protect Jakub than to give you to…"

He looks at me with that boyish face and bright eyes, but his mouth is twisted. "You think I don't know what I am?" He releases a long breath and places his hand on my arm. "If I wasn't with Heinz, then I could be with someone a lot worse."

"Still, I'm sorry."

He smiles at me. "I appreciated your protecting me in the lager. No one has ever done that without wanting something from me. Heinz doesn't beat me. He even tells me he loves me, but he's still SS and I cringe whenever he touches me."

Jakub stands fifteenth in the line, his head bowed, his look one of hopeless resignation, like that of a young man who got slapped trying to steal a kiss.

We watch as Hirt approaches the line. "Damn it, Pole. What're you doing here?" Hirt grabs Jakub by the shirt and pulls him out of line forcefully. "You're going back to work."

He turns his back and starts to leave pushing Jakub in front of him.

"Stop." An SS guard quickly steps between them and us, blocking their retreat. Hirt turns to face the SS officer who had brought Jakub to the ramp.

"What're you doing, Hauptscharfuhrer?" The officer stands over Hirt and glares at him.

"Retrieving this worker, Untersturmfuhrer. He sometimes wanders off, but he's a good worker and one I can trust." Hirt is sweating.

"He's mentally defective, Sergeant. I'm letting the doctor decide whether he should work or be sent for special treatment, for sonderbehandlungen." He looks at Jakub then turns his attention to Hirt. "Our Fuhrer has decreed Germany will be rid of all mental defectives." He continues to stare at Hirt.

The sergeant braces himself. "And I agree wholeheartedly with mein Fuhrer, Lieutenant, but we have much work to do and he's still strong." Hirt is fidgeting. "I thought we should get all the work out of him for the war effort before we give special treatment."

"I understand you, Sergeant. Conflict in your orders, is that not so?" The officer walks to where an SS doctor is selecting people to go to the right or the left, one to work, one to die. He speaks to the doctor briefly as the man continues his motions, and motions for Hirt to bring Jakub to the front of the line.

I strain to see what is happening when Dr. Josef Mengele steps into the small group. I worry now about the two doctors and fear for Jakub.

The German officer continues talking, directing his address to Mengele. "He's obviously mentally defective, Herr Doctor."

Hirt swallows hard, but summons the courage to speak to Mengele. "He is defective, Dr. Mengele, but that's what makes him such a good worker. I wish all my charges were as stupid as he."

Mengele turns to the SS doctor directing the line of people. "Fritz, he will be a good candidate for the sterilization experiments, don't you think?"

Dr. Schuller holds his hand motionless halting the next in line. He looks first at the SS officer then Mengele. "May I?" He points with his head towards Jakub.

"Certainly." Mengele motions for Jakub to come forward, which he does tentatively, forcing the guard to shove him with his rifle.

"I'm Obersturmfuhrer Dr. Fritz Schuller. This is Dr. Mengele." Schuller turns to Mengele and smiles. "They call him Uncle Pepi." He turns back to Jakub. "Can you tell me who I am?"

"Doctor… Sch…" Jakub looks from one doctor to the other and rubs his hands on his hips.

"And who is this?" Schuller points to Mengele.

"Uncle Pepi." Jakub smiles broadly and points. "Uncle Pepi."

Schuller smiles at Mengele then continues. "And what work do you do here?"

"I'm a lauferin. I run for Kapo Filip." His nervousness is lessening and I fear he will say too much.

"And what else do you do?"

Jakub is silent for few moments, then blurts out, "I drive a truck."

Schuller turns to Mengele and the SS officer. "He's obviously defective, but I think he could work." He glances at Hirt and turns back to Mengele. "But I agree with you, he should go to block ten for sterilization."

Block ten is located in Auschwitz and is the building they use for medical experiments. More often than not, once prisoners go in, they come out destined for the crematorium.

Jakub is taken by Dr. Mengele and an SS guard, and the other officer and Dr. Schuller return to the selection. Hirt retreats without being dismissed and returns to where I wait with Jan.

"He's being taken to block ten. He's to be castrated."

I feel miserable. "We must stop them."

Hirt's anger flares and his eyes are the old demonic stare I had first seen. "Remember your place, Kapo, or I'll send you to the line for special treatment."

I lower my head and speak softly, feeling the need to temper his anger. "I'm sorry, Hauptscharfuhrer. I know you've done all you can do."

His shoulders drop and he nods his head. "There's nothing more we can do. Hopefully, he'll survive the experiment and will return to us." He motions for Jan to stand and points towards the inner camp. "I'll watch. I'll bring him to you if I can."

He and Freimark make a hasty retreat from the area and I follow slowly, returning to the Kanada kommando and going to my office. I am at a loss as to how to proceed, thinking I have failed Aron and Jakub. I can't imagine what I would do without thinking of him and my promise, but it feels easier the more I think of it, the more I realize that, without Jakub, I only have to take care of myself.

CHAPTER SIXTEEN

Jakub returns two days later. He walks slowly, preventing his legs from rubbing together, painful with each step. I settle him in my office and quarters with Hirt's knowledge and tacit consent, assuring him I am near and there to protect him.

The damage is severe and needs medical attention, but that means the camp hospital and gas chamber, or returning to Mengele's lab. I can only look at the deep red marks on his lower abdomen, thighs, and buttocks, and the blackened skin of his scrotum and penis.

He is so much like a small child who is terribly sick and doesn't understand what has happened to him. "Uncle Pepi gave me candy. He told me to climb up on the table." He wipes tears from his eyes. "I did like you told me, Filip. I didn't talk too much. I did what I was told."

My heart sinks as he looks at me and shakes his head.

"They tied my hands and feet and I couldn't move." He continues to wipe the tears. "It hurt." He demonstrates his position and leans forward. "Dr. Sch... the other doctor was going to put this long shiny pin in me, but Uncle Pepi stopped him. I didn't want him to stab me."

I want him to stop, fearing I would hear too much, but he needs to tell me.

"They then pointed this machine between my legs." Tears roll down his cheeks. "It made a funny noise, but I didn't feel anything." He wipes the tears. "Then the machine seemed to go faster, like my truck when I forget to change gears. And it was hot. It hurt."

I listen and bite the inside of my lip.

"I tried to move, but I was tied. I asked them to stop, but they just looked at me as if they didn't hear me." His head drops and he wipes away more tears. "It hurt, Filip, and I couldn't stop it." He looks at me. "You couldn't stop it either. You weren't there.

"I bit my lip the way Aron taught me. And I listened to them, trying to understand what they were saying. Uncle Pepi laughed at something the other doctor said." He releases a long breath. "Then the machine stopped."

He lies back and I cover him with a blanket and he is silent for a long time. I remain beside him, feeling helpless, but angry, hoping a day will come when I could see the death of these doctors.

"Filip?"

"Yes, little brother."

"After the doctors left, a man told me I wouldn't be able to make babies with a girl." He looks at me, fear filling his eyes. "What did he mean?"

"I don't know, Jakub." I want to tell him something, but can't think of anything that will comfort him or ease his fear.

He closes his eyes and sleeps, and I stay and watch, thankful he can't see me wipe my eyes. I suppress my fear that I have failed in my promise to Aron.

It is more than the physical pain of what they had done to him, but the damage is also to his mind, too severe to allow him to trust even me. He becomes despondent and won't respond to anything I say or do. He doesn't take the candy or other treats I bring for him, treats which could result in severe punishment had I been caught.

Jan Freimark comes and attempts to reach him, to get him to come out of his depression, but Jakub has learned not to trust anyone. Even as the burns heal and no longer cause him serious pain, he remains unto himself. I insist he return to work and carry messages for me, and, even then, he remains quiet and aloof. He runs faster than ever, not stopping to idle anywhere, completing the tasks asked of him, as a morose temperament settles upon him. Gone is the Jakub of old, the boy who found pleasure in everything, as I watch him step on roaches he used to allow to sit in his palm.

1943 starts as an exciting year, a year that holds a glimmer of hope, a year in which the Germans no longer seem unstoppable, at least on the battlefield. In Auschwitz, they remain all-powerful and exercise that power in extremes unheard of and unimagined in the world outside the camp.

The first news comes from North Africa as we learn the British have defeated a German general and pushed him across the desert. The news of that success spreads throughout the camps and is still argued when we learn the Germans lost a huge battle in the East, at a town called Stalingrad. The Russian POWs celebrate with stolen vodka, exclaiming the Germans will soon find themselves against a massive army.

Even with the brutality of the SS, the spirits of all inmates seem buoyed by the belief that Germany can be defeated and will one day release them, but not Jakub's spirits. He remains like a kitten, skittish and frightened of everything.

The snows still cling to the ground when fifty Russian women arrive at the kommando and I meet Anna Kalitnikova. She was a night fighter, attacking German lines during the darkness to disrupt their communications and disturb their sleep. But she was captured when her plane went down near Kursk, in Russia.

She is taller than average, as tall as me, but thin and sinewy, muscled throughout her body, her hair cut short and wispy, with deep brown eyes and dark complexion. She walks erect, her head high, her arms in cadence with her steps, proud and defiant towards her captors. She is married to a political officer, but hasn't seen him in a year and is uncertain even of the front to which he was assigned. She hasn't received a letter in seven months and fears he has been killed at Stalingrad.

I remember Klara as I watch this Russian and feel more aroused than my memories of my first time. Anna is beautiful, graceful, possessing an almost magical charm, and I want her near me as much as possible. Her command of languages is good, speaking some German, Polish, and Yiddish, as well as her own, and this makes her more useful in the lager. I assign her to be my lauferin, allowing her to search among the Russian prisoners and inquire about her husband.

Her duties bring her to my office, where she comes in contact with Jakub. As spring comes, Jakub responds to Anna, who seems to exude the tenderness she shows him. He begins to laugh again, to enjoy another's presence, a woman's kindness, and he again smiles at me and starts with his joking way, glad to be my runner again.

Slowly, without expressing my feelings, I know I am in love. Anna knows it, too, and welcomes it. Forbidden as it is, it is something we both want, and, loving each other, need. It is an early morning and, as is routine, the SS change guards allowing one group to eat, while the other stands watch. Hirt is in charge of the shift and remains on duty, taking his morning break in the latrine, as is customary for him, very German in his regimentation.

Anna is standing by the door, looking out into the barracks, as I ease the door closed and stand before her. I tremble when I lean forward and kiss her cheek. She doesn't move and I'm unsure what I should do, but she leans forward and kisses me softly on the lips. The excitement courses through my body like a flood and I pull her into my arms and kiss her hard. She, too, grabs me and holds me tightly, pressing our mouths together urgently.

Our first time is rushed, more to satisfy our needs, but we have other times together, times to express the love we feel. All of a sudden KL Auschwitz isn't as much of a hellhole as before.

Jakub, too, seems altered by Anna's love, taking to her as he would his mother, and she responds maternally as if she was. It is becoming a pleasant time with the return of spring, until Hirt brings the word, news that will shatter Jakub and cause a rift between Anna and me.

The Germans report unearthing a large gravesite in the Katyn Forest near Smolensk in Russia. In the grave are more than four thousand Polish bodies, killed with a single bullet to the back of the head. Among the corpses are army officers of all ranks, and the Germans accuse the Russians of the massacre.

Jakub receives the news with a puzzled demeanor, as he seems lost in deep concentration. He comes to me as I sit with Anna, looking at me, then Anna, then at the floor.

"What is it, Jakub?"

"Aron. Is he dead?" There are tears in his eyes.

"I don't know." In my heart I know one of the bodies in the Katyn Forest is Aron's.

"Who is Aron?" Anna's eyes are dark.

"Aron was my best friend and Jakub's brother. He was an officer in the Polish army." I look at Jakub and notice he is watching Anna closely. "He was taken in Brest by Russian troops."

"And you think this brother is one of those found in Russia?"

"Yes." I divert my eyes just briefly.

She picks up on my nervousness quickly. "And you believe these German lies that they were killed by Russians?" Her eyes narrow and I can feel her anger.

"I don't know."

Anna turns towards Jakub and takes a step towards him. "They're lies, Jakub." Her eyes, too, fill with tears, and she bites her lip and shakes her head.

Jakub wipes his tears with the back of his hand. "Aron is dead. Russians killed Aron." He turns and runs from the room.

Anna turns to me. "Surely you don't believe Russian troops killed those officers." She shakes her head. "Not with all you know about the Germans, you can't believe these lies."

"I don't know, Anna." I know she doesn't believe it and I don't want to believe it, too. "I think the Germans are just trying to stir up some problems, more propaganda." But I wonder to what purpose. It is the Germans who have the advantage, and if they had killed them, they wouldn't have made the graves known.

Anna and I continue meeting, continue our lovemaking, but a rift has grown between us, an unspoken distance neither of us knows how to bridge.

But for Jakub it is more traumatic. He reverts to his despondency and nothing seems to affect him. He avoids Anna at all times and avoids me whenever Anna and I are together.

Near the end of spring Hirt comes to my office, his manner solemn, his mood depressed. He looks at Anna. "Leave us, woman."

She leaves without a word.

Hirt looks at me. "We must make some changes."

Suddenly I feel emptiness in the pit of my stomach. "What sort of changes, Sergeant?"

He sits opposite the desk and looks at the blank wall. "There's a man from Berlin, from the Reichsfuhrer's office investigating the functioning of all the major camps." He looks at me. "He'll be coming here and looking closely into overall operations, including the storehouses."

"Ah, not too closely, I hope, at least not here."

"Close enough for me to worry." He rises and walks to the edge of the room before turning again to face me. "I know you don't think I'm as clever as you." He silences me with his hand. "It's true, I'm not very fast with ideas, but I have a plan I think will work."

He gives a mock bow and returns to the chair. "I've been asked to form a kommando to work near the crematorium, constructing a pit for the cremation of bodies." He holds out his hands, palms facing outward. "I've volunteered myself, you, and your entire unit, except the women." He waves his hand, signaling there is more.

"If you and I aren't here, then there's nothing to investigate. Once it's over, we come back."

I swallow hard. "You want us to become Sonderkommandos?"

"No. We'll only be there until after the inspector leaves. Then I'll get us a transfer back to here. Then, with your organizing, I'll become a rich man." He smiles and leans back against the creaking chair. "Now, that's a good plan, isn't it?"

I want to argue, but envisioned the blow to my face when I first met him and remember he is a very dangerous man. "I can't find any faults in it." Except, I thought, that I could be left to the ashes.

"Good." He rises to leave.

"When will I begin?"

"Tomorrow." The mask of the authoritarian has returned to his face. "I'll have blueprints for you tomorrow at roll call."

I find Anna and tell her of the transfer for the following morning, and express my alarm at working in the crematorium. She, too, is concerned and expresses her love for me, promising to sneak any provisions she can to me.

True to his word, Hirt presents me with the blueprints and I explain to the labor unit what we are to do. The news is met with groans and moans, as they have become used to better fare in the warehouses. I, too, have become soft, no longer the ruthless kapo who drives his kommando. I scream for the first time in many months, and prod and slap with my baton, forcing them to move quickly.

Jakub receives the news quietly. His downcast eyes and slumping shoulders indicate his depression has returned.

The site picked for the pit is located outside the fence surrounding Kanada II, Birkenau, in the woods near a massive grave of Russian POWs. The pits are to be very large to contain the bodies, where oil, alcohol, and boiling fat will be poured over the bodies to speed the cremation. It has to have indentations on either end of the pit to allow fat to drain off, sloping the pits from the middle towards the ends.

I push the men to dig quickly and dig it well. The sides are sloped to avoid the banks crumbling, and the dirt is used around the pit to allow for the ease of transporting the bodies and stacking them four and five deep. It takes three days for the kommando to complete the task but, upon completion, we are taken to the edge of the enclosure and instructed to dig another.

I don't see Hirt during these busy, backbreaking days, setting me to worry about my future. Yet, I can do nothing more than keep my unit working and hope we won't become involved in the actual cremation.

But my concerns are borne out. I've been betrayed by Hirt and my resolution to someday kill him is renewed with vigor. He has remained in Auschwitz with the six warehouses and has trained another kommando to do the work formerly supervised by me.

Summer passes into fall when the first bodies are brought by the Sonderkommandos, pushing large, flatbed wagons loaded with the naked bodies of women and children. The bodies are tossed on top of each other and cans of oil, alcohol, and fat are poured over the bodies, while the SS stand by and watch. Finally, an SS man lights the pyre with enthusiasm.

The worst of it comes a while later, as all the bodies have been reduced to ashes and form piles in the pit. A water hose is sprayed over the ashes to cool them, but intact skulls shatter whenever the cool water hits the hot bone, raising clouds of white dust, covering the ground and us. I push my unit into the pit where they shovel the ashes into carts, which are taken for burial. All bones not reduced to ashes are crushed by a roller and spread into composts or into gardens. But there are more ashes than we can spread or bury, piles of ashes that need dispersing. It is then I think of a method of disposal, a way to improve the process and help Jakub at the same time.

"Excuse me, Scharfuhrer, but I have a plan to improve the removal of the ashes."

He yawns, but looks at me with a nod of his head.

"We can use the river to disperse the ashes." I let my words linger for a moment.

"I'll ask for permission, Kapo." Suddenly he snaps to attention and clicks his heels together.

"Permission to do what, Sergeant?" Grabner is walking towards us.

The NCO relaxes as the officer waves his hand. "The kapo wants to take the ashes to the river for dispersal, sir."

Grabner nods and turned to me. "Dump the ashes into the river?"

"Yes, sir." I turn to face him. "We have no more places for disposal, so I think if we take the ashes to the Vistula, the river will disperse them for us, and much more efficiently."

"That's a good idea, Kapo." He turns to the NCO who returns to attention. "Sergeant, get as many dump trucks as you can. Bring them here." He turns back to me. "You'll set up the program and use the drivers that bring the trucks. That way you won't have to train new ones."

"Yes, sir." But I know of one driver who might need a little training and feel this is the way to bring Jakub out of his depression.

Grabner turns to the NCO. "You're dismissed, Sergeant. Go get those trucks."

He motions for me to walk with him, away from the pit and other workers. "The warehouses, the ones you call Kanada, are not run as efficiently since your departure."

His announcement is almost too much for me to contain. "I'm sorry, sir."

I caution myself to not be too bold or to praise my own efforts too much. "The lagerkapo and the kommandos are just learning. Perhaps they'll improve soon."

"I... the Third Reich doesn't have time for them to learn. No, they need firm leadership." He stops and focuses on me a hard look, the look of a man who gets his own way. "As soon as you get this new program started, I want you to take over the position of lagerkapo again. You'll report to Blockfuhrer Georg Hocher."

He slaps his leg. "The material is piling up outside the warehouses, going to ruin from the weather, and left there for anyone to go through and steal. We definitely need more space." He again looks at me. "You do a good job for me on this, Kapo, I'll get you the larger compound." He smiles and slaps me on my stomach. "And then you won't have to worry about the lousy food in this place." He laughs at his humor then smiles slightly.

His tone changes again to one of urgency. "You finish here as quickly as possible and report to Hocher. Don't delay, Kapo." He turns on his heel and walks towards the main camp.

The dump trucks are brought to the work site, and I tell the men to fill them with ashes. I force one driver, a burly Russian, to step out of the cab and hand him a shovel, pushing him towards the pit. I then motion for Jakub to get behind the wheel, as I climb up with him. I hope he remembers our lessons back home, but I go over everything with him.

Slowly, it dawns on him what I want him to do. "I can drive this truck?"

"Yes, Jakub. This truck. You watch the truck in front of you and you follow him. Understand?"

"Yes. I will follow that truck."

"Good. You do what they do. Understand."

"I think so. I think I remember."

"Jakub, you must do this right, or they won't let you drive anymore."

"I'll do it right, Filip." His voice trembles. "You'll see. I'll do it right."

I accompany him on his first and second trips, confident he knows what to do, but I continue to watch to make sure he is okay.

It seems to do the trick. Jakub is no longer depressed and his own cheerful demeanor has returned. Even as I tell him I am going back to the stamlager, the main camp, he seems to accept it without fear, pleased with himself.

He exclaims to the others that he is a truck driver, and the kommando unit seems pleased to have Jakub back to himself, all except the burly Russian who seems to be awaiting an opportunity to get his job back.

Before I leave, I take the Russian POW aside and explain in my halting Russian my intention. I make him a kapo, giving him my baton. I reason that this man, Ivan Meretsky, would rather be a kapo than drive a truck, at least that is what I think.

CHAPTER SEVENTEEN

I report to Blockfuhrer Hocher and learn Sergeant Hirt has been promoted to sturmscharfuhrer, working as SS supervisor in charge of construction at the new complex enlarging the armaments production. Many of the laborers in other camps throughout Germany are sent to Auschwitz to work in the lager. I have serious doubts about Hirt's ability to construct anything, but I am free of him and his treachery.

I know from the amount of material coming from the processing center that more and more people have arrived at Auschwitz-Birkenau. From the Sonderkommandos, I learn more are gassed and cremated, and that the ashes are collected faster than they can be dispersed.

I redouble my efforts as well, as I prepare larger and more frequent shipments to Berlin, entire trainloads of material for the Third Reich. I make frequent shipments, yet siphon off many valuable items to Grabner.

Anna and I renew our relationship, more ardent without Jakub's presence as a reminder of Aron. We are more careful because of Hocher, but as my lauferin, she is able to carry messages to all the warehouses, enabling us to meet in many places.

New transports begin arriving bearing Russian and Jewish women to work in munitions at Auschwitz III, called Monowitz, where the I.G. Farben factory is built. Their treatment is better than others due to the nature and need for their labor, but the living conditions are as bad as camp one.

Anna knows many of the women and talks with some whenever

her chores take her near the lager, or whenever they venture near our camps. Many of the lauferin are able to spread news in this manner, setting up systems of communication and running the items from one camp to another. The Jewish women establish a network between themselves and the Sonderkommandos of Birkenau, with Russian munitions experts who advise them on the use of gunpowder and other explosives.

I learn this from Anna, who also has news of an uprising in the Jewish ghetto in Warsaw, of Poles and Jews fighting back. A Jewish cell in Birkenau springs up, encouraging their own revolt, and Jewish women are stealing and supplying gunpowder to the Sonderkommandos, who are storing the explosives for use at a propitious time.

Runners carry the gunpowder throughout the camps, and I fear Anna's involvement. Lying together behind a stack of battered suitcases, she reassures me with a kiss.

"It's nothing dangerous, my love. Just messages from the big Russian to my friend, Ella. I don't know what Ella does with it."

"I'm afraid for you, Anna. You know these men. They don't need an excuse to kill us, to kill you."

She shrugs and kisses me gently. "I'm a soldier, my Filip. I have lived with death before."

"Your war is over. Now you're with me. We only have to wait until these Germans are beaten." I lean towards her.

"No, Filip." She pulls away. "I'm a soldier. I may be a prisoner, but I'm still a soldier and it's a soldier's duty to fight."

"And die?"

She moves closer and puts her arms around me. "Yes, my love, and die if necessary." She eases away and looks me in the eyes briefly. "But you needn't worry about me. I'm doing nothing that would be considered dangerous."

We make love again, holding each other longer, seemingly more desperate than before. I love her deeply and know she loves me, but I have little control over her and have to accept her assurances.

A message from Freimark distracts me, telling me there is trouble in the Sonderkommandos and that Jakub needs me. I receive permission from Hocher and Grabner to visit Birkenau on the pretense of recruiting workers, and hope to learn for myself the problem.

Jakub still drives a truck and I climb into the cab to listen. "I'm doing an evil thing." His eyes are dry and he concentrates on driving the truck. "I'm helping the Germans kill my friends."

"What friends, Jakub?"

"Dr. Samuel. The Spiegelmans. Zus." Still he doesn't look at me.

"Who's telling you this?"

"The Russian. The kapo. He says ashes are Jews. He says ashes are my friends." For the first time he glances at me, and bites his lower lip.

I sit for a long time and watch him handle the gears of the truck, double clutching between gears with no grinding. I wonder what to say, hesitant to say anything, but he continues to glance at me, his lips tight, his gaze intent.

"Jakub, these aren't the ashes of your friends."

"How do you know?"

I don't want to tell him, but know I have to. "They died a long time ago, Jakub."

He looks at me longer than I think he should, but maintains control of the truck. "How do you know? When?"

"Remember the church we found? You said it was Dr. Samuel's church. Remember?" I struggle to keep my voice calm, hoping to avoid upsetting him.

"I remember." The knuckles on his hands are white.

"I found Dr. Levi's doctor's bag, or I found the clasp."

He sits silently for a few moments. "Is that all? Just some... something or other?"

"As I came out, I stumbled and saw the blackened hand of a

child, her fist tightly holding what remained of her doll." I don't know what else to say.

He doesn't respond as the truck bounces along.

As we near the river, I can't tolerate the silence any longer. "There were people in that building, Jakub, Jews like our friends. They were burned to death by the Germans."

"I know. Just like now." He doesn't cry as I thought he would, but he wipes a single tear from his cheek.

He backs the truck up to the edge and operates the lever raising the truck bed, dumping the ashes down the sloping embankment into the river, which slowly carries them north, crisscrossing a good part of Poland. I think how ironic, that so many of those gassed and cremated at Auschwitz had left towns and villages near the Vistula, and now would have their ashes float past the homes they had left behind.

On the return to the cremation pit, I ask Jakub if he wants to return to the Kanada kommando, but he declines. I ask him if anyone bothers him and he indicates he stays pretty much to himself, except for a punch or shove from the Russian once in awhile, and the taunts the kapo always heaps upon him.

He lifts his shirt, revealing several round, blackened areas covering his torso. "Kapo Ivan doesn't like me."

I want to cry and feel the tears in my eyes, but Jakub's cheeks are dry and his eyes hard, seemingly chastising me for not keeping my promise to Aron. I nod and open the door. "I'll do something, little brother."

As I depart the cab of the truck, Jakub thanks me for my help. He even smiles briefly, leaving me feeling as if he no longer needs me. I return the smile. "You're doing well, Jakub. You drive the truck better than me."

He nods but doesn't say anything.

It is a lonely walk back to the stamlager, a distance of about three kilometers, but my mind is filled with thoughts of Jakub and the horror of all he has been through. I question if I have failed in my promise to Aron, accepting that Jakub is still alive. I want to believe he is happy, but this is Auschwitz and it is unreasonable anyone could be happy in hell.

It starts to snow as I cross through the gate leading to Kanada, and it dawns on me what I can do to protect Jakub. I run into Blockfuhrer Hocher as he is leaving his office, an old bottle of cognac tucked under his arm.

"Blockfuhrer, I need a tough man to work as kapo in my kommando. I saw this Russian, a burly man who used his baton with force and harshness. I would like someone like him." I glance at the cognac long enough for Hocher to notice.

"What's his name?"

"Ivan Meretsky, sir."

"A Russian, you say, as kapo? A Sonderkommando?" He shrugs and hunches his shoulders against the cold. "Maybe. It will be difficult, but I'll see."

He starts to walk off, but stops and faces me. "Grabner is no longer with us."

"Excuse me, sir, I don't understand." I feel my sense of security slipping away again.

"The inspector from the Reichsfuhrer's office filed his report. Grabner has been relieved of duty. He's been recalled to Berlin for suspected crimes of corruption involving the lager's storehouses." He smiles. "And other things, as well." He steps closer to me and taps me on the chest with the bottle of cognac. "We're lucky you and I, Kapo. He didn't find anything about our involvement with Grabner, or, at least, he didn't say anything." He smiles before turning to leave. "Oh, I believe Kramer and Hoss are also involved. They've been reassigned." With that he leaves in the direction of SS barracks.

I feel a combination of relief and fear; relief that I wasn't implicated in Grabner's organizing, and fear that Hocher will use any knowledge he has to sacrifice me. I have endeared myself to two men I loath to guarantee my security in this very insecure world, only to have them either betray me or removed from the scene. But, still, I'm not sharing whatever fate awaits Grabner.

Meretsky arrives the following week, puzzled but pleased to be moved out of the Sonderkommando. I put him to work in the sorting warehouse, one of the easiest places to find all sorts of material, such as vodka, cigarettes, canned goods, and jewels. His appetite goes wild and he can't resist the urge to take and hoard as much as he can hide near his barracks and bunk.

I initiate a casual search through the kapos' barracks, with SS guards beside me, and, not surprisingly, we find contraband items hidden in the straw on the Russian's bunk, items cherished by the Third Reich. They wait until the first shift ends, the roll call is completed, and the prisoners return to their bunks. There they find a thief in Ivan Meretsky. Two SS men lead him away, pushing him into the courtyard between the barracks.

Once outside, the Russian shoves the first guard, then hits the other, taking his rifle. He turns to face the first German who fires the same time as Meretsky, striking the Russian in the side, but his shot kills the guard. He turns and shoots the other as he attempts to flee, but the entire camp is alerted to his whereabouts.

He tries to reenter the barracks, but I close the door and slide my baton through the handle, preventing his reentry. I listen as there are shouts in German and more in Russian. Shots are fired, first from close at hand, then more shots from farther away. They continue for several heated moments and end with a machine gun from a distant post. Then all is silent.

I remove the stick and open the door. I raise my hands when all of the rifles point in my direction. "I'm not armed, sirs." I can feel the sweat pouring down my back and neck, even in the cold air and gently falling snow. "He was arrested for stealing from the lager."

Nothing more is said and the Russian's body is dragged from the scene. I feel a sense of satisfaction that my day ends with the Russian's death, again reassuring myself that the promise is being kept, and that Jakub is again safe.

Jakub continues driving a truck and Anna and I are able to get together on a cold day for the first time in weeks. Her excitement at her part in the activities is obvious, as she waves her arms and smiles brightly. The Jewish underground, she calls it, is actively involved in complex plans. She talks about how they learn to build bombs, using gunpowder supplied by the women from the munitions plant. Between our lovemaking, she talks incessantly of her activities of meeting the Russian expert, Borodin, and passing the information to her friend, Ella. I listen, but am terribly uncomfortable with what I hear, uncomfortable for fear she will be discovered.

"You said it was just messages you were carrying. Nothing dangerous."

"Instructions are messages, lover." She pinches my cheek and snuggles against me.

"You must be careful, Anna."

"Oh, Filip, you don't understand. I'm a soldier. I'm sworn to fight back, to escape if at all possible." She holds both my hands and squeezes them.

"I know you can die for this." I want to forbid her from any more activities, but know she won't listen to me.

"I'm a soldier, Filip."

"You're a woman, Anna, my woman."

She smiles at me and kisses me softly on the lips. "Yes, my kapo, I'm your woman, but your woman is a soldier." She releases my hands and sits up. "Do you know how many missions I've flown?"

"No."

"Six hundred and ninety." She squares her shoulders and looks me in the eyes. "I've dropped many, many bombs on German soldiers. I've personally shot down twelve German planes, and I've destroyed two hundred more on the ground." She took a deep breath. "I've destroyed over a hundred German tanks, and more trucks and trains and other vehicles than I can count. And, my dear kapo, my love, I've killed many German soldiers."

She lies down beside me and motions for me to join her. "I'm a soldier, but I'm also a woman. I'm your woman, for as long as you want me." She puts out her lower lip and whines, "You do still want me, don't you?"

And I do still want her, more than I can find the words to tell her. And, I guess, that is what frightens me most, that I can love a woman so much. But I reconcile that I do love her and that she will continue to play the most dangerous game in the most dangerous place on earth.

We continue together even as winter sets in. The population is gathered for a massive roll call that lasts for hours, almost as long as the one when we first came, but now it is cold and it penetrates to the bone. The muslims, emaciated ones, as the Germans call them, have only a single thin blanket to keep out the cold, and they suffer the most, but the SS want to be confident the coming notices are heard by all.

The announcements come on loudspeakers and are heard in all three camps. "Achtung, achtung. KL Auschwitz is to be divided into three camps, and each will be commanded separately and individually."

"Commandant of KL Auschwitz will be Arthur Liebehemschel, Obersturmbannfuhrer SS."

"At Auschwitz II-Birkenau, the new commandant will be Fritz Hartjenstein, Sturmbannfuhrer SS, and Hans Aumeier, Hauptsturmfuhrer SS, has been appointed camp director."

I watch the snow fall and allow my mind to wander, imagining a life with Anna and Jakub. I realize that I haven't thought of him in a long time and need to visit him.

A long silence follows with a lot of static and crackling from the loud speakers, enough noise to bring me out of my reverie. I become aware I haven't heard the announcements about Auschwitz III-Monowitz, as the voice continues. "New directives will be forthcoming from the commandant's offices and all orders will be obeyed."

An eerie silence trails the announcements as the prisoners stand in the snow and cold. Finally, SS soldiers come and direct us to return to the barracks. We pick up the fallen among us and carry them to their bunks, where their friends rub circulation back into their toes and fingers, hoping, at times beyond hope, to restore blood and circulation and stave off frostbite. Many are successful, but others go to the hospital and directly to the gas chambers. Some of the more fortunate go directly to the ovens.

It is several weeks after the announcements, that we receive visitors to the storehouses. I receive a summons to meet the men, fearful knowledge of my activities on Grabner's behest has been learned.

"Hauptsturmfuhrer Aumeier, this is the lagerkapo for this facility."

I remove my cap and stand straight, nodding towards the camp director.

"What is your name?" His sneer is more authoritarian than any I've seen.

"Lagerkapo Filip, Hauptsturmfuhrer."

"I'm told you're the most experienced kapo we have in managing the storehouses." He continues to look at me, studying me.

"Is there a problem, Hauptsturmfuhrer?" I am fearful.

"No, Kapo, no problem." He walks past me and looks into the warehouse, turns and continues to address me. "You have shipped more material to Berlin than any other kapo. More than any SS officer." He glares at the men with him. "And you keep very good records."

"Thank you, Captain Aumeier." I don't know what to think.

"These barracks are insufficient for our purposes. We're opening a larger sorting and storage facility at Birkenau. There'll be thirty buildings to sort and store the things that are collected."

He looks at his entourage then back at me. "You'll take charge of the facility in Birkenau and function as lagerkapo. You'll maintain reports and file them with my office every day. You'll prepare shipments to the SS Economic Office Administration once a week. You'll see that all perishable items are sent to the administration offices of the camp." He relaxes and slaps his side. "Is that completely understood, Lagerkapo?"

"Yes, Hauptsturmfuhrer."

"We'll start with six hundred prisoners in each shift. You'll select an arbeitkapo to oversee the two shifts, and more if you see the need." He turns to leave, but stops short. "You'll begin now, Lagerkapo."

I know I shouldn't ask questions, but I want to ensure Anna and I will be together. "Excuse me, Herr Director, but may I take my present kommando with me?"

He narrows his eyes and seems irritated. "Take the men. Leave the women." He pauses, more to measure my reaction, I thought, than for a reply.

"Yes, sir, just the men." I struggle against showing my disappointment.

SS guards wait outside to escort the kommando to Birkenau, leaving a few moments to hold Anna. "I'm sorry, love. I'll find a way to get you with me."

"Oh, Filip, I love you so. You're all that makes this place bearable." Tears streak her face.

I kiss her cheeks and hold her tightly. "I'll worry about you, Anna. Please don't keep playing the soldier. I couldn't bear to lose you."

She kisses me hard and whispers in my ear. "I'm your woman, Filip, but I'm a soldier, too."

CHAPTER EIGHTEEN

The prisoners experience especially hard times in 1943. The year began showing us Germany wasn't all-powerful, what with the defeats in Africa and Russia, and the Americans taking Sicily. For some of us, it is the first news we hear of America being in the war, fighting the Germans alongside the Russians and British.

We gain hope from the news of Germany's losses, even when we learn of the destruction of the Jewish ghetto in Warsaw. We believe the conditions in KL Auschwitz will improve, that the SS will see how much they need our labor, and recognize our importance. But the reality is the SS grows more sinister and cruel, inflicting more hardships on the prisoners and laborers.

I learn from an SS guard that the year is 1944. Already I have been in the stamlager for more than three and half years, a long time to survive in this place. I realize that Jakub and I are the only survivors from that first transport from Tarnow, the only survivors of the first hundred prisoners, at least, as far as I know.

On a cold and snowy day more prisoners arrive at the kommando, increasing the staff to more than eleven hundred workers in two shifts. They are a disturbing lot, more near death than life, emaciated and almost too weak to work.

The SS guard smiles at me as I shake my head. "Muslims, Lagerkapo. Walking dead."

Women, too, come to the camp, their heads showing dark stubble where hair is growing. They, too, are in very bad shape, causing me to wonder how much longer they can survive the harshness.

The NCO approaches me, his face a mask of consternation. "Nothing more than schmutzstuck, Lagerkapo. They look ready to die. I doubt they'll be of any use to you."

The first SS guard is still smiling. "Sure they will, Sergeant, tomorrow morning." He laughs at his joke and wanders off, leaving me to puzzle the meaning.

The NCO sees the look on my face. "Here, 'tomorrow morning' means never."

I spread the new laborers evenly throughout the lager, hoping they will find food or other nourishment quickly, anything that will allow them time to rebuild their bodies.

I meet with the new kapos in my office. "From the appearance of your block, you have had a difficult time. It will be easier here." I lean on the desk. "It will be easier because you will not be beating anyone."

"How are we going to get them to work?"

"Yeah, if we don't lay into them once in a while, then they quit working. You got to bash them to get them to work."

"You'll persuade them to work, because if they don't they'll go to work at the crematorium."

"I'm not sure I like this. The SS expects us to beat some of these people to death."

"What's your name?" I stand as straight as I can and look down at the shorter kapo."

"It's Felix."

I glare at the man. "You address me as lagerkapo. You beat any man or woman in this block, Felix, then you will be sent to the Sonderkommandos without your status."

I look at each of the faces watching me. "If any of you beat anyone in this kommando, then you will be sent to work the ovens. If any of you report this conversation to the SS, then I'll use you to show the SS that I'm brutal and treat my charges ruthlessly.

"Any questions?" I watch them as a few smile and others lower their heads. "Go to work. I'll arrange for potatoes in the soup and an extra serving of bread tonight. But for now, look the other way when someone is stealing food."

Nearly thirty find food and engorge themselves, only to have their stomachs seize and contract with terrible pain. These are set in the alleys between the storehouses to be carted to the cremation pits the next morning.

One of the more emaciated prisoners is familiar to me. I don't recognize him at first, as his body is so very thin, his hair white, and his back stooped. That he has been selected to work surprises me, remembering how old he was when we first met. I approach him slowly remembering the last time I saw him. "Father Jan?"

He rises quickly, standing straight and looks at me through cloudy eyes, as his lower lip flutters. "I don't know that name." His mind is racing. "When I had a name, it was Oscar."

His denial of his identity surprises me. "I'm Filip Stitchko, from Katy. I was the constable."

He nods and slowly relaxes into his bent posture. "I remember you. You took care of the moron, the one with a Jewish name." He says the word Jewish in an odd, distasteful way. "I remember his father as well. Not a good Christian. Always associating with the Jews."

"His name is Jakub. He, too, has survived here." I am angry with the priest and his veiled animosity towards Jews. "How long have you been here, Priest?"

"How does one know how long he has been here?" He straightens as best he can and looks me in the eyes. "It seems like many years. Perhaps it's been forever. Maybe it has only been a short time."

"Yes, time only tends to cause more pain."

He nods and looks at my armband. "Are you kapo here?"

"I'm lagerkapo. I look after all of these storehouses." For some reason I want him to know I am more important in this hell than I was in our village.

"And how do you rationalize your crimes?" The self-righteousness he always showed in the village, especially to those who didn't attend his mass or listen to his sermon, makes itself evident, as evident as when he had to talk to me or Aron or any of the Jews. I recall the many times he would glance at me, but look away as he continued to talk, always leaving me feeling uneasy.

The memory of his keeping Jakub from school and me flashes in my mind, sparking old animosities. "Tell me, Father Jan, do you think we should still render unto Caesar the things of Caesar?" I look at him wondering if he would remember that sermon.

"That's from the Bible, I think."

"Luke, chapter twenty, Priest. And you preached we should render unto Hitler the things of Hitler." I bend down to see his face. "You're a thing of Hitler. You must render yourself to Hitler, old man. And as long as I'm in charge of this lager, you'll render unto me."

I don't feel the satisfaction I want to feel, but it doesn't matter. The priest is found in his bunk the following morning. I wonder if he ever regretted giving that sermon.

The New Year brings more news of the war, news that should have brought hope, but everyone is guarded against optimism. Yet in March, the Russians crossed the Bug River, and we know that once in Poland, it won't take long to liberate the camps. But it does, for in June the allies enter Rome, and two days later, they land somewhere in France. But we of Auschwitz remain prisoners of Germany.

Still the news comes, items giving false hope to all of us. We learn we aren't the only ones who hate Adolf Hitler, as some of his officers try to kill him. We curse their failure. And news from Warsaw comes after we learn of the liberation of Paris. The Russian army stands on the banks of the Vistula, the same river on which Birkenau sits, and the Poles are fighting back, fighting the Germans in the streets of Warsaw. Even I want to be jubilant, but I do not expect too much from the Allied armies.

The year grinds on painstakingly and more trains arrive on the siding at Birkenau, pouring the people from the cattle cars to the makeshift showers and clouds of gases that end their lives. And into the lager flows their possessions, clothes, shoes, bags, and suitcases, a flood of material requiring scrutiny, sorting, and shipping to Germany. And with the tidal wave of material comes another contingent of workers, my Anna among them.

Our reunion is blissful, as we caress each other longer than either of us has ever been held. She is thinner, her hair shorn, and her cheeks sunken, but she is as beautiful as the first time I saw her.

She tells me of how they receive less rations from the new kapo at Kanada I, a German criminal who preys upon her and the other women.

"He came at me, too, but I resisted and finally fought back." She intertwines her fingers with mine and lays her head on my shoulder. "It just made him meaner and angrier. He lashed out at me, beating me to the floor of the building, but I stayed conscious, fearing he would take me if I didn't."

I bite my lip and hold her tighter, hatred and anger growing in me.

"He did this frequently. He believed I would eventually consent to his ardor." She looks up at me with those brown eyes, so much darker than I remembered. "But I knew I could never tolerate a German pig touching me." She smiles slightly. "Not alive."

Again I grip her hand and ask softly, "And what of this man now?"

She sits up and looks at me. "He's cruel, my love. Don't try to hurt him."

I try to conceal my anger. "Where is he?"

"He was transferred with our group. He's here in the lager."

I kiss her gently and feel the tremble in her lips.

"No, Filip. I'm with you now. He'll not bother me again."

"No, he won't." I pull her to me and hold her tightly. "What's his name?"

"Kapo Karl." She pushes away and looks at me. "He's big, Filip, too big to hurt."

I release her and lift her to stand, again holding her. "You stay here. I want to have a word with this kapo."

"Filip, don't anger him. He's dangerous."

I pick up my baton as I leave the room and search for the new arrivals. I find them in the fourth building, and he isn't hard to spot. He is big and looks as dangerous as Anna said.

I approach my underkapo for the building. "How are things here?"

He looks at me and shakes his head. "Not good." He looks towards the German and continues. "Already he has beaten three workers senseless for no reason."

"You're oberkapo in this building. Can't you control him?"

"I'm Jewish, Lagerkapo, and he says he will get to me before the day is over."

"Then this man is disrupting the operations here, wouldn't you say?" I look at the kapo as kindly as my anger will allow.

"Yes. We'll not get much work done today."

"I can't allow that." I start for the German.

"Be careful, Lagerkapo. He's a dangerous man."

I study the man carefully, trying to decide on the best strategy to use against him. He is a bully and a rapist. He uses his size and bulk to intimidate, but he is a prisoner here in Birkenau, not a soldier in the most brutal army in the world, obviously unacceptable to the SS.

I stop ten feet from him and put on my fiercest mien and scream at the man. "You, Kapo! Come here!"

He looks at me briefly and glances at my armband, confused for a moment and casually walks to stand in front of me. I recognize him before he recognizes me, the same man I had doused with sewage at Tarnow, the biggest man I had ever seen.

Just as I see the acknowledgment in his expression, I swing my baton upwards, striking him just below the ear, sending him reeling against a sorting table, where he tries to stand on legs too weakened to support him. He falls to the floor and his baton shoots from his grasp, but as he attempts to sit up, I crash my foot into his face. He rolls onto his side and reaches for the club, but I stamp on his hand, crushing it. He screams loudly and I backhand him with the stick, shattering his upper teeth, jaw, and nose. But he still struggles to regain his feet, charges me, and crashes into a table, where I kick with all my might to his groin, again buckling his knees, forcing him to the floor. As he kneels, I slam the baton against the back of his head, and can hear the crack of bone as blood spatters me and the floor.

My breathing is hard as I look around me. No one is looking in my direction, except the oberkapo.

"I saw him attack you, Lagerkapo. You were only defending yourself and disciplining a lazy worker."

"And thief." I wipe the blood from my face and smile at the kapo. "You can call me Filip."

"I'm Leon, Filip."

"Thank you. And I'm your friend."

He is startled, but acknowledges my statement with a nod.

I kneel beside the inert body of Kapo Karl and remove the armband denoting his rank just as two SS enter the room.

"What's this?"

"A haftlinge, sirs, a worthless prisoner. He's fertig, finished in this camp. I'll not tolerate a thief in my lager."

They look at the remains of the man and examine his skull. "Good, Kapo. The camp director will be pleased."

I watch as the body crew drags his inert form to the waiting wagon, and realize I had killed my first German. I can't say it is satisfaction I feel, as my body still trembles with the rage, but I can face Anna and assure her there is nothing to fear from him.

Shortly after Anna and I are reunited, Master Sergeant Heinz Hirt comes to Birkenau, as SS superintendent of the cremation pits. It is a less than jovial Hirt who comes to the lager to see me, demoted to his old rank of Oberscharfuhrer, or staff sergeant. But he is still SS and ranks above me, and I know better than to anger him.

"How may I help you, Staff Sergeant?" I can't help using his lower rank.

"It's how I may help you, Kapo." He sits opposite me, slouching in the chair. "You can see I've fallen a bit since last we met."

"I'm sorry."

"It's no matter. But I must get away from the Sonderkommando. It's too depressing, too dangerous, even for SS." He makes a wide sweep and clasps his hands.

I look at him, unable to guess how I fit in his plans.

"I haven't come up with a plan as yet, but I'll find a way." He continues to hold his hands together, almost in supplication, and points them at me. "Unless you can think of a way."

"Me? You forget my position here." I am surprised and angry. "You also forget how you left me in the pits, of how you took another kommando and used them. You forget this, Staff Sergeant, and now you come to me for help." I stand over him and walk to the door, reminding myself that I'm not this man's equal. "But," I turn to face him, "we have worked well together."

He doesn't move or even try to explain away his past behavior. "And we can work together again. You're lagerkapo now. You have ways to obtain things, ways to get things done. You'll think of a way."

He rises to leave and stops at the door. "That friend of yours, the mentally defective one, is having trouble with a certain kapo."

"Jakub? What sort of trouble?"

"Jakub, yeah, that's his name. As I understand it, it began a week or more ago." He returns to the chair and eases himself into it.

"This friend of yours was driving a truck. It had been raining so the ashes were clumping together." He slumps in the chair. "At the river, he had to break the load with a shovel, and, somehow or other, when the ashes fell into the river, he spotted something that wasn't ashes. He plunged after it."

"The kapo, Tolik, went after Jakub, followed by an SS guard." Hirt sits up, but doesn't look at me. "He started beating him over the head and back, laying into him brutally, but Jakub just bent over protecting whatever it was from Tolik's baton."

"When this Tolik stopped hitting him, Jakub stood and showed them the lifeless body of a baby." The sergeant moves to the edge of the chair. "He carried it up the embankment, where the soldier snatched the small body from him and threw it onto the bed of the truck. It was returned to the pits and cremated."

He takes a deep breath. "Anyway, Jakub refused to drive a truck anymore and they put him to work in the pits. It's dirty, filthy work and he doesn't take to it very well.

"The trucks no longer work, anyway. We don't have enough petrol. The ashes are dumped in the marsh, buried, or spread throughout the area." He rises and starts for the door. "Your man doesn't take well to this new work, and this Jewish kapo is always beating him. I don't think Jakub will last much longer."

"Thank you for telling me." I smile slightly. "How is your pipel?"

"He works in the pits, too. I need to get him out of there as well."

"I'll think of a way. I'll send word as soon as possible."

He nods and leaves as quickly as he had come. And he left me to wonder what I can do to get him transferred to my lager. Him, Jakub, and Freimark. And Tolik, too.

I meet Hirt the following morning after roll call. "Staff Sergeant? I would like to speak with you."

He struts over, pretending irritation. "What, so soon?" He keeps his expression harsh. "You're a clever man, Pole."

"I have information which you can use." I lower my voice. "With it you'll be able to show Captain Aumeier intelligence concerning a possible uprising on the part of the Sonderkommandos." I straighten and watch his eyes closely. I can see the avarice in them and realize I still can't trust him. "The information concerns a Russian munitions expert who is supplying technical information to a Jewish underground."

"Who?" His eyes widen.

"I don't remember, Sergeant. I won't be able to remember anything until Jakub is transferred to my lager." It is a dangerous game to be playing, but it is the only plan I have.

"I can't use that. But I can tell them there is a lagerkapo who knows, and the SS will get it out of you." The fire returns to his eyes.

"Yes, I think they could, along with information concerning an NCO who helped organize in the lager and who organized a lot of money from the Third Reich."

I expect him to explode, but he just stares at me. "Okay. I'll transfer the dummy today." He shifts his feet and stares at me. "I'll send Jan as well."

"And Tolik."

"Tolik?" He pauses. "Why the kapo?"

"As a cover for transferring the other two, and because I want to deal with him myself." I want to neutralize this kapo and show Jakub I can still protect him.

"Done. But you give me the names today."

"Tomorrow. At roll call." I'm not sure why I want to delay giving him the information, except that I hold the power and have the advantage over him.

As I return to my office, Anna bursts in, smiling and waving her arms. She kisses me passionately. "I'm a good soldier, my love."

"What have you done, Anna? Killed the Fuhrer?"

"I wish." She releases me and steps back. "I carried a bomb, a real bomb, from Monowitz to Birkenau. It wasn't big, but the fact that I was able to do it was wonderful."

"Where did you get a bomb?"

"From Timofei. It was small, only to show them how to assemble one." She was very pleased with herself.

"You scare me, Anna. What if the Germans had caught you?"

"I would be dead, and so would the ones who caught me, and any others who were close enough." She kisses me again. "But I wasn't caught."

As she lies in my arms, I realize the risks Anna is taking are too dangerous. It is then I decide to give Hirt Borodin's name.

The others come before Hirt and I greet Kapo Tolik as he pushes Jakub and Jan into my office. He is a short man, stoutly built with big hands and a barrel chest. His face is a mask of frowns and snarls. He reminds me of the criminal kapos that greeted us when we came from Tarnow. I assign him to work outside the barracks, clearing the suitcases and parcels from the alleys and bringing them to the storehouses for sorting.

I give jobs to Jan and Jakub as well, working side by side in the shipping area, packing large crates with items destined for Berlin. Jakub is pleased to see me, but much of the light in his eyes is gone and I fear he has seen too much and lived through more than his mind can stand.

I put Jakub and Jan in the last line of the block and walk to the front and finish my morning count. In the cool air Hirt watches me, pacing back and forth, his impatience obvious. As the prisoners queue for their coffee and soup, he sidles beside me and motions for us to move away from the area.

"Well." His tone makes me realize he is desperate. "What have you got?"

"A name, a given name, but it shouldn't be too hard for the SS to find him."

"You tricked me, Pole." He grabs me by the arm and squeezes.

"There will be an uprising, Sergeant. A Jewish uprising." I don't want to give him too much.

"This whole damn place is filled with Jews, damn it."

"It will be in Birkenau. Among the Sonderkommandos." It is all I wanted to give him.

"I need more." His tone is angry, urgent.

"If you have more, why would they need to assign you to my lager?" I let the question sink in. "You can gather all the intelligence needed if you're in the right location."

"I'm in the right location! I'm in the pits!"

"But the information is in Kanada lager." I am sure he is going to turn me over to the SS.

He releases my arm and nods. "You're clever, Filip. I tell Aumeier I learn it from one of the prisoners in Kanada, and…"

"You overheard it from one of the storehouses in Kanada."

"That I overheard two laborers talking about supplying…"

"Not supplying, not two laborers in my lager. Too dangerous."

"Then what?" He is calmer, but frustrated.

"You overheard two Jews talking about a Russian munitions expert, named Timofei, who is teaching the Sonderkommandos of Birkenau how to build bombs." I relax as I hold his gaze. "And that's all you heard before a kapo broke them up."

"A Russian named Timofei. That's good. I hope it works."

"It'll work, Staff Sergeant. Tell them you think you can find the two Jews and learn more." I lower my head at the approach of the camp director.

"Sergeant, what's going on here? You're holding up this work detail." Aumeier's uniform is crisp and fitted to his physique.

"I was questioning this man about information in his lager, sir." He doesn't even glance at me.

"Are you finished?" The captain is impatient.

"Yes, sir."

"Then dismiss him." The camp director starts to leave.

"Hauptsturmfuhrer? I would like a word with you." He turns to me. "You're dismissed, Lagerkapo."

I bow slightly and watch as Hirt joins the camp director,

matching his pace to the officer's and I wonder if I am doing the right thing.

I visit shipping on my arrival at the lager and find Jakub and Jan working without conversation. I check all the stations and handle some of the items on the table, palming a few diamonds and rubies. I spot a beautiful diamond bracelet and am tempted to take it as well, but don't want to risk being seen.

I take the gems to the kapos' barracks and locate Tolik's bunk. I find the beret he wore with the Sonderkommandos, and carefully insert three diamonds and two rubies into the lining of the cap, leaving it as I found it.

I wait until after the evening count and approach the SS officer assigned to the lager. I tell him I suspect some of the kapos have been stealing and recommend a search of their barracks. He agrees as he welcomes the opportunity to harass the laborers.

He carries the search further than I want, bringing in additional SS and beginning in the laborers' building. He and I go directly to the kapos' barracks and begin the search.

I watch as an SS private pushes Tolik aside and searches the bunk. The German picks up the beret and finds its contents.

The lieutenant rips the lining from the cap and watches as the five gems tumble to the floor.

"Those aren't mine." Tolik's response shows his incredulity.

The German just stares at him. "Where is your bunk?"

Tolik points to his bed, then the jewels. "Those are not mine, sir."

The officer looks at the young soldier. "Where did you find this?" He holds out the beret.

"Hier, Untersturmfuhrer." He points to Tolik's bunk.

The German holds the cap in front of the kapo's face. "Whose beret is this?"

"It's mine, Lieutenant, but those aren't my gems."

"You're right, Jew. They belong to the Third Reich."

Tolik is taken into custody, screaming his innocence.

I am pleased until two more of the kapos are taken for having stolen canned goods and cigarettes from the lager.

As we leave the barracks the SS officer is pleased and congratulates me for recommending the search. We walk into the courtyard and are met by the SS contingent and seven members of my lager. Tolik, who seems totally defeated, the other two kapos, and four laborers, including Jan Freimark.

"This has been a good night, Lagerkapo. Your cooperation will be noted to the camp director." He points to Tolik and Freimark. "These two are the most ambitious. The kapo had these gems, but this one," he holds up the diamond bracelet, "this one has an eye for beauty."

I am stunned. In my desire for vengeance, I have gotten Jan arrested. It will be a sad time for Jakub, but Sergeant Hirt will take it worse than any of us. I fear the man's anger and know he holds the power of life or death in his hands. I wish it wasn't mine.

CHAPTER NINETEEN

Staff Sergeant Hirt arrives the following morning. Five of those arrested are sent to Sonderkommandos and Tolik and Freimark are held at SS headquarters.

Hirt is pleased to be assigned to Kanada, and exhibits the best demeanor I can recall, very pleased with his performance for the camp director. "I told the captain that I had stopped to light a cigarette when I heard two men talking. I explained how I listened and heard them talking about bombs and that the Jewish Sonderkommandos were going to start an uprising like the one in Warsaw."

He paces the room with quick steps, his arms waving about. "I described how I heard the kapo beat them and force them back to work, and of how I entered the storehouse and found the two men who were nursing a recent beating. I informed him that they were Jews."

"And now you're here."

"Yes. They want me to gather as much information as I can. They want the identity of this Russian named Timofei." He stops in front of me. "And you're going to tell me who he is."

I feared he would take this tone. "You have all I have. I can get the name of the Russian for you, but I would take my time surrendering your intelligence." I need to stall him. "If you make it look easy, they'll think you were making it up just to be reassigned."

"Possibly." He squints at me with a scowl on his face. "But you're going to give me the name of this Russian now."

He is prepared to beat it out of me. "His name is Borodin. Timofei Borodin, but I don't know where he works." I watch as the sergeant holds his menacing stance. "I think he's new to Auschwitz."

"So?" He continues to hover over me.

"When assigned to work, he was given a number, which was probably tattooed on his arm." I don't want to look at his evil face and hold my head down, looking at the floor.

"You don't have a number or a tattoo." He just knows I am lying to him, just as he will lie to me whenever it suits him.

"Number forty-four." I raise my head to look at him. "They weren't doing tattoos when I came."

"All right, so he has a tattoo." Confusion has again crept into his eyes as he looks about and avoids looking at me.

I enjoy his denseness. "You have a tattoo, Staff Sergeant. Why?"

"They record my blood type and other things in case I'm wounded."

"And a tattoo for a prison laborer records name and whether he is a Jew, a Pole, or something else." I relax and look at him for a few moments, waiting to see if he would come to the conclusion I intended. "Match his name to a number, then you will know where he's working and can find where his barracks are located."

He nods and pulls up a chair. "How long do you think I should wait before I give them this intelligence?" Not surprisingly, he ignores the information I have given him.

"A week, no more."

He sits quietly, pondering his situation, and I decide it is time he knows about his pipel. "I've some bad news."

He hardly responds, keeping his eyes on the floor. "What?"

"There was an inspection last night. They found stolen property on seven of the lager. Tolik was one and Jan was another."

He jerks his head up and bounds to his feet, upending the chair.

"The little fool. I told him I would get him more rations once I joined him."

"It wasn't food, Oberscharfuhrer. It was a very beautiful diamond bracelet."

I reason the bracelet had been intended for the sergeant, something more than a gift, more akin to a bribe, but doubt he will acknowledge it.

He rights the chair and sits, his head in his hands. "Where is he?"

"I can only guess. Five were transferred to the Sonderkommandos, but Tolik and Jan are being held."

"The basement of SS headquarters." He raises his head and bites his lip, and I can see tears in the corners of his eyes. He strikes his chest and speaks softly. "God help the poor bastard." With that, he bolts from the room to express his grief alone, I guess, and curse his helplessness, for there isn't a thing he can do.

Jakub is next to learn the bad news. I tell him as gently as I can and he accepts it without saying anything. Even his eyes are dry.

A siren rings at mid-shift and all the laborers from the lager are assembled in the large courtyard adjacent to the Kanada barracks. Nearly a thousand men and women stand in the cold as the portable gallows is towed into place by the SS personnel. There are three nooses hanging from the top bar and three chairs set beneath them.

The three men, Tolik, Jan Freimark, and another I don't know, climb the steps to the platform, pushed by an SS guard, and followed by Camp Director Aumeier, who steps to the front of the gallows and addresses the lager.

"These men stole from the Third Reich. This will not be tolerated. You'll see what we do to anyone who attempts to steal from Germany." He steps back and motions for the nooses to be placed over the heads of the prisoners. "Any more attempts by anyone in this lager to steal anything will result in the entire camp trading places with those in the Sonderkommandos."

From where I stand at the rear of the formation, I can see his news has a tremendous impact. Then it suddenly grows worse.

"Lagerkapo, come forward." The camp director is looking at me, and I trot to stand in front of the gallows. "Yes, Herr Director?"

"Two of these are part of your lager, Kapo. The other was caught sneaking through the wire with cigarettes. Your work is lax, Lagerkapo." His face is stern, but he seems to be enjoying himself. "Come up here."

My heart seems to stop, but I struggle with wobbly knees to climb the steps to the platform, where a guard reaches for my baton, startling me. I stand before Aumeier, my head bowed. "Yes, Herr Director."

"Don't be so down, Lagerkapo. This is only a lesson to teach you to be stricter, harsher with these people. You must treat them ruthlessly or they will take advantage of you, just like this vermin. I want the lager to fear you, Kapo."

I relax and breathe a sigh of relief knowing my life is not yet over. "Yes, Herr Director. I will make them fear me."

"Good, but just so you'll remember this, you'll hang these men."

I jerk my head up and stare at the camp director, who is smiling at me, a sinister, evil expression covering his face. "Don't think about it, Lagerkapo, just stand in front of them and push the chairs backward. It's as easy as that. Just do it." He walks from the platform and stands in front of it, along with the guards, leaving me alone with the three men.

I stand there and look at them. Only once have I killed anyone, and I did so then out of anger and the realization that he could have killed me. I have struck them, beaten them, even manipulated their deaths, but the Germans have done the dirty work. Now I must kill men who are no threat to me, to kill as ruthlessly as the SS. I can't bring myself to look at them, especially Tolik, nor can I bring myself to move.

"Lagerkapo. Do this now or you'll join them." Aumeier's voice carries its authoritarian edge, but he softens it and speaks in an almost whisper. "Don't think about it, Lagerkapo, just do it."

I step in front of the stranger and push the chair hard, upsetting it and forcing the man to dangle, kicking with his feet and twisting his body. I move to Tolik and have to look at him. He is staring across the plains of the camp, his eyes glazed and his lips moving, a silent prayer, coming with his last breath. I kick his chair with equal force, and he falls hard against the rope, which stills him immediately.

I hesitate before I move to Jan, and as I stand in front of him, I look at his face. He is smiling and his eyes sparkle. He whispers, "Danke, Filip. Thank you."

I push the chair quickly and allow him to fall against the rope, but his body isn't heavy enough to choke him. I can hear the rasping and wheezing of his struggle to breathe, as he twists his body and kicks with his legs, trying to tighten the rope around his neck. He fights with it, his eyes wide, still alert, still alive, but filled with fear and terror. As hard as he fights, he can't tighten the rope, and he continues suspended, still breathing, still kicking and twisting occasionally, as the lager is forced to witness his slow death.

I hear Aumeier chatting with the men around him, as Jan's breathing becomes more labored, raspy and wheezing, but I can't look at him, too afraid to see the anguish in his eyes. I stand with my head bowed, looking at the planks of the platform trying to block out the sounds of strangulation, of a slow death. Finally, after interminable minutes, a long slow breath escapes Jan's body and he becomes quiet. I look at his open-mouth face, the eyes fixed on a distant horizon, just as his head relaxes and flops to his chest with lifeless eyes staring at me.

I turn and slowly walk down the steps to be halted by Aumeier. "I hope this is a lesson to you, Lagerkapo. Let's not have any more theft from the storehouses." He steps back and looks at me. "Any more and it'll be your neck in the noose. Understand?"

"Yes, Herr Director." I tremble as I look at him and try as I can, I can't stop it.

"Now, back to work. Los! Hurry!"

The SS guard throws the baton at my feet, and I quickly retrieve it and run towards the unit.

Aumeier stands by the gallows and watches as I trot to the front of the lager, screaming for the oberkapos and arbeitkapos to take them to work. They run all the way and disappear into one of the thirty buildings that make up the lager. I have never been so frightened in my life, and, once out of sight of Aumeier, I stop and throw up, ending with dry heaves and the recurring vision of Jan's breathing and his accusatory eyes.

Anna is waiting for me when I reach the office, my face drained of blood, my stomach still twitching. She wraps her arms around me and holds me.

There isn't a lot she can say to ease my burden, but her eyes tell me she understands my pain.

As I sit next to her, I ask the question foremost in my mind. "How do you get the pictures of death out of your mind? You're a soldier, how do you do it?"

"I don't. They're still there, but I never killed anyone like that. I never saw the damage I did." She strokes my forehead, pushing my hair back.

"I was sick. I am sick. I knew two of those men. Jan was even a friend, more to Jakub than to me, but a friend."

"I know, my love. I'm sorry, but you'll learn to live with this. We all do."

I open my eyes and Jakub is standing there, looking at Anna with a frown, then me. "I'm sorry, Filip."

His eyes are hollow and I can see the bones of his shoulders pressing against his skin, and realize for the first time that he isn't eating the things I have given him. "Thank you, Jakub. I'm sorry, too."

He nods and leaves. I chastise myself for not looking after him better, and wonder if he is still working in shipping. I promise myself that I will speak to the kapo of that department and make sure Jakub is treated kindly.

I resume my duties as Anna continues her activities on behalf of the Sonderkommandos, making deliveries to the crematoria and talking with the Jewish women who are supplying the gunpowder. I have told her about Hirt, of his investigation into a suspected uprising, leaving out my role. I urge her to quit, but she always kisses me and tells me it is what she does, that she is fighting back.

The workload at the Kanada lager increases terribly after this time, as more and more suitcases, parcels, and bags are delivered and stacked against the outside walls of the storehouses. More prisoners come to the lager, bringing the total of workers to over nineteen hundred. The accumulation continues as mountains of unsorted belongings clutter the lager, and the buildings overflow faster than we can manage.

I plead for trains to take all of the crates and boxes to Berlin, only to be told there is a war and all trains are needed elsewhere. But I can see where the trains are, shuttling people from the various ghettos to the gas chambers and crematorium. It is more than I can handle, but the camp director insists I remain at the job. He relaxes his stance on stolen goods, allowing the workers to take canned goods and other foods that are not destined for the SS. He even allows them to drink wine, as there is more than the German army can drink.

But still the work piles up. I move crates and boxes bound for Berlin to the outside, stacking them between the buildings and moving the unsorted material into the buildings, yet the work continues to increase, as more and more transports come with Jews and their belongings.

It is one of these transports, one in which able-bodied men and women are selected to work, that news from Warsaw is received. We learn the Russian army did not cross the Vistula, and the

Polish home army surrendered Warsaw to the Germans. We learn, too, that Warsaw is being razed.

I never saw the capital city, but Aron had said it was large and crowded, but beautiful and clean, always busy with people flitting about like bees and dragonflies. Sadness fills me when I hear the news and realize that we have been disappointed again.

But, for the Sonderkommandos at crematorium four, it signals a time to strike back. A truckload of SS arrives early in the morning, and the Jews of the crematorium guess their turn in the gas chamber has come. They pelt the Germans with stones and any other weapons they have, forcing the SS to withdraw from the area. They put into operation their plans for escape and destruction of the crematorium, setting fire to the building and placing a bomb in the oven. It detonates and causes a great fire throughout the building.

The explosion and smoke prompts the Sonderkommando at crematorium two to also revolt. They overcome their German oberkapo and an SS guard. After pummeling them both, they throw them screaming into the oven. A third guard they overcome and beat to death. All of the Sonderkommandos attempt to escape, some making it to a barn in a nearby village, which the SS surrounds and sets ablaze, shooting any who try to escape.

The Jewish fire unit responds to the fire at crematorium four, and is cut down by German machine gun fire, reprisal for the attack on SS soldiers. None of the escaped prisoners make it, bringing it to a total of more than two hundred and fifty killed for their involvement. Another two hundred were lined up against the wall and shot as a reprisal. We try to learn how many of the SS have been killed, but the Germans say little about it.

Staff Sergeant Hirt isn't around during this time, neither is Anna. I try to find her, but have responsibility to ensure no one of my lager will be involved in the uprising. I force all of the laborers into the buildings and fasten the doors to keep anyone from leaving. All the kapos, oberkapos, arbeitkapos, and I patrol the buildings to make sure no one tries to leave the compound or participate in the uprising.

But mostly, I worry about Anna. Jakub is secure in building number one, and I remain close to that building in case Anna returns. I pace back and forth and wish for a cigarette, even as the SS are mobilizing their forces in preparation of a larger revolt. They come en masse to the lager, led by an SS officer, followed by the camp director.

"What are you doing out here, Lagerkapo." The SS man steps aside at the director's question.

I stand at attention. "Ensuring none of the lager leave these buildings, Herr Director. I've ordered everyone inside and secured the doors. My kapos are patrolling the area to make sure no one leaves the buildings."

He glances around the compound and can see the kapos standing in the alleyways keeping watch. "Very good, Lagerkapo." He turns to the SS officer. "Station a man at each building. Make sure no one leaves.

"You, Lagerkapo, get your men into the buildings. Make sure you remain there until you are told to leave."

"Yes, sir."

He departs and starts pointing to where he wants the men. I do as ordered, stressing to the kapos to secure the buildings completely. I warn them against making mistakes.

We remain in the buildings until the next morning, when we are called to assembly for the morning count. I am distressed when the kapos report the numbers to me, with one missing person, and that one is Anna. I fear her recklessness has finally caught up to her. I debate whether I should report a full count, but don't think I should risk it. I give the NCO my count less one, reporting that Anna Kalitnikova, a Russian POW, is missing.

I know what I should feel, but I feel nothing. If I had been braver, I would have lied and given the count as complete, but I'm not that brave. I don't know where she is, or even if she is alive, and I want to be angry with her, but am just too numb to feel anything.

The count is taken and delivered to the camp director's office, and we are kept standing for a long time. Finally, the NCO returns. "You can go to work, Lagerkapo."

I nod, but don't move. "Excuse me, Scharfuhrer. Should we recount?"

"No. The Russian has been arrested. The Gestapo is interrogating her now."

CHAPTER TWENTY

I have no heart to return to the lager, no desire, but I return more by habit than anything, return to my office to continue with a routine forced on me by my German masters. I am a slave, just as indentured as any of the two thousand souls in my lager, or the thousands of others spread throughout the three main camps or those in the more than forty sub camps. I am as much a slave as any of those led to the gas chambers, buying time with my labor, a luxury not afforded to those facing the gas. But I reason my turn is coming, that I will see a day when I walk down the steps and crowd into the room with hundreds of fellow slaves, as the gas pellets emit their poisonous vapors choking off my breath.

I awake, startled with the image, my chest tight and my breathing labored, until I realize it had only been a nightmare, only it isn't night and I wasn't asleep. It seems quieter than normal, more still than a day in the lager should be, a quiet and stillness suddenly broken by the shouts of SS guards.

I rise to investigate, only to meet a tall man in civilian dress, wearing a long, black leather coat with beads of water clinging to it.

"Lagerkapo? Gestapo. You will come with us." Two SS guards step behind me and motion for me to follow the agent.

I feel I am still dreaming. "May I ask where I'm to be taken?" The blow is sudden and smashes into my shoulder and neck, sending a bolt of lightning through my shoulder, arm, hand, neck, and head. I stumble and sprawl in the doorway, barely conscious, barely alert enough to hear the Gestapo agent scream at the soldier.

"You oaf! Imbecile. He's not under arrest. Do you want to carry him?" He taps me with his foot. "Can you stand?"

Hands on either side lift me to my feet and I stand facing the German. "Can you walk, Lagerkapo?"

I nod slowly. "Yes, Herr..." I search for his name, but can't remember him giving me one. "I can walk."

"Good. I'm Sturmbannfuhrer Hoffman." He smiles and nods his head. "If you'll follow me, we can proceed."

He extends me civility, preparing the goose for basting, I surmise, suspicious of German compliments. My head throbs and there is numbness in my left shoulder, extending to my fingers, and I'm not able to walk very fast, but it doesn't matter, for there is a car waiting outside the gate. I lower my head to enter the vehicle and notice for the first time that it is raining gently, almost imperceptibly, reminding me of gentle spring showers and green fields stretching as far as I could see.

The car moves slowly, its wipers sluggishly moving across the windscreen, stopping whenever the car speeds up, only to resume its pendulum movement, sweeping only a few raindrops in its path. The Gestapo agent turns in his seat and extends his hand to me. "Would you care for a cigarette, Lagerkapo?" He offers me one, holding a white pack with a red circle on it. "Americaner. Very good."

My mind wanders back to my days in school, a time when Aron and I were friends, always together, always helping each other. He had studied Homer, Plato, or one of the other Greek historians, I don't remember which, and was holding class for me and Jakub. I remember a line Aron gave us, "Beware of Greeks bearing gifts."

"Thank you." I accept the cigarette and put it between my lips as he holds a lighter to the end of it. I take a draw and cough, and the smoke makes me feel dizzy, dizzier than I already was. I take another draw and find it easier than the first and remember Aron's words, "Beware of Germans bearing gifts." I am sure he had said Germans, but my head is too fuzzy to know for certain.

I become afraid as we pass through the gate into Auschwitz and I recognize block eleven. It is there the SS likes to interrogate prisoners, in the basement, just before they bring them to stand against the black wall. I exit the car, toss my cigarette aside, and turn to face the German. "Thank you, Sturmbannfuhrer, for the cigarette."

"You're welcome." He takes my elbow and motions for me to precede him into the building.

An SS guard holds the door for us and I am directed to an office on the left. There is a large desk and an ashtray filled with cigarette butts, with one burning, the ash long and hanging into the tray. There is a large leather chair behind the desk and a picture of Adolf Hitler directly behind it. I sit and watch as the ash from the cigarette falls, slowly burning into nothing, much like the ashes from the pits.

There is no more light coming through the window, and I don't know how long I have waited, but it doesn't seem long. I sit as erect as I can, my mind still fuzzy, and try to remember why I am sitting in front of Father Jan's desk, trying to remember what mischief had brought me here. And where is Aron? I am always the one that is caught, but he never makes me accept punishment alone, always confessing and taking whatever was our due.

"So, Lagerkapo, we have reason to meet again." Camp Director Aumeier is sitting at the desk, lighting a cigarette.

I shake my head and blink several times, trying to recall why I am sitting in the office. I stand quickly. "I'm sorry, Herr Director."

He looks past me to someone standing there. "Is he well?"

"A thousand apologies, sir, but one of the guards, an oaf, clubbed him on the back of the head. He seems a little slow since then." It was the Gestapo agent, a name I can't remember.

"He probably has a concussion." The director purses his

lips and shakes his head.

"That'll work to our advantage, I would think." The Sturmbannfuhrer steps to my right and I can see him.

"Perhaps, you're right." Aumeier leans forward and rests his elbows on the desk. "Sit down, Lagerkapo, I have some questions for you, and I expect your full cooperation."

"Yes, Herr Director." My head is clearing and I feel my life is in danger.

"How did you come by the name of Timofei Borodin?" He isn't smiling, but his face doesn't carry the menacing expression I have seen so often before.

My mind races. I can tell them Anna told me, which would condemn her if she hadn't told them anything. I wonder from where they learned that I know the name, concluding it was Hirt. "I had heard the name several times about the lager. First, when I was summoned to the cremation pits, then in the lager, with one of the new kapos. He was a Jew named Tolik." I think it's best to give them the name of a dead man, and I don't think he would object.

"Who asked you to come to the cremation pits?" His look is becoming more intense.

I don't know what they are after, not with this line of questioning, but it is an opportunity to cast their attention away from me. "Scharfuhrer Hirt. He was the SS superintendent of the Sonderkommando at the time. He asked me to take Tolik to my lager." It is very narrow ground on which I tread, where a mistake will be my death either way, but I want to involve Hirt any way I can.

"And you agreed?"

I answer slowly, shaking my head a couple of times, finally lifting my left arm to my head, and feigning continuing problems as a result of the rifle blow. "Yes, sir. How could I refuse, he's SS." I let my arm flop to my lap and look at it. "I thought it irregular, but there's no one to talk to about such things."

"Do you know Anna Kalitnikova?" The question comes from the side, from the Gestapo agent.

I delay my answer, uncertain how to answer, but rationalize they know about the two of us. "Yes, sir."

"You were slow to answer. Why is that?" His tone is vile, filled with cunning and suspicion.

"I was afraid."

"Afraid? Because she is a conspirator?"

"A conspirator?" It is as I feared, but I doubt she involved me. "I don't know anything about that. We were lovers. I was afraid to admit it, afraid I would be..." I let the words hang, hoping one of them will take it.

"Shot, Lagerkapo?" Aumeier smiles at me and lights a cigarette with the butt of the old.

I know now who is directing the interrogation. "Yes, Herr Director."

"I'm not interested in some dalliance between my kapos and some Russian whore." He stands and stares at me, then the Gestapo agent. "I want to know who is responsible for blowing up my crematory.

"You, Lagerkapo, aren't telling me the whole truth." He throws the cigarette at me. "Perhaps, you would like to go to the basement and let the Gestapo learn what it is you aren't telling me."

"Please, Herr Director. I'm telling you what I know. I'll answer any question you ask of me, truthfully." I realize I had best stop trying to guess what they want and answer their questions as fully as possible.

Aumeier returns to his seat and motions for the agent to continue. "What did you and this woman, this Anna Kalitnikova, talk about?"

"Many things, Sturmbannfuhrer Hoffman," his name suddenly flashes into my brain, "but I wasn't interested in talking."

"I can imagine." Aumeier winks at Hoffman.

"But, still, there was some talk, wasn't there? With women, there's always some talk." They both laugh.

I keep silent, allowing them to enjoy their little joke. "She talked mostly about being a soldier, flying against German lines at night, attacking planes and tanks, and strafing German positions." I pause for a moment and clench and unclench my left hand. "She was very proud to be a soldier."

"Did she ever tell you what she was up to in the lager?" Hoffman's eyes are penetrating.

"She told me she had talked to several Jews who were planning an uprising, but I didn't think anything about it, Major."

"Did she know Tolik?" I sense a trap is being laid for me.

"I'm uncertain. She was my lauferin and carried messages from me to the oberkapos under me. There were times she left the lager, but I didn't say anything, because, because we were involved." I wish I knew what they know.

"And you didn't want to lose your whore, right, Lagerkapo?" Aumeier smiles broadly and wicks at Hoffman.

I become angry at his calling her that name, but I remind myself to stay calm. "No, Herr Director."

"But you don't know if she knew Tolik or not?" Major Hoffman is relentless.

"It's possible, Sturmbannfuhrer."

"Wasn't it she who told you about Borodin?"

I begin to feel trapped. "I don't remember, Major, we talked about a lot of things. She mentioned a Russian expert on explosives, but if she mentioned his name I wasn't listening."

"But you remember Tolik talking about Borodin?"

"I overheard the name. I remember them talking about an uprising." I start to add that they were copying the one in the Warsaw Ghetto, but remind myself to not give them too much information.

"You told Staff Sergeant Hirt that the man was a Russian munitions expert, didn't you?" Hoffman's eyes are narrow as he pulls a chair next to me and glares.

This is not the way Hirt had reported his conversation with Aumeier, and he had been boasting about the way he handled it. I again feel a trap is in his questions. "I volunteered information to the staff sergeant that I had overheard talk concerning a revolt, or an uprising, and that the only name I could give him was Timofei Borodin."

"And that name came from Albin Tolik?"

I hadn't given them Tolik's given name. "Yes, sir. Kapo Tolik, that's all I remember about his name."

Major Hoffman leans away from me and continues to study me. "Would you like another cigarette?"

"Yes, sir." My hand trembles when I accept it and place it in my mouth.

He is smiling as he holds the flame to the tobacco. "And what other things did you and this Russian woman, this whore, talk about?"

He is trying to goad me into losing my temper. "Nothing, sir. Just her combat experience and killing Germans." I say it on purpose, hoping to get a reaction, but they are too well trained. "I'm sorry, sirs."

"Did this woman have any friends in the lager?"

"I'm sure she did, but I don't know any of them."

"You weren't interested in that aspect of her life, were you?" Aumeier sits behind his desk in a cloud of gray smoke, his arms resting in his lap.

I lower my head. "No, sir."

"Tell me, Lagerkapo, did she ever mention the name of Rosa?"

"No, sir, not that I recall."

"How about Josef?"

"No, sir."

"Hershel?"

"No, sir."

"None of these names mean anything to you?" His voice is

raised and he speaks tersely.

I remember my father's advice to speak softly when others are angry, and I keep the edge off my voice. "No, sir."

Hoffman looks at Aumeier and shrugs.

The camp director leans forward and flicks his ash. "Before we return you to your kommando, Lagerkapo, is there anything else you can remember that would help us?" His mood is relaxed, his face a mask of simplicity.

"Any names you can recall from your romantic escapades with the Russian?" Hoffman springs on me, surprising me.

"Ella comes to mind." I speak before I think, realizing they tricked me into giving more than I wanted to give, but I am trapped. "Ella."

Hoffman relaxes. "And who was this Ella woman?"

"A Jewish woman she knew from some other place." I struggle to keep my composure, certain I have made a serious mistake.

Both Aumeier and Hoffman look at each other, a look of satisfaction on their faces.

It is Hoffman who continues. "What did she say about this woman?"

"That she visited her regularly. That they were old friends. Mostly women's stuff, really." I want to make as light of the relationship as I can.

"Where did she say they visited?" Aumeier asks the question very casually.

I know they can trace the movements of the Jewish woman and would discover a lie if I told it now. "Monowitz, I believe."

The Gestapo agent looks at the camp director, then back to me. "Does the name Ella Gartner mean anything to you?"

"No, sir."

"Did it ever occur to you that this Russian woman was carrying gunpowder to the Sonderkommando at Birkenau?" Hoffman's sneer is malignant.

"No, Sturmbannfuhrer. Why would I even consider such a thing?"

Both men rise at the same time. Hoffman lays the cigarettes on the desk and a box of matches. "Help yourself, Lagerkapo." They leave together and silence fills the room.

I try to remember the questions they asked and the answers I gave, but my head throbs and my eyes hurt. I try to reason what it is they are after, thinking I had once been a policeman and should fathom what it is they want from me. I only hope I have given them enough to be satisfied, but not enough to hurt Anna.

Anna, my beautiful, loving Anna. I wonder if I will ever see her again, if I will ever hold her in my arms, kiss her lips, and make love again. I wonder if I will ever lie beside her and listen to her breathing as she sleeps, satiated with our lovemaking, content in the embrace of each other. I sit there thinking of her, as warm feelings course through my body.

I sit in the chair and smoke Major Hoffman's cigarettes, wondering what they're going to do with me. I hope, I pray, they won't come back and repeat the same questions again, a technique we were taught for police work in Brest, a technique I had never had to use in tiny Katy.

Tiny Katy, I think, of how I had never thought of our village as small, but, after the war, after Auschwitz, it would be tiny, wonderfully tiny. I want to return to that little village more than anything on earth, return with Jakub, and light the lantern that serves as a beacon in the night. Perhaps, Jakub and I will run the store, but mostly, I want our lives unfettered with Germans or Russians. I want the vast plains of wheat and the quiet streets of a little town, away from swarms of soldiers and slaves, and I want to be free again, no longer a slave of Germans.

Suddenly, I understand that for which Anna was fighting. She had courage. She was a soldier, but, what's more, she had a clearer vision of our world, one where we obeyed, or one where we fought for the freedom they wanted to take away. Anna was fighting for that freedom. So were the Sonderkommandos, fighting to show the Germans we were not like some animals to be eradicated from the earth.

Light shines through the window and greets me as I stir from a slumped-over slumber, my back aching, and my head throbbing. There are no more cigarettes and I search through the ash in the ashtray hoping to find a butt with only a tiny bit of tobacco. But as I stir the ash, I envision the ashes from the pit and realize it is like trying to find a living person in those ashes.

AN SS guard enters the room and orders me to stand. "Lagerkapo, you're ordered to attend an assembly in the alleyway." His expression is like all German soldiers, devoid of emotion or even an ounce of compassion.

I follow him as he turns the corner and is greeted by Aumeier and Hoffman. "Morning, Lagerkapo. We have arranged a little entertainment. Watch, you might see someone you know."

Four prisoners are herded out into the courtyard and are marched up the steps of a gallows. Anna stands beside three women with the yellow Star of David sewn on their uniforms. All of their faces are badly bruised, their lips split open, and strangle marks around their necks. Anna's once beautiful face is broken, her eyes almost shut, and I hope she can't see me, lest she think I have betrayed her. They all look defiant, all proud and uncowed by the proceedings, even Anna, the soldier.

Aumeier turns to me. "I wanted you to know, Lagerkapo, that we appreciate your assistance."

I hesitate and don't know how to respond, fearful they are trying again to entrap me. "Thank you, Herr Director."

Hoffman offers me a cigarette. "Without your information on the Gartner woman, the Jew in the middle," he pointed to her, "we would never have been able to connect Kalitnikova to the uprising." His face is a sickening, smug grin.

I accept the light and draw in a deep draught. I start to say something, but can't find the words, thinking they never needed evidence or justification to kill anyone here.

The chairs are kicked from beneath them and I watch, smoking my cigarette and wishing it were me swinging from the rope instead of Anna. I have killed her. I hadn't meant to, but she is dead.

Maybe I'm dead, too. I don't feel anything and don't even remember walking back to the lager. It is a long walk, and I make it for no other reason than there is no other life for me. I make it because I belong in Auschwitz, and it is here that I should die.

As I enter the Kanada lager, Jakub comes to greet me. He looks worried, biting his lip and cheek and reaches for my hand. I, too, become worried. "What is it?"

"I was scared, Filip. I was scared they had taken you to the pits." His eyes are filled with tears, the first I had seen in a long time.

"I'm all right, Jakub. I'm here."

He wipes the tears with the back of his hand. "I was afraid I would be all alone. I didn't want to lose my best friend."

He touches me, like no other time in my life. I realize he is more than a promise for me to keep. He is the only friend I have in the world.

CHAPTER TWENTY-ONE

Things begin happening rapidly after the Sonderkommando uprising at Birkenau. Large trains suddenly become available for the shipments from the lager, and I receive orders to crate and pack only items that can be turned into gold or material for weapons. Aside, they tell me to forget leather goods, shoes, hairbrushes, eyeglasses, and even some food items. We pack boxes of currency from every country in Europe, including English pounds, Swiss francs, and American dollars. Box after box of jewelry and loose stones are loaded onto the boxcars that once carried the owners of the new treasure. And we sack and box many cases filled with gold teeth, coins, small bars, tableware, and plates.

All of the crates are destined for Berlin, but I observe some of the addresses have been altered for places like Vienna, Paris, Bern, Geneva, Rome, Budapest, Helsinki, Stockholm, and, most unusual of all, cities of which I'd never heard, Buenos Aires, Montevideo, São Paulo, and Ascensión. A shiver runs down my spine when I think of the implications, realizing the Germans are spreading out, running to every corner and crevice on earth, running away. They are defeated, at last, and it is only a matter of time before we will be liberated.

It turns cold, but not as cold as my heart when I see the train pull sluggishly into Birkenau. My hopes are dashed as I see all the people, the men and women, the children pulled from the cattle cars, milling around like mice in a box with nowhere to go. I am thankful I am too far away to hear the commands of the soldiers or listen to the cries of alarm caused by the massive shepherds which strain at their leashes to attack.

"That's the last of the trains, Lagerkapo." Staff Sergeant Hirt steps beside me and stares at the crowd. "Those zugange, new arrivals, will be gassed and cremated. Then we'll all put on our walking shoes and march away."

I look at him; no expression and dark circles under his eyes. I wonder if he is still as dangerous as he was when we first met.

"Is the SS leaving then?" I want to keep my voice as calm and matter-of-fact as I can.

"The SS, you, me, everyone who can walk." He continues to stare at the transport. "The rest? Who knows? For them it'll probably be nacht und nebel, nothing more than night and fog, like those poor devils there, into the gas and up in smoke."

I'm too stricken to say anything, but wish I had something in my hand with which to kill him.

"No, Lagerkapo, you and I march away and leave the sick and wounded, the musselmanns, the garbage, who are too weak to walk, to fend for themselves. See if they last long enough to greet the Russians." His tone is so final, so lacking in any remorse, but laced with despair.

"And what of your fortune, Scharfuhrer, is there nothing left?"

"I left everything in Warsaw. The Russians have it."

I understand his manner. "Sorry, Sergeant." I am still playing the role, and will as long as he wears that uniform. "What brings you to my lager?"

"You, Lagerkapo." He smiles at me and nods. "You and I have worked well together."

A tremendous sense of dread sweeps over me. "Yes, Scharfuhrer."

"You can dispense with the rank, Filip. I'm Heinz." His smile is knavish, the gleam in his eye evil.

"Dare I?"

"Yes, I insist."

"Then it's Heinz." It sticks in my throat and I want to vomit. "Why the honor?"

"We're going to work together again."

"That almost got me killed last time. You get the fortune, Heinz. I get a rope around my neck."

"It's different, now. The SS and Gestapo are all packing their bags and making a clean getaway, now, before the allies encircle us."

"And why would I help you if I'm soon to be liberated?"

He looks at me, his eyes narrow. "Because, you little Polish shit, I can still kill you." He relaxes and shakes his head. "I didn't mean that, Filip. I just have a bad temper."

He leans against the fence. "Because I can protect you from being forced out of the camp to be taken to another camp in Germany. There are many still functioning and they're a long march from here, I assure you. Bergen-Belsen, Mauthausen, Theresienstadt, Buchenwald, Nordhausen, Ravensbrück, Dachau, Sachsenhausen, and hundreds more. And the plans call for forced marches. How many do you think will be able to hold out on such a march? Do you think Jakub could survive?" He continues to stare at me. "And what do you think the SS will do to those who can't keep up?"

He looks away for a few moments then turns his vision back on me. "You don't look so well fed either, Lagerkapo. Do you think you could survive?"

As I watch the train back away from the ramp, I realize the truth in his words, for I certainly don't have the heart to walk home, much less to another camp. "No, Heinz, it isn't something to which I would look forward."

"Then, Filip, you must steal, excuse me, organize as much as you can; gold, gems, and money, for me. I'll find a way to get it out and store it." His eyes sparkle with the thoughts of so much wealth.

"How will you keep me and Jakub from being forced on a march?"

"I'll let you know when a lapanka, a sweep of the lager, is coming, then you and Jakub can be somewhere else, or find a place to hide."

I still don't trust him. "How will you keep from going on a march? I'm certain the SS is conducting this little exercise."

"I'll worry about that, Filip. You just concentrate on getting me my little nest egg. And get one for yourself, too. There's no point in your being poor after all this, is there?"

The first dragnet of the lager comes in the afternoon. I suspect it is a lapanka as soon as I see so many SS and dogs coming through the gates. I gather as many as I can, including Jakub and push them into shipping, forcing them to pack boxes with anything they can find, even junk, but to be busy.

I walk behind them yelling and creating the proper atmosphere for the SS, all the while whispering encouragement and warnings telling them what will happen if they suspect we aren't working hard.

The first man through the door is a tall SS officer, an untersturmfuhrer, with two Iron Cross decorations on his tunic. "Are you lagerkapo here?"

"Yes, Lieutenant."

"All of these people are to be moved out now."

"To where, Untersturmfuhrer? We have much work to do and have been ordered to prepare all of these crates for shipment to Berlin." I want to muddle his thinking and get him confused about his orders. "Already a train is sitting by the loading ramp waiting for these crates and boxes. I wouldn't want to disobey the orders of the camp director."

He looks around nervously and is at a loss, needing someone to bully and intimidate. "We are..." he is searching for the right words, "breaking up this camp. I must proceed with my orders."

I need to take a risk. "These are confusing times, Untersturmfuhrer. I'm sure your orders are mistaken. Or perhaps, they were intended for the storage facilities in the stamlager. I'm certain all the material from there is on the way to Berlin."

He moves his hands from his hips and looks at the stacks of boxes and crates all labeled for the SS Economic Administration in Berlin. He studies the address and notes the description of contents. "This says medical supplies."

"They all do, Lieutenant. My instructions."

"Yes, I see." He walks past me and looks into a half-filled box of eyeglasses. "These aren't necessary to the war effort."

"No, sir. We stopped packing non-essential items when the orders came to rush the shipment. That has just been left there, and we've had no time to remove it." I am thankful my mind is working.

"I see." He motions to his men to leave and turns to me. "I'll check on my orders. In the meantime, you keep working."

"Yes, sir. We'll continue to follow orders, and, please, sir, let them know how much there is to process. We still have more coming from this morning's train."

With that, he spins on his heel and is gone. Everyone in the room breathes a sigh of relief and several congratulate me.

I discover most of the lager milling about in the alleyways and call the kapos to me. I instruct them to keep everyone busy for it is the only way to avoid the forced marches. I also instruct them to ship boxes of useless items to Berlin to be rid of them, and mislabel other shipments as non-essential. It is the first time I purposefully undermine the Germans' ability to make war.

I encourage the lager to eat what foods they find, concealing as much as possible from the roving guards, and to build up their strength just in case. I suggest they put on additional socks and find good shoes as further insurance. Lastly, I caution them against theft of small valuable items, as the SS will surely punish them if the things are found on them. But there are ways of concealing such small items, and the lager knows them all, and they know I won't be looking.

It becomes quite hectic throughout the closing months of the year, as it is apparent the Germans are fighting a strategic withdrawal, taking whatever they have stolen with them. But it is also dangerous as SS detachments sweep through the lagers and force many onto marches, to who knows where. I continue to bluff my way through with different young SS officers, thankful no officer comes twice.

There are no more gassings after the day Hirt came to me. I haven't received word from him of any dragnets or orders affecting the Kanada lager, nor have I received word of what to do with the currency, gold, and jewels I hold in a box labeled 'hairbrushes'. I think, perhaps, that his luck has run its course and he has been ordered on a death march, which I think would be justice, but I harbor an old grudge and want to dispense justice my way.

A crematorium continues functioning, pumping its white plume into the cold air, the remnants of long-suffering slave labor from the camps. These are the ones who no longer have the stamina or desire to last a moment longer, even as we approach the eve of liberation.

All of the administration has disappeared, including Aumeier and the Gestapo, Hoffman included. Rats on a sinking ship, I surmise, leaving the slaves to run the camp alone. And we do run it, run it as we always have, without the batons and sneering kapos pummeling us, forcing us to work. We work to stay alive. We work to keep as many alive as possible.

But there are SS about and we work to avoid them. They are busy with orders from the Reichsfuhrer, I later learn, to destroy the gas chambers and the crematoria, to demolish all traces of the work that went on here. In victory, they bragged of their accomplishments, of the splendid system of camps producing labor for the Third Reich. In defeat, all of their accomplishments become crimes, and they labor to destroy all evidence of their misdeeds.

The dragnets are increasing. All through December, in the cold and snow, without blankets or coats, the remnants of Auschwitz, Birkenau, and Monowitz are herded onto the icy roads to take their last steps. Shots are heard even before the long lines pass through the gates, and continue until they are a great distance from the lager.

Kanada has been evacuated, leaving stacks of suitcases and other non-essential material piled in mounds to the ceiling. Jakub and I wait for a long time, wait until I am positive there is no one about, before we make our way from beneath the valises, our hiding place.

I'm surprised to see Hirt walking about the room calling for me, his voice a whisper. His eyes grow bright and he smiles when he sees us. "I knew it. I knew you were too clever to be forced out of here."

He is wearing the uniform of a captain in the SS, decorated with Iron Crosses on his left pocket and around his neck. "So, Hauptsturmfuhrer, promotions do come rapidly in these last days, don't they?"

He smiles and waves his hand over the medals. "Decorations, too. I thought it would be better to be an officer than a lowly staff sergeant."

"I imagine it would." I'm not going to anger the man, but I think that lowly staff sergeants kill as easily as captains. "And I take it you have deserted?"

"Yeah. I got caught and was sent out with a bunch from Monowitz. A couple of the women broke away from the line and escaped into a field. I told the officer in charge that I would bring them back." He is fingering the boxes, glancing inside and closing them again. "A soldier and I took off after them, but out of sight of the column, I killed the bastard and made my way back here. I went into headquarters and found this uniform, replaced with civilian clothes, I'd wager. I found these medals as well and thought I deserved them."

"I see." He amuses me with his complete amorality, and I guess he is looking for something of value.

"Well, where is it?" His countenance screams his impatience.

"It's in a safe place, Heinz. Very safe." I don't trust the man.

"Don't play games with me, Polack. Give me my fortune." He is becoming angry, but it is my game to play.

"I'm not playing games. I'm just being practical."

He unsnaps his holster and points the pistol at Jakub whose eyes are round and he steps backwards. "Tell me where you have put my stuff." He grimaces at me, showing his dirty teeth, teeth unlike an officer of the Third Reich.

"Don't be afraid, Jakub. He won't kill you."

"And why won't I kill him?"

"Jakub doesn't even know what we're talking about. Only I know where everything is hidden."

He quickly points the pistol at me. "Then you tell me where it is."

"You won't kill me either, Heinz. If you did, you would end this war a very poor man. They'd probably arrest you and you'd be hung." I smile at him and push the pistol away. "Put it in your holster, Heinz."

He holsters the weapon and has the look of a child who had just been punished. "You know I can't leave here without that treasure, don't you?"

I walk away from him and turn to face him. "I'm quite tired of your bullying, Heinz. It all started with you in Katy, when you punched me in the face. I haven't forgotten that. I won't be intimidated again, not by a German. You point that pistol at me again, then you had better use it, because I'll never give you one damn diamond. Understand?" I push it further than I intended, but my temper has got the best of me.

Hirt stares at me, his hand on the pistol, his eyes darting

between me, Jakub, and the floor. Slowly he moves his hand away from the holster and holds it out as a sign of peace. "Okay, Filip, no more guns."

"How long do you think you're going to fool someone with that uniform?"

He shrugs.

"No German officer, particularly SS, would let his teeth go as badly as yours. And your hands show signs of work. You'll be spotted first thing. And let's face it, Heinz, neither of us is a gentleman, and we wouldn't know what to do in gentlemen's company." I finger his medals. "Don't get me wrong, but you're wearing two Iron Crosses, second class. It should have a cluster shouldn't it, denoting the receipt of more than one? And isn't the second class medal awarded to common soldiers?"

He looks at the medals and runs his tongue across his teeth. "You're right, Filip, but what can I do?"

"Another uniform, Heinz, and no food until the liberation."

"Why no food? What uniform?"

I pinch the fabric of my uniform and pull it from my body. "One like this. You are about to become a Pole."

Confusion reigns in his expression. "The SS won't be looking for an SS NCO in lager dress, particularly wearing the yellow star or the purple P. You can hide right here in the lager."

"Okay, but not the yellow star. I'll not be a Jew for anyone."

I smile. "Then you can be Polish."

He acknowledges my suggestion. "Why no food?"

"You've eaten too well to be a slave laborer, Heinz. We need to get a little of the fat off of you." I enjoy his discomfort.

"And the treasure?"

"Not until we can leave together." I want to tell him "tomorrow morning," to see if he would enjoy the joke, for I have no intention of giving him the jewels and gold I have stowed away.

CHAPTER TWENTY-TWO

These first weeks of the New Year are terribly fearful and hectic for the lager. The SS has run dragnet after dragnet through the camp and has gathered all of the laborers for a forced march to the west. They are also busy destroying the last of the crematoria, before they push another group on a long march to nowhere.

It is then we learn the news of how serious the war is going for Germany, as we learn the Allies are closing a giant pincer around the Third Reich, and they have already lost most of Italy, including Rome, and have surrendered Warsaw to the Russians. The American and British armies, with French and Polish units are set to cross into Germany itself. All around them, their enemies are preparing to strike the final blow to the heart, ending the terror of the Nazis. They are defeated, but they still want to destroy us. It makes no sense.

Jakub, Heinz and I continue the cat and mouse game with the SS, hiding throughout the lager and making the Germans look for the needles in the warehouses. But they are losing their enthusiasm, making only cursory searches, spending more time looking through boxes and unsorted suitcases.

When idle, the three of us search the valises, keeping the things we find of value, wishing for pockets in the uniforms. There are others who are also clever enough to elude the sweeps through the lager and we encounter them searching as well. But we leave them to themselves and keep to ourselves, knowing there is more here than the few of us can ever search.

Heinz keeps track of time, marking dates and days, watching the eastern horizon for Russian tanks, and scanning the western expanse and hoping to spot American tanks. And in between his frequent urges to scan the horizons, he tears into luggage like a frightened burglar, tossing useless items in every way, scattering the contents throughout the camp.

And he is growing impatient. "When are you going to give me my treasure?"

I am tiring of putting him off, tiring of him. "Right now, Heinz. Let's go get it."

His eyes widen and he clasps his hands together. "I can't wait to see all the things you have collected."

"It's this way." I hope he will be too distracted to see what else I have for him.

I look around carefully, more for Heinz's benefit, than any suspicion that we are being watched. We make our way to building twenty-six and climb the steps. "It's down here. Second door on the left." I creep ahead and stop to pick up a small bar.

"What do you need that for?" He backs away from me, his eyes narrow.

"It's a crowbar. It's to open the crate." I shake my head. "You're too distrusting, Heinz."

I lead the way into the storeroom to the middle section. I pull a few boxes away from one I have especially prepared and marked 'utensils'. I pull the heavy box into the center of the floor. Carefully I pry open the lid, and, holding the bar, lay the box lid on the floor. I pull out some of the packing straw and motion for him to see for himself.

"I don't think so." He pulls a pistol from his waistband. "Drop that crowbar. Now back away." He points towards the end of the room.

I turn my back to him and do as instructed, chastising myself for underestimating his suspicious nature, realizing I may have lost my one chance to kill him. As I turn to face him, I see the pistol aimed at my head and can see his finger move to the trigger. Then I see Jakub.

The shovel hit the sergeant squarely on the head, forcing him forward onto his face, sending the pistol against my foot.

"I've never been as glad to see anyone in my life, Jakub. Thank you."

He smiles. "I watch over you, Filip."

I pick up the pistol and embrace my friend, kissing him on both cheeks.

We stand over the inert form of Heinz Hirt and study him. "Did I kill him?" Jakub's face is constricted and he is biting is lower lip.

I kneel and feel for a pulse on his wrist. I don't feel one, so I check the one in his neck. He is dead. I glance at Jakub and see the tears in his eyes and tenseness in his face. "He's okay. He'll live, I'm afraid. But he'll have a headache."

Jakub backs up as tears flow down his cheeks. "He'll kill me."

I shake my head. "No, Jakub, no one is going to hurt you again." I point the pistol at Hirt's temple and pull the trigger, jarring the head, causing it to bounce from the floor. I pull it again, and a third time, each bullet smashing the man's head, bouncing it from the floor, spreading blood over the boards, splattering it on me.

I turn to Jakub who is just watching me. "He won't hurt anyone ever again." I stoop and tear the left sleeve from the dead body, exposing the SS tattoo. "Now when he's found, they'll know he got what he deserved."

Jakub smiles, relief covering his face. "I think," there is a sparkle in his eyes, "he wake up tomorrow morning."

I look at him, then laugh and he laughs with me, enjoying his joke.

I rise and punch him on the arm. "Let's go." I turn to leave, but he stops me. "The box? The treasure?"

I smile at him. "Rocks. Heavy rocks. I never intended giving him anything."

Jakub beams and punches me in the arm.

All of the activity is in and around Birkenau, which is to be expected with its size and its evil purpose. I gather what things we have and pack them into a small duffel. Jakub watches me as he baths, a ritual he continues to follow the whole time in Auschwitz.

As he finishes, he comes over to me and I can see his ribs pressing against his skin. He speaks first. "What are you doing?"

I can't stand to look at his emaciated torso. "Packing. We're going over to the stamlager tonight."

"Why?"

I remember asking that question once and was told that wasn't a question asked in Auschwitz. "I think we have a better chance of avoiding the SS there."

"I see." He returns to his bath, the vertebrae of his spine protruding grossly from his back.

Tears well in my eyes as I look at him. "Jakub?" I wipe the tears, refusing to acknowledge the pain. "You're too thin. You're not eating."

He doesn't turn around or answer me for a long time, but I continue to watch as he splashes water onto his face and body. "It hurts."

"To eat?"

"Yes. I don't feel good when I eat."

"It hurts in your stomach?"

"Maybe. Yes. No." He shakes his head quickly and his voice is higher, strained. "It hurts everywhere, Filip. I don't like to eat."

I release a long breath and remember others who had felt the same way, and remember laying their bodies in the alleyways for removal. "Jakub, you'll die if you don't eat."

The silence becomes a burden, a heavy pall hanging above both of us. Finally, he speaks, almost a whisper. "This isn't a good place. It's bad. Bad people hurt us." He splashes water onto his skinny legs.

He is quiet for a few moments, continuing his ritual, and then speaks softly, his words clearer. "Remember the bird I found?

Remember what Aron and Papa said. They said we couldn't let animals suffer." He continues bathing. "I'm not a bird, but I suffer too. I don't... want to suffer... anymore." Sniffles and deep breaths come between his words, hiding his tears.

"It's almost over, Jakub. Soon we'll be able to go home. Then you won't suffer anymore."

He is quiet and still for a long time and I feel uncomfortable with the silence, which is broken with a sob.

Slowly, he catches himself and releases a long breath. "I've done wrong, Filip. I should die like my friends." His words are clear, crisp.

I'm frightened at his confession, frightened for his life. "Jakub?" I want him to face me, to look at me, but he stands at the bucket of water, his head bowed, silent. "And should I die as well?"

"No, Filip. You must live." I can hear the tears in his throat as he keeps his back to me.

"I don't want to live without my best friend." I swallow hard. "We've been through a lot, you and I. I can't return home alone."

Still he doesn't turn to look at me. "Will we ever go home? Will we live in Dr. Levi's house?" He stays quiet for a few minutes. "Can I drive a truck?"

"I want us to go home, Jakub, even if we have to walk. We'll find a place to live when we get there. Just you and me." I stand. "And we'll find you a truck, a new truck. You can have any truck you want, Jakub."

Again he is silent for a long time. "I don't think I'll drive a truck again."

"Why not?"

He starts crying, his body convulsing with sobs. "I don't want to carry anymore babies to the river."

I don't know what to say, but I need him to want to live. "No matter. No truck. We'll open the Spiegelman's store. You can help me there."

"I liked the store. I swept the floor and helped women shop."

"You can do that again. But we must get to Katy and will probably have to walk." I want to see his face. "But if you don't eat, then you'll not be strong enough to make it."

"I could steer a horse." He turns to face me. "We could get a wagon and horse. I could hold the straps and steer the horse for home. I won't drop them now." He smiles. "You could show me the way to go."

His mood picks up and he seems a little better as we wait for the opportunity to leave. I fear another sweep through the lager and decide to conceal ourselves under the valises in building one. It will be nearer the gate and we can also collect the treasure I have accumulated and placed in a box marked 'hairbrushes'.

As Jakub clears the entrance to our hiding space, I go to where I left the box. The area has changed since I was last here, and several of the boxes are torn open. I search them, tossing them aside like a blustery wind, arousing Jakub's curiosity. I curse and kick boxes when I find the right one.

"Empty. Everything gone. That was to be our future, our earnings for the suffering we've gone through."

Jakub walks over to me and stares at the empty box, then looks at me. "Hair... brushes. Hairbrushes?"

"I marked it that way to keep anyone from looking. I outsmarted myself." I sit down on the floor and feel like crying.

"I don't understand, Filip."

"All the gold, jewels, and money we were going to use was in that box." I thought I had told him that.

"I remember." He sits down in front of me. "Not hairbrushes."

I think he is being a little dense until I notice the gleam in his eye, and realize he is joking with me again. "Yeah, not hairbrushes."

"Not good place to hide things." He just looks at me with a stern expression on his face as if he is lecturing me.

"I know that now."

"I find better place." He gets up slowly and goes to our nook, crawls in and returns with our winter coats. Without a word, he tosses a coat to me.

"This is heavy. This is very heavy."

Jakub is smiling. "My coat is heavy, too."

"You're telling me you sewed everything into our coats?"

"Not everything. Just money, jewels, and some gold bars. No German money."

"How did you learn to do this?"

"Meister Jan showed me how. He taught me to sew."

The carpenter, I thought, and am again ashamed of taking the soap from him.

Jakub produces a sack. "More gold here. I don't know what to do with it."

I look in the sack and it is filled with hundreds of gold teeth. "Let's take the sack and hide it somewhere."

He nods and the gleam returns to his eyes. "Not hairbrushes."

It is dark by the time we finish packing and there is no movement in the lager. There are no floodlights or guards in the towers, no patrols with dogs and machine guns. It is time to leave.

In the light by the gate, stands a lone sentry leaning against the post with his collar turned up to keep off the wintry breeze. His rifle looks new and is propped against his leg and, by his youthful appearance, the soldier is as inexperienced as his rifle. I pull the blanket tightly around Jakub, blocking out the cold wind and motion for him to stay behind. I leave our duffel and the sack with gold teeth and check for Hirt's pistol in my coat pocket. I finger the safety just to assure myself that I can release it quickly with one hand.

"Halt. Come forward slowly." He isn't as asleep as I thought. "No prisoners are allowed out after dark. And you should not be here."

"But I'm here, Private." I point in the direction of Auschwitz. "And I want to go there."

"No one goes through this gate. I'm to arrest all Jews. Those are my orders." He continues to hold the rifle on me, but I can see the safety lever is on and it is unable to fire.

"I'm not a Jew. I'm Polish. And I want to go through that gate." I feel very tired, and I am sick of Germans telling me what I can't do. "If you will lower that rifle, I'll be on my way."

"No one is to pass through this gate. Those are my orders!" His words are sharp and loud, like most of the SS soldiers I have met.

"How old are you, boy? Sixteen? Seventeen?"

"My age is of no concern to you." He stresses his point with a small thrust of the rifle in my direction.

"Fifteen? Fifteen, I bet, maybe fourteen." I wait and stare at him.

"Sixteen." His eyes are angry.

"Too young to die, but many young men have died. Germany did that."

He bristles at the accusation and grips his rifle tighter. "No one passes through this gate. Those are my orders." His words lose the crispness.

"I'm going to ask you to do something, soldier, I'm going to ask you to think."

He looks at me with a shake of his head, loosening his grip slightly and turning the rifle away from me.

"Germany is defeated. You're guarding this gate for no reason other than it was an order." I put my hands in the coat pockets, grasp the pistol, and release the safety. "Germany and her Fuhrer will soon be dead."

He again aims the rifle at my midsection and pulls the trigger, but nothing happens. He quickly glances at the bolt and doesn't see my fist coming. He lands on his back, leaving the rifle in my hand.

"Stand up, German." I point my pistol at him. "Open the gate."

He stands. "I can't. I have my orders!"

"Think, you bastard. How many people must die so you can follow your orders?" I slam him against the gate and level my pistol at his heart. "I'm giving you a choice, Private. Open the gate or die. Obey a stupid order or die. It's your choice and I don't have all night."

He is frightened and I'm certain he never dreamed obeying orders would be so difficult. The dilemma shows in his eyes and he doesn't know what to do.

"Well, Oberschutze, what is your decision? Think about it. Germany has lost too many of its sons. Don't be one of them." I hold the pistol aimed at his heart and will him to open the gate. "Well, Private, are you going to open the gate?"

He straightens himself to his full height and clicks his heels together. "No one is to go through this gate. I have my orders."

The crack of the pistol is the only noise in the night. The guard's body crumples against the gate and rolls away from it, spilling his blood on the snow.

I pick up his rifle and open the gate, motioning for Jakub to join me. We run for a few minutes until I realize Jakub can't keep up. I loosen the sling of the rifle and throw it over my head and shoulder, and take the bags and extra blankets from him.

He smiles between his panting. "Where… we… go?"

"The old warehouses in Auschwitz. It'll be a good place to hide. If the SS come looking for us, they'll think we tried to escape to the woods."

A heavy snow begins to fall and I am thankful, for it will wipe out all traces of our direction and give us time to sneak into the stamlager. I find a large stone and shift it, with Jakub's help, breaking its bond with the frozen earth. I flatten the bag of gold teeth as best I can and set the stone over it. I carefully note the various landmarks, making certain where we are. I know the snow will cover the stone and sack, and protect it from prying eyes until the first melt. Hopefully, by then, we will have recovered it and be in Katy for the spring planting.

Jakub is exhausted by the time we reach the main camp. We are within a hundred meters before I see all of the activity through the falling snow and I'm disturbed by the presence of guards in all the towers. It is as if it were beginning all over, with new arrivals and fresh SS troops to guard the prisoners. I crouch in the snow and look at the activity, befuddled in my thinking, and too tired to think of a way out. Jakub, too, is too tired to go any farther.

I remember a drainage ditch outside the fence and motion for Jakub to follow me, which he does slowly. We crouch low and find the ditch less than twenty meters from the fence. All the lights from the towers are pointed into the interior of the camp, but, suddenly, a light shines in our direction, scanning rapidly for any movement or for something out of place.

I shove Jakub into the ditch and jump in after him, lowering our heads and letting the light pass over us. It scans back and forth several times and I wonder what prompted the guard to search the area.

The snow continues and I cut a niche in the drift with the butt of the rifle, digging as quietly as I can, making it big enough for me and Jakub to nestle together for warmth, allowing the snow to cover us and all of our tracks. I vow I will wake before dawn and plan our escape then. But, now, we need to avoid those searching for us and Jakub needs to rest. Our escape will have to wait.

CHAPTER TWENTY-THREE

Jakub wakes before me. It is daylight and I can see his eyes in the dim glow of our niche through snow-filtered light. They are wide and still.

"What is it, Jakub?"

"A lot of noise. People crying. Soldiers shouting. Trucks. Sounds of rifles." He continues to stare straight ahead.

I can't believe I slept through so much commotion. I listen carefully. "I don't hear anything." I strain and can't hear movement or noise of any kind. Then I hear the caws of many crows.

Slowly I pull back the blankets covering us and peer through the opening to the fence and compound beyond it. There is no movement. There are no guards in the towers, no signs of life anywhere. I widen the opening and scan more of the area, still finding nothing. I raise up on my elbow and look towards the gate nearest us and see the crows huddled around dark lumps lying in the snow.

Confident it is safe to come out, I sit up and push the rigid blankets aside, and am struck by the frigid wind, which cuts into my face like needles. I motion for Jakub to join me, and he shrugs and turns his face away from the harsh wind.

"They've gone, Jakub. The SS have left the camp."

The fear is gone from his eyes, but so is the spark of the day before, and I realize he is freezing. We gather our things and make our way to the camp, past the bodies of those who tried to walk, but surrendered to the bullets of the SS. Neither of us look, both having seen too much death, hard-pressed with our own need to survive, which means getting warm and finding something to eat.

I stop Jakub as we approach the fence, fearful it is still electrically charged, and fearful what that will mean. I toss the rifle against the wire, but nothing happens. Slowly, hesitantly, I gently touch the wire and find it cold. No electricity, which means there is no power anywhere in the camp, and, hopefully, no Germans.

We make our way to the southeast corner of the lager, towards the commandant's office, main guardhouse, and Gestapo headquarters. I hope these buildings will be warmer than the prisoners' barracks, and pray they have overlooked any foods, canned goods, or anything we can use to quell our hunger. I move slowly, matching my pace to Jakub's, allowing him to rest often and gather his strength.

As we plod along, I hear the sound of an engine, a deep growl coming towards us. We take cover against the nearest building, lying still in the snow. The vehicle speeds past us and stops near the corner of the camp, near the administrative section for which we are headed.

I whisper to Jakub. "SS. We'll go to another area, maybe the warehouses at the other end of the camp."

Jakub nods, but I can see the lack of resolution in his eyes, the fatigue and near hopelessness.

"Jakub, you must hang on. Think of home. Think of the store and waiting on some pretty girl."

Tears well in his eyes and pour down his cheeks. "I can't."

I silently curse myself for not remembering what they had done to him. "I'm sorry. But don't give up. Think of the fields of wheat. Think of all we can do together."

He wipes his tears and looks at me, his eyes as big as a puppy's. "Like what?"

"Do you like fishing?"

"I don't know." He is struggling, but I need that from him, need to have him grasp hold of something else to think about.

"I can teach you. We'll go the river and..." I stop at more tears, and realize he wouldn't want to go near a river again.

"There's a pond..." I stop, realizing it is near the burned synagogue.

I sit back and realize how much we have gone through, and realize Jakub had gone through more than me. I wonder if he is ever going to find something that doesn't remind him of all this. He sits there looking at me, wanting from me something I can't give him.

"I'm sorry, Jakub." I put my hand on his shoulder.

"It's okay, Filip. It's not your fault. You're my friend." His smile takes all of his effort, as he leans back against the building, his eyes half closed. "I'm your friend, too. I'm your best friend, Filip. Just like Aron."

I let him sleep as I watch for any more traffic or signs of SS. I try to think of something to tell him, something that will give him a reason, a desire to live. I listen to his breathing, thankful he is still alive, and try to formulate a plan, something to keep us alive until the Allies, Russian or American, liberate the camp. I hope it will be the Americans.

And I think of us, of the distance we have traveled, short in measurement, but vast in experiences. I watch him breathe and am ashamed of ever thinking my life would be easier without him. Now, I can't, and don't want to think of a life without Jakub.

It takes us most of the morning to make our way past the barracks to the warehouse area, in the north sector of the lager, just outside the fence. We skirt around building after building, slowly becoming aware that there are many people still here, prisoners with no SS to guard them. I think they were left behind, either because they had hidden or were too sick to make the march. I'm surprised they are still alive, but then there are too many of them.

Once we reach the fence, it takes several minutes to find the gate, and then it is fastened with a large lock and chain. I'm thankful for the rifle, as I use it to twist the chain and break a link. I put the chain back to make it appear everything is intact.

We search several buildings and find one with many crates and boxes stacked to the ceiling. There is an old stove at the rear which will allow us to have heat, and, if I find food, a way to heat it.

Jakub is still very morose and little I do cheers him. I settle him in front of the stove and go in search of food, finding canned goods and pots in which to cook. I find an old coffee pot with used grounds still in it, which I use several more times, getting some weak, but tasty coffee.

I search the building used as a kitchen, the place they used to prepare the tasteless soup, but others had been there before me. The cabinets had been broken into and cans overturned, spilling the contents over the floor. Even the camp's garbage had been searched, scattered about hoping for something to eat. But they left the potato peels. I gather up all that I can see and hide them inside my shirt. Even if I make a soup equal to the fare given to us in Auschwitz, it would be better than starving.

I find more canned goods in the other warehouses and offer much of it to the people I find, but I keep enough for me and Jakub, insisting he eat as much as his stomach can withstand. I save the potato peels for a time when we have less. I sit and watch, urging him to eat and drink the weak coffee.

I remind him of stories of Aron and us when we were boys, of the mischief we got into and the jokes we played on our neighbors. I even told him about Klara, thanking him for suggesting she stay for breakfast. He smiles and nods, but I can't bring the sparkle back to his eyes.

We sleep close to the heater, wrapped in blankets I found in one of the buildings, packed and crated for shipment to Berlin. They are musty and smell bad, but it isn't any worse than many nights we spent in this place. We don't have bunks, but the floor isn't any harder than the bunks we slept on for more than four and a half years.

A long time, I ponder, as I watch Jakub sleep. I wonder what life would be like in Katy now. I wonder if the village would even be there, after all, even the priest had ended up in Auschwitz. I wonder if I could get my old job back, deciding I don't want to be a constable, don't want to do anything where I have to wear a uniform or make people do what they don't want to do.

While just sitting and thinking one day, I hear footsteps outside, running steps rushing quickly past our building, only to stop suddenly. I quickly pick up the rifle and hide behind some of the boxes, watching the door, hoping it won't open. I listen intently as the stairs creak under someone's weight, the sounds far apart, the movements careful and slow. Whoever it is wants to surprise us, to catch us off guard.

I know it isn't SS, as they would have burst in on us, weapons ready to cut us down. I watch, the rifle aimed carefully at the door, expecting it to open at any moment, hoping I won't have to fire it. The creaking stops and the door opens slowly, so slowly I am tempted to fire through it, but I wait, wait for someone to step into my line of sight, to find out who is scaring me.

His head peers through the crack and quickly withdraws, but the door remains open, leaving me more alert, more curious as to what someone so young would be doing in the lager. Then the door opens a little wider and the boy peers in, looking carefully around the room, but not seeing me. I relax my grip on the rifle, aware of the tension in my hands.

The boy can't be more than nine or ten, but he is cautious beyond his years, something Auschwitz undoubtedly taught him. He creeps into the room, followed by a girl, similar to him in all their features, probably brother and sister, I reason.

As they near the stove, Jakub stirs and opens his eyes. He sees them and sits up, frightening them and frightened at the same time.

The boy breaks the silence. I don't understand him, but I'm reasonably certain they are speaking Italian.

With no response from Jakub, the girl tries, also in Italian.

Jakub studies them for a long time, leaving them to wonder if he has heard them, as they exchange glances. Finally he speaks softly. "Where's Filip?"

"Here." Both of the children jump back against the wall. I ask them if they speak German.

The boy nods his head. "We're cold."

The girl stares at me for a few moments before speaking. "And hungry."

I motion for them to get near the stove. "I'm Filip. This is Jakub." There isn't a need to say anything else as our uniforms with the "P" say it for us.

Jakub digs into the crates and produces two blankets, which he hands to the children. "You keep warm. Jakub take care of you." He smiles.

I notice a spark has returned to his eyes, as the children have done what I can't.

As I sit watching, Jakub moves closer and plays the role of host, speaking just enough German for them to understand. "What are your names?"

The girl speaks first. "I'm Maria. He's Mario."

The boy adds, "We're from Milano. We're twins."

Jakub rummages through the boxes I have brought back from my forages, finding two cans of soup. He doesn't even look at me, as he takes a knife and saws through the metal as easily as if I was doing it. He pours the contents into a pot and places it on the stove, then turns to them. "You eat in a minute."

As the soup heats, we listen to the twins' tale of coming to Auschwitz and being separated from their parents. They talk of being taken to a building that looks like a hospital with doctors, but there weren't any nurses. They were examined and probed by several men, none of whom spoke Italian, and none seemed to care that they didn't understand. Whenever they didn't do what they were told, or if they moved too slowly, they received a slap. They talked about the main doctor, a tall man who seemed kind and gentle.

Jakub interrupts them. "What was his name?"

The boy answers, "Uncle Pepi is what he asked us to call him."

Jakub turns his head and spits on the floor. "Bad man."

The girl nods and also spits, followed by her brother.

I enjoy watching them and listening to the conversation between them and Jakub, pleased he has found a reason to live, relieved that my burden is lighter because of it, but heavier because of the children.

They describe some of the grotesque experiments Mengele performed on them, some painful, and some embarrassing. "He would give us candy or other treats and talk sweetly, but then Uncle Pepi offered us a ride in his car."

Mario looks at his sister. She continues the story. "At first we were thrilled, but remembered others who had taken a ride with the doctor. We never saw them again."

"The doctor put us in the back seat, but was interrupted by an orderly." Mario picks up the story. "He told Herr Doctor there was a phone call for him. He gave each of us piece of candy and told us to wait."

"The driver was talking to another soldier and smoking a cigarette." Maria looks at us. "They weren't watching us."

"It was cold and had begun to snow. The rear door had been left open, so we crept out and crawled beneath the building." Mario nods and motions with his hands. "We were careful and wiped out our footprints and hoped the Germans wouldn't find anything and would search somewhere else."

Maria crouches against her brother. "There were wide posts

under the building and we hid behind them, keeping still and quiet."

"We heard the doctor shouting at the guards. He was terribly angry and threatened to have them take our place." Mario's eyes widen. "We were so scared they would find us."

"Where we were was too small for the soldiers, but they shone torches in and searched." Maria looks at her brother. "I wasn't as afraid as Mario."

He glares at her. "Were, too. You almost screamed when the light came near you."

"How long ago was that?" I am curious to know if Mengele and the SS are still at Auschwitz.

Mario looks at Maria and shrugs. "Maybe three months, maybe four."

"No, Mario, it's more like three."

"Three months? You two have survived all that time alone?" I am surprised. "You've been running and hiding ever since?"

"Yes." Mario just looks at me and shrugs his shoulders. "We found food at a place on the other side. We hid and were careful."

Maria also looks at me, her eyes a little more expressive. "It was easy, until SS started rounding up people and searching everywhere." She looks at Jakub and Mario and her voice rises. "We had to go outside the fence and burrow in the snow. We did that until we thought it was okay to come out."

Jakub looks at me, his smile wide, and turns to Maria. "Filip and I did that, too. We dug a hole in the snow and hid from Germans. It was cold."

The four of us settle in to wait for liberation or confrontation with the SS if they return. Jakub is eating again, particularly when Maria insists, and both seem to accept him as children often do. He is a child again, happy and carefree, the horror of his experiences slowly suppressed and, hopefully, forgotten.

The twins aren't the last. Everyday, we encounter cold, sick and hungry survivors scavenging for food, blankets and warmth. It is a difficult lot, as Mario and I forage more often, struggling, praying to find enough to feed the group entering our building. Wood is plentiful, but it still has to be broken into smaller pieces to fit in the stove, and has to be gathered from wherever we can find it.

There are more than a hundred people gathered in our building, and several hundred more in buildings near ours. Mario and some of the men and women help me forage as I set up a systematic search throughout our compound and branch out farther and farther each time, always on the watch for SS or other prisoners so desperate for food they will attack us and take it. But we aren't finding a lot.

Mario and I search everywhere, even in buildings where little remains. We salvage scraps of wood, tearing apart cabinets and walls, hoping to find something, keeping the pieces and bits of wood for our stove. I find a cabinet, but it's empty, cleaned out by other scavengers or the SS. I kick the door, breaking it, separating the veneer from the wood, and several scraps of paper fall out. Mario and I pick them up and he is gleeful to have paper to start fires.

I glance at one and notice the handwriting. I show it to Mario and he shakes his head. I can't read the words, but decide I'll save them until I know they're nothing.

We lay the scraps of wood by the stove and Mario hands me the papers we found. I show them to old Abraham, a Jewish man who has joined us.

He studies each piece carefully, comparing the handwriting, as tears begin rolling down his cheeks. "They're poems. I think they were written by two, maybe three people."

"Will you read them to us, Abraham?"

The people gather around him and he wipes his cheeks and rubs his eyes. He holds the first high, allowing the light to hit it.

"This one is titled, 'The Ruse'." He clears his throat and begins reading slowly.

Down from the train
the ruse begins
words of cheer
amid the guards
facing guns
fearing dogs.

To the showers
the ruse portrays
no diseases here
crowding together
walking slowly
upon the ashes of kin.

Into the bleak room
the ruse reigns
stripped and bare
holding babies
waiting for cleansing
abandoning hope.

None of us stir. I'm filled with admiration for the poet, as I look and see the wet cheeks. Jakub, too, is crying, nodding his head and accepting the hands of the children.

I remember our first day, the lies they told and the poorly concealed laughter when they told them. And I think of Grabner and the slap, wishing I could have my revenge.

Abraham looks at another and nods. "This one is titled 'Ashes to the Vistula'."

Suddenly I want to stop him, but don't know how and I lean back against the wall and remember my time in the pits.

We knew it as the Wisla
A noble river flowing north
The waterway beside our homes
Bringing nourishment to our crops
Meandering through fields of wheat
And bringing us refreshment on summer days.

It was called the Vistula
When we saw it again
Down south near Krakow
At a little place called Oswiecim
A small community they called
Auschwitz-Birkenau-Monowitz.

It is there we learned the cruelty
Of men, of evil beyond imagination
Of things such as red houses
Where we entered innocent
And breathed our last breaths
To die together in chambers of gas.

It is there beside the Vistula
Our broken bodies and lost lives
Were pillaged and plundered
And we were tossed like scraps
Into the ovens to vanish in smoke
And our memories reduced to ashes.

It is there our ashes
Were taken to the river
Dumped into it to join the current
As the Vistula carried us north
Carried us down the river
Past our farms on its banks
Taking us home again.

The silence is frightening. Mario and Maria sit next to Jakub holding his hands. The others stare at the floor and old Abraham sits quietly, wiping the tears from his cheeks.

Finally, he speaks. "This is too painful to read. Too painful to hear. But someone, one of us, risked his or her life to save these poems. And the poets risked their lives to write them. The least we can do is witness their heroism." He wipes his eyes and looks at the paper.

I settle back and lower my eyes, wiping the tears welling there, and I listen as Abraham continues.

Nacht und Nebel

Fog hugs the still night
and darkness holds its secrets
hidden in the recesses
of its bosom
protecting them
from those who don't know
covering the crimes
of those who skulk in the fog
and hide in the night.

And yet another train passes
beneath the arch
its false slogan an irony
promising freedom for work
as workers cling to hope
grasping their children
holding them to their bosoms
unaware of the secrets
hidden in the night.

Arbeit macht frei
for those who don't know
who cling to silly notions

of the honor of men
who believe they will be free
giving them hard work
to die under the strain
as their children are chosen
to vanish in night and fog.

Again the old man stops and wipes his tears and looks up to meet my eyes, but I can't look at him, won't allow him to see my pain.

He continues. "This one is titled 'Selection'."

To be chosen
Left or right
One to the showers
One to the barracks
One to die
One to waste away.

Past angry dogs
amid the ruse
massed together
clutching children
walking the trail
to selection.

One to the left
one to the right
one to the showers
one to the barracks
one to die
one to waste away.

Selection
is the mere motion
one to the left

one to the right
one selected to die
one selected to live.

One to die
one to live
no hope for either
no choice in selection.

He doesn't cry this time, but he is silent for a long time. The room is quiet, more quiet than I've ever known. I'm quiet, too, and am barely aware of the air coursing through my lungs.

I remember Jakub standing alone in that long line, scared, as he came close to being selected to die. He was selected to live, but at a terrible cost.

I look up and see the tops of people's heads and feel the need to end this, to shout, to know our lives will be better, again, but Abraham coughs and wets his lips.

He studies the next poem, wipes tears from his eyes, and lowers his head to his chest, allowing deep sobs to escape his body. Finally, he quietens, takes a deep breath, and looks up. "I'm from Kiev. I escaped before the Germans came." He holds up the paper. "I know this place. I made love for the first time in this forest, in this very spot." He rests his hand on his knee. "I did not marry her. But she married a friend and they stayed in Kiev." He wipes the tears from his eyes, looks at the poem and begins softly.

The Ravine

In the pristine forests
north of Kiev
is a ravine
undisturbed beauty
a peaceful place
renowned in the world

as Babi Yar.

There is little to hint
of what happened there
no graves or signs
or markers like those
of their forefathers
they passed on the road
to Babi Yar.

There is peace in the woods
north of Kiev
but ghosts haunt the valley
restless souls of thousands
of innocents
roaming the ravine
at Babi Yar.

In the pristine forests
north of Kiev
there is no peace
for those who know
what happened
in the ravine
at Babi Yar.

I remember smashing a man for exclaiming the victims were only Jews and it didn't matter. I remember my dislike for the Jews of Katy and I'm deeply ashamed. I push away from the wall, wanting to leave, but Abraham looks at me, his eyes glistening with tears.

"I would like to keep these, Filip. To protect them."

I swallow hard, and release a breath. "Yes, protect them and see that the world reads them."

I pick up the rifle and summon up the courage to venture towards the administrative sector, to the SS barracks, Gestapo building and commandant's office. They are mostly picked clean, either by the SS, or those inmates braver and more desperate. I find canned goods and some moldy cheese, but little else.

We manage to make a thin soup from the sparse supplies, adding the potato peels and shaving the cheese into it for flavor, and nourishment, dispensing it at a rate of a cup a day. It is precious little, but it is more than nothing.

We have been together for more than a week and hear a loud explosion, too singular to be artillery, unaccompanied by other noises. I climb with Mario to the top of the building, crawl onto the roof and survey the area carefully. We see a large cloud of dark smoke to the north and can make out the movement of men and trucks through the Birkenau complex.

I am more concerned about the trucks than the dark smoke, fearing they are coming towards us. Exiting through the gate, they turn south and head for the stamlager. It is as I fear, for it appears the SS are making a final sweep through the camps and destroying anything or anyone they find.

As I watch them, I realize how helpless I am, for there is nothing I can do to save this many people, and it is doubtful Jakub will leave them behind to come with me. I hold by my promise to Aron and my feelings for Jakub and I won't leave him, nor will I save myself unless I can save everyone of the survivors under my care.

Mario and I watch as the truckload of SS turn into Auschwitz, then head for the storage facility. I reason they have seen the smoke from our chimney and are heading directly for us. Furiously, my mind starts working to come up with some way to stay alive, not through confrontation, but negotiation. But these are SS, bent on erasing the evidence of their crimes, leaving me no alternative but to kill as many of them as I can.

I open the breach of the Mauser and count the bullets. Five. I can kill five SS before they kill me. As I start back down the roof, Mario stops me. "Look, Filip. They aren't coming here."

The truck turns away from us and shoots down the main street of the camp. "I wonder what they blew up." I look at Mario and he just shrugs.

Watching as the truck exits the camp and heads west, I assume that the explosion was the last of the crematoria, the one used to destroy the last of the corpses from the camp.

"The Russians must be near, Mario."

"No, Filip. The Americans will liberate us."

"The Germans are going west. Probably to avoid the Russian army."

"Maybe." He looks at me, a look of anticipation about his face. "When do you think they'll be here?"

"I don't know. The sooner the better. We don't have any soup left." I look at him and can see the disappointment in his eyes. "Tomorrow, Mario, the Russians will be here tomorrow."

CHAPTER TWENTY-FOUR

Mario looks at me as he awakens. "Are they here?"

"No."

He narrows his eyes, shakes his head, and lets out a long sigh.

"The day isn't over, Mario. They may come yet." I can only hope they will, for I don't know how long any of us can last.

There isn't anything to occupy our minds, no place that hasn't been searched more than a hundred times, no nook or hiding place that we haven't seen a dozen more. Yet there is nothing else to do.

I organize the able-bodied among us and instruct them where we are going to search. There are groans and curses, epithets as to my heritage, and querulous behavior throughout the building, but they span throughout the lager and search. I realize it is a half-hearted search at best, but it isn't my intention to find anything in the camp, just to busy those of us who are able and keep alive something akin to hope. It serves as well to keep our minds off our empty stomachs.

Mario and I are searching the administrative offices when we hear a low rumble, much like thunder a long ways from us. We continue to listen and realize the noise is constant and not intermittent, a low rumble of many vehicles, powerful engines driving heavy machines. As we listen, the noise increases, coming closer.

We run towards the entrance and see a line of tanks a thousand meters from the camp coming towards us from the town of Oswiecim. And across the frozen field, in the direction of

Monowitz, come more tanks, more than I knew existed, followed by troops in trucks and on foot.

I send Mario to tell the others, as I wait for the arrival of the liberating army. I lean the rifle against the fence, stand by the gate and wait, my heart beating more rapidly than anytime in my life, and I release a long breath, accepting that I am about to be liberated.

As the tanks approach, I can make out the Russian red star and remember the last time I had seen Russians. I can only hope this time will be better than then.

I want to sit, but stay on my feet, ready to receive the conquering army, showing my respect. They seem as strong and powerful as they seemed in 1939, but I'm sure they have been tempered to something harder and stronger after these years of war.

A large tank stops alongside me and a man jumps from the turret, alighting in front of me. He smiles and salutes, making note of the 'P' on my uniform. "Privet." He stops himself and begins again in Polish. "Hello. Would you like a cigarette?"

"Yes, I would like a cigarette." I smile and accept it from a white pack with a red circle on it, just like the last. I hold it to my lips and accept the light, inhaling deeply, coughing furiously. "Americaner. Germans have these, too."

The officer laughs at my information, and he translates what I said, to the laughter of those gathered around. We exchange introductions.

"What place is this?" His question alters his expression.

"Auschwitz." I took another draw on the cigarette and point to the different camps. "Monowitz." I turn and point north. "Birkenau." The tears come and roll down my cheeks and I try to stop the flow, but it is too much.

The Russians look embarrassed and some turn away, but the officer grips my upper arm and nods. "I have seen many camps. I was at Maidanek near Lublin. Very bad."

I don't know the name, but know it was near our home. "Many,

many people die here. Many, many are still alive, but will soon die without help. We need food, blankets, and medicine. Please, we need doctors to look at our sick."

He looks over me and scans the buildings. "How many, friend?"

"Thousands. Several thousand." With that I sit and pull my legs to my chest, fold my arms over my knees and rest my head on my arms.

I cry and remember a time, a century ago, when alone I followed the old priest, a mere child left to face a world gone mad. I had promised I would never cry again or let anyone see my fear or pain, and I had kept that promise during a lifetime in Auschwitz, holding back tears when Jakub was tortured, biting my lip when I kicked the chair from beneath Jan Freimark, and stiffening myself when Anna, my lovely Anna, was hung.

But now it just burst through, and I no longer feel brave.

The officer barks orders to the gathered contingent who are crowding around to get a look at me. I am in much better shape, compared to others they will see, better fed with more flesh, even if it is just hanging from my shoulders like a time-worn, threadbare old coat.

The officer asks me to show him where they will find the survivors, as he puts the pack of cigarettes and matches into the coat's pocket, and finds the pistol. He withdraws it and looks at it carefully, then at me.

"You kill someone for this?"

"He was about to kill me. I got the pistol and killed him."

He removes the clip and counts the bullets. "You shot him four times?"

"Three. The fourth was for a young sentry who chose to obey orders."

He beams, put the clip in the pistol, and shoves it into my pocket. "Two dead Germans. That's good."

Jakub and the twins join me as I am showing the Russians the various buildings where they can find survivors. I smoke my third cigarette and am feeling fuzzyheaded, but I enjoy it and don't want to stop. We walk with a bounce in our steps, something missing since all this began, stretching back to Katy and to Brest, with the arrest of Aron.

I hesitate to talk about it, but it preys upon my mind and fills my heart with dread. As Jakub moves ahead of us, I turn to the Russian and inquire. "A friend of mine," I point to Jakub, "his brother, was an officer in the Polish army. He was arrested in Brest by your army the day they reached the city." I want to say invaded, but decide it is best to use tact.

"Yes. They arrested many Polish officers and civilians. A sad time, my friend, enemies one moment, allies the next." He continues to watch me.

"I understand they were taken to Russia to work." I turn my body to look at him. "Is it possible for you to find out through your channels where he is?" I purposely avoid letting him know the Germans had told us about the Katyn Forest.

He is quiet for a few moments, looking first at Jakub, then turning back to me. "I'm sorry to give you such terrible news." He again looks at Jakub before addressing me. "All of the Polish officers and important political persons were taken to a prison in Smolensk. I understand there was talk of releasing them, but there was also talk of sending them farther east to work in our industries.

"But the Germans invaded before any decision was made." He lights a cigarette and continues. "The Nazis had these roving military police units called Einsatzgruppen, death head units. When they reached Russia and Smolensk, the army found the prison. These para-military units took all of the prisoners outside the city to a forest called Katyn. There they killed all of them and buried them."

He draws on the cigarette and his face shows his concern. "Afterwards, the German propaganda machine started spreading falsehoods, saying we Russians had killed these men." He continues with the cigarette and looks at Jakub. "They were trying to win the loyalty of the Polish people in this awful struggle, by blaming everything on us.

He grinds out the cigarette. "I'm sorry, Filip. I hope you can explain it to the brother."

I wonder what I can tell Jakub that would make Aron's death easier to take, especially now that he has accepted it. And I'm not sure I believe the Russian, although it would be very much in character for the Germans to use it as a propaganda ploy. But my senses say there is another explanation, one nearer the truth.

He leaves me at the gate and goes back to his unit, as swarms of Russian medics, doctors and nurses begin gathering the ill and crippled and transporting them to safe places. Cameramen, too, are bustling about taking pictures and talking with survivors, documenting the horror of what went on at Auschwitz.

The day isn't finished when a tall Russian man dressed in a non-military uniform, one vaguely familiar to me, approaches. I remember that day in Brest when such a man appeared at our table and directed the officer to shoot Aron. This was a commissar, the political officer of the detachment.

I remain seated even as he stops in front of me. "You. What is your name?"

I thought I had left such tones behind me, but they seem to follow me. "Filip Stitchko."

"You're Polish, are you not?" I glance at his face to see the haughty sneer of the SS.

I point to the 'P' on my uniform. "Yes."

"And were you not a kapo?" The man's demeanor suddenly sends a chill through my spine.

I stand to look him in the eyes. "Yes."

"You worked in the crematorium?"

"No. I worked in many places, but not the crematorium." I feel cold on the inside, as if I am facing something more than questions.

"May I see your tattoo?"

"I don't have a tattoo. They didn't use them when I arrived, but my number is forty-four." The feeling of dread is becoming more prominent. "You can check their records if you wish. But I came in 1940, from Tarnow."

"What date?"

I don't like this man and don't want to cooperate with him. I remember the date we left Tarnow, arriving at Auschwitz the same day, the fourteenth. "I don't know. I didn't keep track of days then, but I'm certain it was June."

"How do you know it was June?"

"It was the day Paris fell to the Germans." I am bewildered as to what he is after. "And the heat. The hours of daylight. The new wheat, still green, in the fields." I remember all of those things. "It seemed more like June than May, and too early for July."

"And you're certain of this?"

"Yes, it was June."

"Were you a farmer?"

"No. I was a constable in a small village."

His eyebrows rise slightly. "How is it they didn't kill you?"

"I don't know. Maybe they thought I would be more use to them alive."

"Precisely. As a kapo. Their tool to keep the prisoners in line." His sneer is contemptuous. "Do you know the name of Leon Grabowski?"

"No. But that's not surprising. We don't use a lot of names here."

"Do you know the name of Albin Tolik?"

I start to become alarmed. "Yes. A cruel, evil man who would batter anyone to death. A thief."

"And do you know Jan Freimark?"

The hanging. "Yes. I knew him. He was my friend."

"Your friend? Witnesses say, Kapo, that you hung those men.

244

I'm told you pushed the chairs from beneath them and caused them to strangle to death." His face is as hideous as any I had seen in the stamlager. "Is this not so?"

"Yes, but there is an explanation."

"Arrest him. You can give your explanation to your judges, Kapo. Then we'll hang you just as you hung those men."

They confine me to a hastily constructed fenced enclosure with four Russian soldiers armed with machine guns watching me. I am alone.

Jakub and the twins come and are allowed to approach the fence. Their cheeks are wet and their faces contorted with pain. Jakub starts to ask a question, but stops himself.

Mario speaks for him. "Why are they doing this?"

"I was a kapo. I was forced to hang three men from my lager." I shrug to make light of it. "The Russians consider my actions a crime, and I must stand before a tribunal."

"What will happen, Filip?" Jakub's lower lip trembles.

"I don't know, but I won't be with you for awhile. You must rely on each other." I look at the three of them.

Maria starts crying and Jakub puts his hand on the back of her head and pulls her to him, gently hugging her. Mario grabs Jakub's hand, a scared look in his eyes, but determination shows as well.

"Children, listen to me." I bend over and look at the twins, then straighten to look at Jakub. "No matter what happens to me, the three of you must stay together. Understand?" I look at Jakub. "Take care of the twins. Don't leave them, ever."

He nods. "I understand, Filip." He stands as tall as I have ever seen him.

I clear my throat and notice one of the guards looking in our direction. "Jakub, help them find their parents."

"Mario. Maria." I have to hurry as the guard is walking towards us. "Promise me you'll stay with Jakub and keep him with you, even when you find your parents."

The guard walks between them and me. "Time enough. You leave now."

Frightened, they back away from the Russian. "Promise me, children. Promise you'll stay together, always."

The fence has large open sections, and the guard wheels and punches me in the face, knocking me off my feet.

Jakub and the twins start towards me, only to have the guard turn and aim his machine gun at them. I want to get to my feet and strangle this man, but know the other guards would just kill me. I look at Jakub and the others, imploring them with my eyes.

Mario understands my look. "I promise, Filip. Always."

"Me, too. I promise." Maria is crying.

Jakub's eyes fill with tears, but he has hold of the children and won't let go of them. "I promise too, Filip."

CHAPTER TWENTY-FIVE

"Your name?" There are three men sitting on the panel, two commissars and a senior military officer.

"Josef Grabowski."

He is very thin. I remember him from the lager.

"You are Jewish?"

"I am."

"What is it you wish to tell this tribunal?"

"My brother, Leon Grabowski, was hanged by this man, Kapo Filip."

"You saw this? With your own eyes?" I recognize the questioner as the political officer that freed me when I was in Brest. I struggle to remember his name.

"I did. He hung him in front of the entire kommando unit. We all saw it, we all saw him kick the chair from beneath him." The witness glares at me as I sit in the chair provided.

"I have no further questions."

Punin, I think to myself, pleased I can remember.

The military officer begins. "Will the witness tell us why your brother was hanged?"

The witness doesn't answer the question and seems irritated with it.

"Did you hear the question, Mr. Grabowski?"

"For stealing cigarettes." He is fidgeting. "But he didn't steal them. He was carrying them back to his barracks."

"Who stole them, Mr. Grabowski?"

Again he seems nervous and delays answering the question.

Finally, he speaks in a much-muted voice. "I did."

"Did I hear you correctly? You stole the cigarettes and gave them to your brother?"

"Yes."

The judges confer with each other before the military officer continues. "What was the prescribed punishment for stealing cigarettes?"

Grabowski shrugs his shoulders and doesn't answer.

I tire of sitting and not participating. "If I may speak on this issue, your honors, it will enlighten the court."

Again the three confer, and Punin, who appears to be the senior among them, addresses me. "You may speak only on the question at hand, but do not attempt to address this court on any other issue. Understand?"

"Yes."

His eyes are harsh and strict. "What was the prescribed punishment for stealing cigarettes?"

"Punishments in Auschwitz varied. They could be as mild as a lashing or as serious as a hanging." I hold out my hands. "One never knew what punishment the SS was going to give."

Punin turns to the witness. "Is this true, Mr. Grabowski?"

He is hesitant, but answers in a soft voice. "Yes."

The other judge speaks up. "Do you have anything else you want to add to this hearing?"

Grabowski's tears run down his wizened face. "I loved my brother. He didn't deserve to be hung."

A Russian guard leads the man away and the tribunal looks at me. Punin begins. "Defendant Kapo Filip, we'll turn to your defense. Do you have anyone to represent you before this court."

Victor Punin I think to myself, as I remembered the note he had given me. "No, sir, but I would ask that I be allowed to appoint a spokesman."

The tribunal confers. "Agreed. Who do you want?"

I feel strangely numb about the proceedings, almost oblivious that I may be condemned to die. "I would like Victor Punin to act as my representative."

Both of the other judges look at the senior man, and he has a look of incredulity on his face, looking at one then the other, shrugging his shoulders.

"Do I know you, Kapo?"

"We met in Brest when the Russians were the allies of Germany." I warn myself to be careful not to go too far, lest I condemn myself to death.

"I don't recall our meeting."

"My appearance is somewhat less than it was." I start to add that he looks as healthy as when I first met him, but heed my own warnings. "I was arrested with a Polish officer and confined to an alleyway." I pause to allow him to associate the scene with my words. "My friend, Aron Galinski, a major in an artillery unit, complained that officers should not be detained with peasants."

"I remember. A very arrogant man. He didn't speak well of you."

"A ploy, your honor. We were best friends and had been since childhood."

As soon as I say it, I know it is a mistake, as he seems to bristle at the knowledge that I once duped him.

"So, you lied?" He glances at both judges. "I'll decline to represent you. Is there another you'd like to ask?"

I am in deep already and decide to forego any chance at saving myself. "Yes, your honor. I would like to have Aron Galinski speak for me."

The military officer just looks at me. "And where is this man?"

"I don't know, your honor. The last time I saw him, he was in the hands of the Red army." It is becoming a dangerous game. "I understand he was taken east to Russia, perhaps all the way to Siberia." I feel strangely elated. "I don't mind waiting until he can be brought here, your honors. I'm in no hurry." There are some giggles from the crowd.

There are no smiles from the tribunal, no appreciation of my humor.

I walk to the back of my chair and lean upon it. "Ask Commissar Punin. Perhaps he knows what became of my friend."

The commissar stands and addresses the onlookers who are watching the proceedings. "All Polish prisoners during that time were taken to a prison in Smolensk. But, when the Germans invaded, they sent out units called Einsatzgruppen and found the prison. These para-military units took all of the prisoners outside the city to a forest and killed them all."

He takes a sip of water and continues. "Afterwards, the German propaganda machine started spreading lies, saying Russians had killed those men. They were trying to win the loyalty of the Polish people in this awful struggle and blamed everything on us."

He sits down and looks at me. "I suppose your friend was one of those found in Katyn. For that, I'm sorry. Is there anyone else, someone neutral and alive?"

"No, sir."

As the judges confer, I conclude the Russians are lying about the massacre of Aron and the others. Twice I had heard their explanations and both times it was nearly identical, too similar to be anything other than a rehearsed script from their own propaganda machine.

"Prisoner, you'll remain standing and answer the questions of this tribunal. I caution you to not address any other issue. Just answer the questions. You'll receive an opportunity to speak for yourself later." Punin is staring at me, but it isn't hatred or animosity I see in his look. "Understand?"

"Yes, sir."

Punin turns to the other political officer. "I'm Vladimir Melankov." He shifts his chair and settles firmly in it. "Did you ever kill anyone, Kapo?"

Punin interrupts. "I think that question is improper, comrade. He's accused of killing three men."

"Sirs?" I want it understood I had killed Germans. "I would like to answer Comrade Melankov's question."

Punin looks at me shaking his head. "So, answer it then."

"I voluntarily killed SS Sergeant Heinz Hirt with three bullets to his head."

There is applause from the gathering and some cheers.

"I also killed an SS guard who thought his orders were more important than his life." I relax and study the eyes of the panel. "And I would willingly kill Adolf Hitler."

More cheers and applause from the crowd.

Melankov leans forward and rests his elbows on the table. "Did you ever strike a person hard enough to cause a bruise or damage to his body?"

I remember Kapo Karl and the blood, but choose not to mention it. "My job as kapo was to make people work. If they didn't work, then the SS was going to kill them."

Melankov interrupts. "Answer the question, prisoner, and do not try to rationalize your behavior."

I stare at the commissar. "Yes, I struck many workers…"

"That will do." Melankov glares at me.

"But…" I am determined to finish my statement.

"Stop it!" The commissar jumps to his feet and appears threatening, dangerous, like a man who is used to having his way through force. He would have made a good Nazi, I think.

Punin motions for his associate to sit down, then whispers something to him.

The senior judge turns to me. "You may finish your answer."

"I struck many laborers in my care, but no man was ever taken from my lager, my camp, for not working." I take a breath. "But there are many who died because they couldn't do the work. There are many who died of starvation. There are many who died of thirst. There are many who died because they lost hope, and there are many who died because they just didn't want to go any further." I wipe a tear from my eye. "But no one died because I beat them to death, or injured them so badly they couldn't go on."

Punin interrupts. "That's enough. I ask you again to control your comments. Answer only the questions asked of you."

"Yes, sir. And thank you."

"Eloquent, Kapo." Melankov sneers. "But the facts remain. Three men were hanged by you, and nothing you've said disputes that fact." He doesn't pursue the statement any further.

Punin turns to his right. "You may ask your questions, Colonel."

"I'm Colonel Belinkin." He looks at the notes he has been preparing. "You have heard the testimony of the witness, Josef Grabowski. Were you the man he saw push the chair from beneath his brother?"

"Yes."

"And you did the same to two others?"

"Yes."

"And why did you do it?"

"Because I was ordered to do it. It was a lesson to teach me to be harder on my laborers, because the camp director thought I was too lenient." I suddenly feel the weight of that day on my shoulders. I release a long breath. "I did it, because if I hadn't, then I would have been hung alongside them, and the lager would have been in for a rough time."

Melankov interrupts. "You did it to protect this, this lager?"

"Yes, sir. With me gone, the camp would get another lagerkapo, perhaps one as cruel as Tolik."

There are some calls from the gathering, some applause.

"If you don't believe me, sir, I suggest you ask some of them."

Punin interjects. "Quiet. Address only the question asked of you and add nothing further. We'll decide how this tribunal will be conducted."

"Yes, sir." His expression puzzles me, for it bears no animosity.

Punin holds out his hands to his associates. "The witness Grabowski? Was he in your labor gang?"

"Yes, sir. He was in the lager."

"If you had caught him stealing cigarettes, what would you have done?"

"I would talk with him and ask him to stop. If he refused, then I would transfer him out of the lager to protect everyone else."

The colonel addresses me. "Transfer to where?"

I am afraid of this question and slow to answer. "To the Sonderkommandos."

"These are the prisoners killed occasionally, just to be rid of them?"

"Sometimes."

Melankov interjects. "Sometimes, Kapo? Weren't all the prisoners of those units gassed and cremated?"

"No, sir. Some transferred to other work. Tolik was one and a Russian named Meretsky and Jan Freimark."

"Two of the men you're accused of hanging. Is that not so?" Melankov obviously doesn't like me. "And the Russian, what happened to him? Did you hang him as well?"

"No, sir. Ivan Meretsky broke away from two SS guards, killing them both, took their rifles and fought against other SS who finally killed him."

The commissar's smugness quickly leaves him and he sits back in his chair.

"Is there anything you would like to add to this hearing?" Punin's face is a mask, but his eyes lack the harshness I had first seen.

Colonel Belinkin speaks to Punin who nods. He stands and addresses the group gathered for the hearing. "Is there anyone among you who has testimony they wish to give the tribunal? It can be evidence against or for him. Please come forward."

Jakub and the twins are first. Mario begins and tells of finding us and of how we took them in and cared for them. Maria talks about the organized search and the many people that we fed.

Jakub also speaks. "Filip is my friend. He taught me to drive a truck. He protected me from Germans. He got me out of cre… er, pits. I drove a truck to the river." He is lost for anything else to say, then blurts out, "Please, don't kill Filip. He's my best friend."

Others from my lager testify how I overlooked their stealing food, and how, in the last days, I encouraged more theft, even of money and gems. Two told of how I misdirected shipments and sent useless items to Berlin or to the addresses given to me. Many from the last week came forward and also spoke on my behalf, stressing how I had organized the searches and found more canned goods, and of how I had prepared soup to feed more than two hundred, keeping them alive. They explained how I had broken into the German stores and stripped them of blankets and heating materials, providing more heat than they had ever found in Auschwitz.

Finally, a thin man I recognize steps forward. "I'm Leon Safirsztain and I also worked in Kapo Filip's lager." He straightens and glances in my direction. "I am also Jewish. I also know of this man." He again looks at me and smiles slightly. "There is one incident of which the defendant hasn't spoken."

"What sort of incident, Mr. Safirsztain?" Punin's words are terse and there is an edge to his voice.

"One in which a man was beaten to death by Kapo Filip."

I feel colder than at any moment in Auschwitz.

Melankov leaps to his feet. "A murder, witness, you saw this man deliberately kill a prisoner?"

Leon straightens. "If I may be allowed to proceed, I'll tell you what I saw."

Punin motions to his fellow commissar. "Proceed, Mr. Safirsztain."

"This German, a kapo, was a cruel man. He raped the women under his charge, Russian women, soldiers they were, then he would beat them until he was sated. This German was an evil man, a man as large as a mountain, a man who prided himself on his wickedness, a man who delighted in clubbing people to death, the kind of man you seek."

He shifts his position and steps in my direction. "Our building lived in fear of this German. I lived in fear of him as well." He holds his hand towards me. "Kapo Filip wasn't afraid of him. He confronted the giant and attacked. Like David, he killed the man."

"And how did he manage to kill this man?" Melankov snarls from behind the desk, glaring at the witness and me.

"With his baton." He turns to face the Russian. "He was faster than the German, but received several blows from the evil man, yet was successful in striking the man on the head, killing him."

No one speaks for several moments as the three judges confer. Finally Punin addresses the witness. "Do you have anything else to say?"

"Yes. I was a judge in Krakow. I know the law, German law, Polish law and Russian law." He takes several steps towards the tribunal. "Kapo Filip defended his life against a malicious assault, killing his attacker." He turns towards me. "At the same time, he freed the lager from the evil of this German, this devil among men. Kapo Filip has committed no crime. Ask anyone of the thousands in his lager and you'll see you're wasting your time."

They follow Leon Safirztain's suggestion, but no one comes forward to accuse me of a crime or to condemn me for my actions on the gallows.

There are many more in line waiting to speak, when Punin rises and raises his hand above his head. "We have heard enough. The issue before this tribunal is whether or not Kapo Filip Stitchko did willfully and without hesitation hang the defendants Grabowski, Tolik and Freimark."

The other judges also rise and Punin confers with them, and then turns to face me and the crowd. "We will confer and render our decision. We'll return in one hour."

I wonder if only an hour is enough to decide my innocence or guilt. But it seems, at the time, that the Russians are in a punishing mood, and I can feel my neck in the noose, as the face of Jan Freimark appears in my mind.

CHAPTER TWENTY-SIX

It seems more like an eternity than an hour. Jakub and the twins stay with me, talking about their family, Milano and their plans of going home. Jakub, too, talks of going home, to stay only briefly, to see if anyone returns, to see if Dr. Levi, the Spiegelmans, Malbin or Aron are alive. Then he smiles and talks of going to Milano with Mario and Maria.

"What if I'm found innocent? What will you do with me?" I look at the three of them, catching them off guard, as I think they have become so adapted to death in Auschwitz, that they are unprepared for my living.

Jakub's eyes glow and he beams. "You come with us, Filip."

"Yes, Filip, you come to Milano with us." Mario smiles and reaches for my hand.

"No touching!" The Russian guard comes over quickly and motions for them to back away. He glares at me. "You may not touch anyone."

Maria watches the guard as he retreats. "They're as bad as the Nazis." She turns back to me. "You and Jakub can be our big brothers."

I nod and think of their parents, hoping they are alive and strong enough to survive the death march. Yet I know if they return we will lose the opportunity to care for them, something I fear for Jakub more than myself. "I would like that. I never had any brothers or sisters, except Jakub, of course."

"And Aron." Jakub smiles, the sparkle back in his eyes. "It'll make me happy to take care of all of you."

I am pleased to see his exuberance has returned, that he has found in the twins a desire to live. Yet, I still have a foreboding, perhaps borne of my existence in Auschwitz, which tells me to not have hope, that it is hope that led us to this miserable place, hope that things would improve.

But it has improved, at least for Jakub, yet confined in this enclosure, I have to answer for my deeds in the lager, looking at the possibility of death, or more prolonged confinement. But after Aron, after learning of the Katyn massacre and my belief that the Russians had committed the crime, I have no faith in hope. I believe they are looking to punish someone, to balance the scales, even against innocents perceived as wrongdoers. I hold no hope that I will go free, nor live, even in a labor camp.

I watch Jakub and the twins as they play outside the fence, laughing and enjoying each other, little evidence of the tortures they suffered, other than the loose-fitting clothes, the emaciated bodies and the scars of Mengele's experiments. I rejoice at the recuperative power they exhibit to get beyond the memories of their immediate past, of their ability to become children again.

They will survive, with or without me, with or without the return of the twins' parents. Theirs is a perspective of innocence, free of guilt, unsullied by their efforts to live, untainted by the horrors visited upon them. They will have memories, unpleasant visions come to mind occasionally, less frequently the further time takes them from here, but they will survive.

But will I? I know I will awaken many nights to the look on Jan Freimark's face, of his not judging me, of his words thanking me, relieving him of an existence more horrid than the prospect of death. I know I will awaken to the sound of Jan's rasping and wheezing efforts to breath, and look into those lifeless eyes as they stared at me.

I will always know of the things I did, unknown to others, things that would deservedly put the noose over my head. I will remember Tolik's face and efforts at prayer, of his innocence of the crime, and I will remember it was my guilt that placed him on that chair. And it was my guilt that drove Meretsky to kill the SS guards and fight back, to forfeit his life. But it is Anna I will remember most, her beautiful face broken and marred by my betrayal, hanging from the gallows breaking my heart.

As I watch them play, scenes flash before me, of Father Jan, broken and dispossessed of all dignity, and I taunted him rather than offer him a few gentle words of compassion. And I will relive the blood spattering my face as Kapo Karl sprawled on the wooden floor, his worthless life and death accusing me of murder. And how many others were there? I remember the faces, but time has taken possession of their names. Perhaps, I reason, time will eventually take the memories too.

I convince myself that I am guilty of many things, things the Germans didn't force me to do, things I chose to do on my own. I rationalized it then as my duty to protect Jakub, to keep my promise to Aron, but I wonder how much of it wasn't due to my love of the job, the love of power. The Germans gave me that power and I accepted it willingly and used it forcefully. I think, perhaps, that I do deserve to die, but I do so want to live.

Jakub and the twins see Punin before me. I turn in his direction as he walks with his head down. I look for the other judges, but they aren't there. Maybe, I think, he has other questions of me.

"Kapo, come here." He stands holding his hand on the fence. "Your name is Filip, isn't it?"

"Yes, Commissar. Filip Stitchko." I feel cold all over, a deep cold one feels in the anticipation of bad news.

"We have voted two to one for your acquittal." He smiles. "Mind you, there are a lot of unanswered questions about the happenings in this camp. But in the matter of the hanging, you're not held accountable." He motions to the guards to open the gate and allow me to leave.

The big soldier that struck me earlier stands to the side as his companion holds the gate for me. I stop in front of the big man and look up at him, meeting a steely gaze. I speak firmly. "No man should hit another." With that I smash his nose as hard as I can, sending the Russian sprawling on the ground.

He reaches for his machine gun and pulls it to the front, aiming at me. Suddenly Punin steps in front of me and addresses the soldier. I don't understand all of his words, but the big soldier gets to his feet, salutes and leaves the area.

Punin turns to me. "Today you're a lucky man. I could have let him kill you. As it is, Filip, be careful he doesn't catch you alone somewhere. He'll be looking for an opportunity to even the score."

"Thank you, Comrade. And thanks for voting for my release."

"Yes, well, let's just say I didn't believe you were completely guilty." He stops and looks at his feet, and continues in a softer voice. "And, perhaps, I owed you something."

As I watch him walk away, I believe he knows the Russian story of the Katyn Forest is a lie, but I am thankful. I am also mindful that he never indicated he thought I was innocent.

We wait in the barracks at Auschwitz, wait as medical teams treat the more seriously injured and malnourished amongst us, and wait as clerks take our names and numbers, asking question after question. Others, legal clerks who have their own questions, follow those clerks, questions of who beat whom, and who among us deserves to hang.

I fear the last round of questions, not of any answers I would give, but of the responses of others pointing a finger at me, forcing me to undergo another tribunal. Our Russian liberators are as paranoid as the SS, as their internal police, the NKVD, their Gestapo, spread throughout all three camps with their own suspicions and their own brand of questions.

More prisoners begin arriving at Auschwitz; Jews, Poles, Russians, and others from across Europe, survivors of death marches, those who were brave enough to flee and elude the SS as they were led to their deaths. And it is in a late afternoon that a truck filled with former prisoners arrives at the lager.

I see them as he leaps from the truck and reaches for his wife, a couple who couldn't have been much beyond thirty, but who appear much older with wizened cheeks, hollowed eyes and cracked lips. Gone from their uniforms are the yellow stars, replaced by its outline, darker than the material surrounding it, partially hidden by the large coats protecting them from the cold.

They approach a Russian guard who indicates he doesn't understand them. She looks around, wrings her hands and bites her lower lip as he puts his arm around her. I take the opportunity to help them, introduce myself and learn they speak some German.

"How is it you return here?"

He begins. "We were marching west, I don't know to where. We were hungry."

His wife interjects, "There was no food or water."

I can see the remnants of her beauty and think I recognize something in her features.

"On the second day they put us in a barn and closed the doors with a heavy bar across it. There was a lot of hay which we could use for warmth."

He licks his lips, attempting to ease the dryness. "We found some loose slats, and peered out of the barn. Sentries were posted in the front and rear to watch for an escape attempt from those directions.

"There was a lot of snow, with some drifts against the side of the building, deep enough for the two of us." He puts his arm around his wife. "I worked all night digging a hole in the snow, just big enough to allow us to crawl in and lay with my feet to Kati's head, covering the hole with the broken slats, snow and hay."

Kati shivers in the cold air and wraps the coat tighter around her. I know they should be inside, but they insist on completing the story. "A friend, who was on the march with us, was too afraid to attempt an escape. She piled straw against the inside wall, covering the broken slat."

He begins again. "We felt confident we wouldn't be missed as they hadn't counted since we left. But, that morning, they counted. There was much confusion and I could hear the SS arguing amongst themselves. They weren't certain how many there were of us, but they wanted to make sure no one remained in the barn."

"Then I became really frightened." Kati looks at her husband. "They were sticking their bayonets into the straw, probing to see if anyone was hiding." She accepts his nod and continues. "The knife hit the wall near my face, frightening me terribly. I almost cried out."

"But she didn't." He picks up the story. "They continued longer than I thought necessary and I feared there was something which caused them suspicion."

He releases a long breath. "But the two finally stopped and talked about how useless all of this was."

Kati looks up at her husband, her eyes bright. "We waited a long time, then Michel crawled out and checked."

"I was so relieved to find us alone, so wonderfully alone." He kisses his wife on the forehead. "We headed back here. A Russian patrol happened upon us and brought us the rest of the way."

"I'm happy for you both. You've shown a lot of courage." I step aside and motion for them to follow me. I take them to the building used as a hospital, hoping to talk with them further.

"Here, you'll get medical attention and some food."

"Thank you. I'm sorry, but I forgot your name." He offers his hand.

I start to say lagerkapo, but stop. "I'm Filip Stitchko." I shake his hand.

"I'm Michel Caprizio. This is my wife Kati." He smiles. "Katarina."

She looks at me with her fingers intertwined and held forward. "Where do they keep the children?"

"Everywhere." She bites her lip and looks down.

"Don't worry, Kati, we'll just search until we find them." He looks at me, shakes his head, and I can see he fears the worst.

"Tell me about your children."

"Twins. Mario and Maria." Kati smiles at me, an uneven smile on her face and a slight tremble of her lower lip. "Maria is older than her brother, but she lets him boss her around."

It is, I thought, the similarity between the twins and their mother. "I'll help you look. But, first, you must eat and gain some strength."

I leave them and my head fills with mixed thoughts, matching my heart. It is going to be wonderful for the twins to reunite with their parents, but it isn't going to be so wonderful for Jakub. I wonder what I am going to do, wonder how he will react. But, I reason, God sent the twins to give Jakub something to live for, and I allow myself to hope Jakub will again find a purpose and a reason to live.

I tell Jakub before I tell the twins. He is happy for them, but I can see the sadness in his eyes.

"Mario, Maria, you're needed in the clinic."

Mario glances at me quickly, his lips part, but halts his question. "Sure, Filip." He smiles and grasps Maria's hand. The look between them is one only people close to each other can share, one born of a special bond. "Come with us." Mario smiles.

The twins lead the way hurriedly, forcing Jakub and me to run to keep up, but we want to be a part of their happiness.

They wait just outside the clinic for us to catch up. "You're slow, Jakub." Mario is smiling.

"You, too, Filip." Maria reaches for my hand. "Are you going in with us?"

I want to tell them I wouldn't miss it. "If you want us to, we will."

They both smile and Mario takes Jakub's hand, as Maria pulls me along.

As we step into the building, their parents aren't where I left them. We walk and find them in the kitchen area, waiting for their bowls of soup, their backs to us.

I look at the twins as they turn their heads to look at me. "I've a surprise for you."

Their eyes light up. "Something sweet?"

I can't stop the tears filling my eyes. "Sweeter." I look at their parents and nod for them to look too.

They are puzzled at first then realize it is their parents. "Papa! Mama!" They both call at the same time and release our hands.

The Caprizios turn quickly and Kati drops her empty bowl. Their faces seem to erase the trauma of their ordeal, as they glow with the joy in their hearts. Kati runs to her children, unable to speak, tears and emotion choking her, silencing words of happiness.

Michel follows closely on his wife's skirt, sweeping Maria into his arms, also unable to express his relief, his utter delight at finding his children.

The reunion lasts many minutes, as the parents find their voices and praise their children, expressing the love and relief at their safety. The children, too, are excited, more than anytime since they sneaked into our building.

All of them turn to us and the twins make the introductions. We sit and listen to them share the stories of how they had survived, of the good fortune of escaping the SS, and of finding friends. It is a joyful time for the Caprizios, an exceptional reunion to bond the family together for eternity.

It appears to be a good time for us as well, as Jakub smiles and demonstrates his fondness and affection for the twins. The family sees the warmth in him, but I know him better, and I can see the disappointment, the growing sadness in his depths, and I shudder to think he will again lose the desire to live.

That night we share barracks with the Caprizios as a strong wind blows outside, and a Russian officer enters. Snow covers the soldiers' uniforms and they carry their rifles slung across their shoulders.

I rise to greet the officer, offering my hand. "I'm Filip Stitchko. Welcome. Come in and warm your hands."

Without removing his glove, he reluctantly accepts my hand, his grip weak, his expression both awkward and pensive. "Thank you, but no. We won't be here long enough."

I turn to introduce the others in the room, but the Russian stops me.

"Which of you is Jakub Galinski?" His expression is a mask of his thoughts and feelings.

Jakub rises. "I am." There is something in his eyes I had never seen, something that frightens me.

"What is this about, Captain?" I feel a terrible dread in the pit of my stomach and feel if my heart is going to stop beating.

He ignores me and motions the two soldiers towards Jakub. "Jakub Galinski, you're under arrest."

I shake my head and step towards the officer. "For what?"

He looks at me, then turns to address Jakub. "You're charged with collaboration with the enemy."

The charge frightens me, knowing that it is one they use to hang wrong doers. "This is ridiculous."

The captain faces me. "There'll be a tribunal tomorrow. If you wish to speak on behalf of the prisoner, then you'll have to request it." He eases me to the side and walks past me, motioning for the soldiers to follow with Jakub.

"Jakub, don't worry. Stay calm. I'll find a way to free you."

CHAPTER TWENTY-SEVEN

Jakub is isolated in a separate barracks, one that contains a room for observation. There are two other men with him, hardened men from another lager, kapos who proved cruel in their attitudes towards all men. For this I fear for Jakub, but guards are present and will stop any abuse the prisoners try to visit upon one another.

After a restless night, a night of wondering what evidence they can have against Jakub, a night of preparing the arguments I can use, the tribunal begins the following afternoon in a light snow that falls slowly.

All three of the prisoners come out, their hands tied in front of them, guards with machine guns on either side of the column. Jakub is last, his eyes bright and watching the crowd, looking, I suppose, for me and the twins, with a slight smile. I can only wonder what is going through his mind, but he isn't despondent and has found something for which to live, something unknown to me. I fear he doesn't understand what is happening.

The tribunal moves swiftly, listening to the testimony of witnesses and soliciting rebuttals. They listen as well to the defendants' responses, patiently asking questions for clarification. As quickly as the evidence is given, the tribunal sentences the kapos to twenty years at hard labor in Siberia.

The sentences of imprisonment are encouraging and I feel hopeful Jakub's sentence will be as fair.

"The tribunal will now hear the case against Jakub Galinski." The senior jurist is Melankov, the man who voted to find me guilty. It doesn't bode well.

Jakub remains seated and looks at the court.

"The prisoner will stand."

Jakub doesn't understand, and I walk to the front of the enclosure and address the tribunal. "May I, sirs, speak for this man?"

Melankov stares at me. "If you wish, Kapo." His words are terse. "But first, have him stand, and have him remain standing until he is told to sit."

"Yes, sir." I turn to Jakub. "Stand up, Jakub. Do as this man says, understand?"

He nods, but still holds a crooked smile.

I turn back to Melankov. "What are the charges against my friend?"

Melankov smiles. "In good time, Kapo. Will the defendant state his name?"

I turn to Jakub and nod.

"Jakub Galinski."

"And you're prisoner ninety-eight of the Auschwitz complex?"

"Excuse me, sir." He reversed the numbers.

"Do not interrupt me again, Kapo." Melankov glares at me. "The prisoner will answer the question."

I turn to Jakub and shake my head. "You were number eighty-nine."

"No, sir. I was number eighty-nine." He continues with the smile and I fear he doesn't understand the seriousness of the proceedings.

There are several chuckles from the crowd.

Melankov marks in his notes and looks at Jakub. "Eighty-nine, then." He pauses. "Prisoner Galinski, you're charged as a collaborator with the German SS. Do you understand the charge against you?"

I turn to talk with Jakub, but he answers the question. "Do

you mean I helped the Germans?"

"Yes."

"Yes, sir." He still smiles and looks at me, before turning back to the judges. "I helped the Germans."

"No! Your honors, this man doesn't understand the nature of the charges against him, nor does he understand the consequences."

"He seems to understand, Kapo. We'll allow him to speak for himself." Melankov smiles and raises his chin. "Now, Kapo, you seat yourself and we'll conduct the tribunal."

"Your honors," I appeal to the military men at the table, "this man has the mind of a child. He is kind-hearted and gentle, but he doesn't understand the complexity of life. He is naïve and trusting, and wants very much to please people."

"Sit down, Kapo, or I'll have you detained." Melankov is showing a vindictiveness and cruelty equal to the SS.

"I'm not a kapo! My name is Filip!"

"Guards, take this man and prevent him from any further interruptions."

Two rugged soldiers come and accompany me to my seat, standing on either side of me.

Jakub is watching me and searching for the twins and, finding them, he waves with his hands still tied together.

"Prisoner Galinski? Turn and face the tribunal."

Jakub doesn't move at first, then realizes the judge is addressing him, and he slowly turns and looks at the commissar.

"The evidence against you is unimpeachable." Melankov looks over at me, then proceeds. "But I'll ask you questions. You answer the questions, understand?"

Jakub looks at me, and then turns to face the judge. "Yes, sir."

I cringe to think what is going to happen, and I know Jakub doesn't understand everything he hears.

The Caprizios join me, their faces etched with lines. "Filip, what's happening?"

"I don't know, but Jakub is going to have to handle this by

himself. They won't allow me to speak for him."

"Then I'll speak for him, just like I did for you." Mario's cheeks are wet.

"Surely they can't believe he's guilty of such a thing." Michel Caprizio is as distraught as the rest of us.

"Prisoner Galinski, did you tell one of the doctors treating you that you helped the Germans?"

"Yes, sir."

"How did you help them?"

"They let me drive a truck. I drove to the river, dumped the ashes, and drove back. I did this all day. I was a good driver. Filip told me so." He is strangely pleased with himself and shows no signs of fear.

"Did you drive this truck willingly?"

Jakub doesn't answer the question, but doesn't look at me either.

"Did you want to drive this truck?"

"Yes, sir. I wanted to a lot."

"And the Germans let you do this, to help them?"

"Yes, sir."

"So these Germans were your friends?"

Jakub hesitates. "No, sir."

I breathe a sigh of relief and tighten my grip on the twins' hands.

The three judges confer before Melankov continues. "Why did you drive the truck?"

"Because I'm a truck driver. That's what I do."

"Is that all you did for the Germans?"

"No, sir. I helped build these buildings. I ran errands. I carried messages. I talked to guards."

I snap my head up with that statement, unable to imagine to what he is referring.

"What did you talk with the guards about?"

"I tell them who doesn't work. I tell them who steals my bread. I tell them who steals from the warehouses."

"Who did you tell this to?"

"Staff Sergeant Hirt and Max. Max was my friend. He saved me from going to the gas."

"That would be Untersturmfuhrer Maximilian Grabner, I believe."

Jakub shrugs his shoulders. "He told me how he liked me. He told me how he wanted me to work for him." He turns and looks at me. "He told me he was my friend. That he wouldn't send Filip to the sonder... er, to the ovens."

He turns back to the judges. "Filip didn't want to work there."

My heart sinks to think he was protecting me better than I was protecting him.

"And you gave Max the names of men who stole things?"

"Yes, sir."

"Tell us, prisoner, what happened to these people you reported to Max?"

Jakub shrugs. "I don't know. They weren't there anymore."

"I'll tell you. They were sent to the gas chamber and murdered."

"You don't know that!" I leap to my feet, upending the children with my sudden movement. The guards quickly grab me and slam me to the chair.

Melankov just glares at me. "Isn't that what happened to them, prisoner?"

Jakub's eyes fill with tears and he lowers his head. "I don't know."

"Or is it you don't want to tell us." Melankov's talent surpasses any evil I knew in Auschwitz. "Those men died because of you. Didn't they?"

"I don't know." Jakub starts crying softly.

"You do know. Admit it. Max punished those men. He punished them because of what you said to him. Isn't that the truth?"

"I don't know." He turns to look at me, his eyes pleading with me to help.

Melankov sips from the glass and is calmer. He waits for a few moments and speaks more softly. "Prisoner, answer these questions."

"Yes, sir." Jakub also is calmer.

"Did you tell Max about men stealing?"

"Yes, sir."

"And these men then disappeared?"

"Yes, sir."

"Then, as they say in Auschwitz, these men were 'nacht und nebel'. Have you heard this expression?"

"Yes, sir."

"It means 'night and fog', doesn't it?"

Jakub shrugs his shoulders and shakes his head. "I don't know."

Melankov pauses and looks at Jakub. "What does it mean to you?"

"It means... er, those who go into the red building become smoke."

"The red building? What happened in this building?"

"People go to sleep. They don't wake up."

"Who told you this?"

Jakub looks at me a long time, holding my gaze with his, then smiles. He turns back to the tribunal. "A kapo. A sond... a man who worked the pits."

He wants me to know something about that time, to understand he is protecting me, but from what I don't know.

"Then it means people are killed. Isn't that right?"

Jakub is silent for a long time. "I guess so."

"Then, prisoner, let me lay out the case for your conviction. First, you gave information to Max. This is true?"

"Yes, sir."

"Then these men were like 'night and fog', gone, into the 'red building', the gas chamber, where they went to sleep, where they died. This, too, is true?"

"I guess so." I can see his hands trembling.

"Then it can be stated that, by giving information to Max, you helped kill those men. Isn't this true?"

Jakub is silent for a long time. "I drove a truck. I carried ashes to the Vistula."

Melankov looks at his fellow judges and they confer. "Prisoner, did you help the Germans kill anyone else?"

"No, sir."

"Just the ones you talked to Max about?"

"Yes, sir."

The judges consult again, and then Melankov stands. "Prisoner Galinski, the three judges of this tribunal conclude, by unanimous vote, that you're guilty of collaboration with the German SS, and furthermore, that you stand guilty of murder."

"Who did he murder?" I scream from my chair, glaring at Melankov. "Tell me the name of just one person he murdered." The guards hold their hands on my shoulders, preventing me from rising.

Melankov nods to the other judges and walks towards me. "So, Kapo, you want names. I don't need names. By his own testimony, he has shown us his guilt. Now he'll hang." He smirks at me. "Unless," he smiles wickedly at me, "you can give me intelligence that will lead to the apprehension and punishment of war criminals." He stares at me, boring into my mind. "Otherwise, Kapo, you open your mouth again and we'll find some fresh charges against you."

I watch him stomp off followed by the guards, leaving me with the Caprizios. I turn to them. "I don't have anything to give. I wish to God I did."

"You were lagerkapo, Filip, surely you know something they would want?" Michel looks at me with his head thrust forward and his hands in front of him.

"I'll rack my brain, Michel, but I don't see what it can be." It is then I remember the gold teeth. "I could bribe him."

"Money greases many wheels, my friend. It works well in Milano." He looks at his kids and smiles. "Mario and Maria are very fond of Jakub and you too. We would be grieved if we lost either of you."

Michel and I find the sack of gold teeth, and I think of the coats, lined with more wealth than Melankov has ever seen. If he doesn't take it, then I will offer it to Punin.

As we walk slowly back to the camp, Michel shows his concern over my plan. "Filip, I think talking with Melankov would be an error."

I look at him. "Why?"

"He doesn't like you, Filip. I think he would take the gold and report you for trying to bribe him. Then, off you go to Siberia, or worse. And we still lose Jakub."

"Punin, then?"

"Yes, my friend." He looks up at me. "Still, I think he is also dangerous, unpredictable. But, yes, Punin would be my choice."

"Thank you." We continue to the camp without talking, both lost in our own thoughts.

As we pass through the gates, I see Commissar Punin walking towards me, a severe look about him. I send Michel on to the barracks and walk towards the political officer.

"Filip, I would like a word with you."

"Yes, Commissar, I would also like to speak with you."

"I'm sorry about your friend." He shakes his head. "He talked too much. Our doctors, some clerks, and some NKVD agents heard him confess to working for the Germans. He was condemned by his own words."

"Sir, he was nothing more than a dupe for Grabner and Hirt. He was too gullible. He's childish, slow in his thinking. Surely you can see how they took advantage of him."

"It's of no matter now. The case is finished. The sentence will be carried out tomorrow morning."

"Please, Commissar, there must be a way to alter the verdict."

He shakes his head. "No. It's done."

I hesitate as he studies me. "I can pay." I bring out the sack of teeth and prepare to show him.

"Stop." He is silent for several long moments, looking at the ground and shaking his head. "I can have you shot for this, Filip." He glares at me. "Put it away and don't ever suggest such a thing to me again."

"I'm sorry, Commissar." I probe further. "Would such a gesture work with Melankov?"

His face remains severe. "Only to get you killed. I'm being generous."

I feel my chances slipping away. "This can't be the end of it. I must save him. I promised his brother. Am I to fail now? Are the Russians going to kill both him and his brother?"

Punin steps back and his eyes flash. "You go too far, Pole. I'm tempted to have you arrested. How dare you accuse us of injustice?"

I chafe under his glare and his temper.

"For your information, the boy's brother was an enemy of Russia. And he was an enemy of Germany. For that, they killed him. As for your friend, he committed crimes against humanity and for that he will die."

"Staying alive, then, must be a crime against humanity." I pause and look about the camp. "He was just so eager to please. Please anyone." I feel the tears in my eyes.

"Yes, he was and he pleased the wrong men." He, too, looks at the camp. "First the Germans, then Melankov."

I look at him. "Melankov?"

"I listened to the testimony. Yes, I was there."

"And what did Jakub do to please the judge?"

"Didn't you notice your friend's smile? He wanted to please the tribunal, so he gave them answers that he knew they wanted."

"You mean he lied? Surely we can get him another hearing." Hope is again surfacing in my thoughts.

"No, Filip, I don't think he lied. It's just that his answers weren't vague enough to create doubt. He was direct and gave clear answers, almost as if he had been rehearsed."

"Do you think he's guilty of what he is accused?"

Punin pauses and nods slowly. "Yes. I think he's guilty of giving information to the SS and I think that intelligence led to the death of some men."

"If Jakub is guilty of a crime, then I think we all are."

"I would agree. I think that everyone who lived in this camp for a long time and survived, must have cooperated with the staff in some fashion." He turns to look at me. "That includes you as well."

"Until you sleep in a barracks at Auschwitz, taste the tasteless soup, beg for the miserable bread and drink the rancid coffee, then you'll not understand." I suddenly feel very tired.

"I can't imagine. But I want you to think of this. Your friend, in his own simple mind, believed he cooperated with the murderers of his brother. He feels that cooperation makes him as guilty as those who ordered the crimes committed." He pauses and looks at the sign above our heads. "And his revelation of his activities in taking the ashes of the innocents to the Vistula, made him feel as guilty as those who pushed the victims into the gas chambers.

"And another thing, Filip, many people died here. Their ashes are everywhere, covering everything, including the people who are responsible and the people who survived. And it covers us, the liberators, as well." His face is stern. "Those ashes cry for justice. Was your friend the only one who worked with the Germans? No. But he is the only one who came forth and admitted it."

He turns and looks at me for a long time. "Filip, I want you to understand something." He waits until I look at him. "Jakub's behavior is more honorable than any I've seen in this war, on either side." He glances at the camp and turns back to me. "His accepting the responsibility for his actions shows a maturity, wisdom and honor beyond anything you or I have ever achieved. Remember that tomorrow."

CHAPTER TWENTY-EIGHT

I think of Punin's words every day of my life. Jakub was an uncomplicated man who saw things a little differently than you or I. He didn't rationalize his behavior to avoid responsibility, nor did he attempt to escape the consequences thereafter.

In Katy, he was even simpler, less understanding of the world, less knowledgeable about things like courage, honor, responsibility and consequences. Auschwitz taught him all of that. When many around him were finding their more immoral instincts, Jakub was finding traits that lay dormant in his personality, traits I'm uncertain even I possessed.

Amid the evil and amongst the cruelest, most insane men the world has ever seen, Jakub found wisdom and, perchance, a deeper understanding of life and the roles men play in it. When all of the baser instincts were the rules of the camp, Jakub demonstrated kindness, generosity and altruism towards all men, including his jailers.

And he developed an understanding beyond that which he had brought to Auschwitz. In his testimony, when he glanced at me, wanting me to understand, he concealed a name that would have resulted in my again facing the tribunal; the name of Albin Tolik. Tolik hanged, not for stealing, but because I wanted him punished for hurting Jakub. Jakub knew this and understood the consequences of giving the kapo's name, so he didn't and he protected me.

I don't fault anyone who survived Auschwitz or any of the other thousands of camps. Neither would Jakub. Like me, all survivors have memories they wished weren't in their heads, pictures of that time, that horror, pictures of the misery of humankind, portraits of unparalleled cruelty, unimaginable torture.

Yet, the memories exist as does the responsibility; the duty to keep those memories alive beyond our deaths. The millions that died from that conflagration of humanity, cry to be remembered, demand their spirits be honored with truth, and anoint us, the survivors, as the possessors of those memories. It's our duty to pass those memories to all those who come after us, so that even as the reality, the horror, the terror of the Holocaust fades from our text books, the memories will live on to remind all of posterity that it must not happen again.

I shared these thoughts with the Caprizios a week later. There were tears in all our eyes and fear, too.

"What will you do, Filip?" Michel already has regained his strength.

"I don't know. Jakub wanted to go home just to see if any of our friends survived. But I think I'll wait until the war ends, then I'll find a place." It strains me to think of what was to be, so different from Auschwitz where it had been decided for me. "What of you and the family?"

"Milano. We all want to go home." He smoothes the sand with his foot. "If there is no home for us in Italy, then maybe we'll go to America."

"That's a long way from here."

"Yes, a long way." He looks at me, tears welling in his eyes. "Home seems a long way from here. Everything seems so far away."

"Yes, even last week seems far away." We both become silent.

"This was Jakub's. I want you to have it."

"We have coats, Filip." He smiles and runs his fingers across the material. "And I think this coat has seen better days."

"Take it, Michel. Get the feel of it."

He twists his head and squints, but takes the coat, feeling its weight. "It's heavy. It's very heavy."

"When you have an opportunity, out of view of others, you'll find enough wealth to keep you and the family for a very long time." I smile and place my hand on the coat. "Perhaps, it'll help you get to America."

Tears roll down his cheeks and he wipes them with the coat. "I can't accept this, Filip. What of you? You'll need this."

"My own is equally heavy. Jakub hid everything we took from the lager and sewed it into these coats." I smile at him. "He would want you and your family to have it. It would be like he's looking after you."

He blots his cheeks again. "Yes, he would like that. The twins will always remember him."

"Yes, I would like that."

He takes a deep breath. "You also have the teeth. That should be worth something." He returns my smile.

"I didn't keep the teeth. A little ghoulish, I thought." I shrug. "No, I gave them away."

His eyes widen and he shakes his head. "To whom?"

"Melankov." I smile. "Then I informed Punin, of course."

"Why did you do this?"

"I concluded Melankov and Punin were political rivals, so I placed the bag of teeth in Melankov's car and wrote Punin a note. He accused Melankov of accepting a bribe and the gentleman is on his way to Moscow, in the company of their secret police."

Michel waves his hand. "For Jakub, then."

"Yes, for Jakub, and for me."

We are silent for a long moment, with no more words to be spoken. I exchange hugs with Kati and the twins, saving Michel for last. "Go swiftly, my friend. Escape this place and find peace."

"I should be saying those words to you." He hands me a piece of paper. "This is an address in Milano. They'll always know where we are. Write to us, Filip, visit us."

I accept the paper and put it in my pocket. "Thank you, Michel."

I wave as the truck passes through the gate and acknowledge that I will never see them again and, after what I had done, I'm sure they knew this was a final goodbye and was for the best.

I pull the coat around me a little tighter and can't remember seeing it snow this much, but then I realize the chill is inside me. As I look around I know my time here is done. There is nothing to hold me any longer, but I don't have any place to go.

The insanity of this war has robbed me of everything I knew and loved. My past is as useless as my existence in Auschwitz. I remember my promise to Aron, to stay close to Jakub, to protect him. Up until the end, I had done a poor job and I would have been ashamed to tell him of all the pain his brother suffered. But in the end, I lived up to that promise and did more than was asked of me.

The sky was clear, the air crisp. I walked with Jakub from the barracks that was his jail to the gallows, our steps slow and measured, almost reluctant. There was so much to say, things that had gone unsaid too long, things that I would never be able to say to him.

"Jakub?" He turned his head and looked at me. "Why did you tell the Russians the things you did?"

He was silent for a moment. "Because I did them."

"Oh, Jakub. I wish you hadn't."

"But, Filip, I did them. I was wrong. Now I must... er, a... atone, that's the word. Atone. That's what Dr. Levi told me. I remembered, Filip." He smiled and looked down. "I remembered."

We walked on in silence, the burden of our time resting heavily upon us.

"Killing will end suffering." He turned and looked at me. "There's no suffering for dead birds." He smiled.

"I don't understand."

"Remember? I found the injured bird. Papa killed it to stop its suffering." He looked at the ground, his cheeks sunken, his eyes set deeply in their sockets.

He had suffered greatly.

"Jakub, are you afraid?"

He looked at the ground. "A little." He turned to look at me. "Will I see Aron?"

"Yes, my friend, Aron will be there waiting for you. So will your parents, Dr. Levi, the Spiegelmans, and Zus." I put my hand on his shoulder. "Tell Zus I'm sorry I gave his name to the SS."

We continued, walking slowly, grasping the last moments we would have together.

"Filip, I'm sorry I was mean to Anna."

"Maybe she'll be there too. You can tell her. She loved you."

Tears streaked his cheeks. "I'll tell her."

"Tell her for me, too. And tell her I love her still."

"I will."

We paced ourselves wanting to say more, wanting to have more to say.

"Filip? When you come, I'll be waiting for you."

Tears streamed down my cheeks. "I love you, Jakub. I'll be so lonely without you."

"I love you, too." He looked ahead to where Melankov and Punin waited, along with a burly Russian man with his hand on the noose. Jakub saw him and turned to me. "Filip, go with the twins. You can watch over them."

We embraced and I took his coat.

"Give me Aron's letter. It's in the pocket."

I found the letter, battered and stained, but the writing was still legible. "After all this time, through everything, you've managed to save this?"

"Yes. I always keep his letter. I always hope I learn to read his words."

I handed the envelope to him and patted his face.

He smiled. "Thank you, Filip. You have been a good brother."

He walked to where the noose hung above his head. He was so frail, so delicate. Even in the end, he was giving away his food, choosing to make others happy, to please them.

Michel came and stood beside me, boosting my courage.

They read the indictment in Russian and spoke to Jakub in Polish, but my mind was in the small classroom in Katy as a skinny kid announced he would be my friend. And I saw him standing close to me, his eyes sparkling with mirth, always willing to joke, always my friend. In the briefest of moments, I relived our entire life together, and watched as the noose was put over his head and tightened.

Jakub was helped to stand on the chair and looked at me and smiled, his features free of fear, more courageous than his jailers, his judges or me.

Melankov turned in my direction and glared, then motioned for the chair to be pulled from under Jakub, to slowly strangle him, allowing his body to fall, tightening the knot around his neck. But he was too light to cut off his air, much like Jan Freimark. His eyes filled with anguish and continued to look at me, pleading for me to help, to protect him.

Everyone had turned away, except Melankov. I rushed forward and grasped Jakub by the legs, lifting him as high as I could, ignoring the cries of the Russian to stop me. I then put all my weight into my arms and back, and jerked as hard as I could, forcing the rope around Jakub's neck to bite in awkwardly. I heard the snap and knew Jakub's neck was broken, just before I blacked out from a blow to the head.

I awoke beneath the gently swaying body of my friend, his brother's letter in front of me. I reached for it and realized I had lost my two best friends, the most courageous and most honorable men I would ever know.

I stood and looked at his face, unprepared to see the peacefulness in his features, and accepted his suffering was done. But I was alone, even more alone than when I sat on the rickety, squeaky bus taking me to Katy, and I knew in my heart I would be alone forever.

Character List:

Historical

Henrich Himmler, Reichsfuhrer SS
Josef Mengele, 'Uncle Pepi', physician
Rudolf Hoss, Sturmbannfuhrer SS, Major
      Auschwitz commandant, 1941-1943
Josef Kramer, Obersturmfuhrer SS, Lieut., 2nd to Hoss
Arthur Liebehemschel, Obersturmbannfuhrer SS, Lt. Col.
      Commandant, Auschwitz I, 1943
Maximilian Grabner, Untersturmfuhrer SS, 2nd Lieutenant
Hans Aumeier, Hauptsturmfuhrer, Captain
      Camp Director, 1943
Blockfuhrer Georg Hocher, SS officer, Kanada I
Rosa Robota, Jewish conspirator
Ella Gartner, Jewish conspirator
Timofei Borodin, Russian munitions expert, conspirator

Fictional - In Katy

Filip Stitchko, policeman (b. 1917)
Jakub Galinski, young Polish man (b. 1920)
Aron Galinski, officer in Polish army (b. 1916)
Zus Malbin, schoolteacher
Dr. Samuel Levi, physician & guardian of Jakub
Marek and Marta Spiegelman, merchants
Father Jan, Catholic priest, schoolteacher
Maria Chapulski, foster mother
Joseph Melichek, brother to Maria
Rabbi Jakim Zacharz, schoolteacher
Klara Walusky, young girl

Fictional - Auschwitz and other places

Heinz Hirt, Oberscharfuhrer SS, Staff Sergeant
Victor Punin, Russian commissar
Dr. Fritz Schuller, Obersturmfuhrer SS, Lieutenant
Ivan Meretsky, kapo, Sonderkommando, ash pits
Jan Freimark, pipel
Albin Tolik, Jewish kapo
Anna Kalitnikova, Russian POW
Mario and Maria Caprizio, twins, escapees

Terminology

arbeitkapo	work overseer
arbeitslager	labor camp
aussenlager	external camp
Einsatzgruppen	SS and secret police
fertig	finished
Gestapo	secret police
haftlinge	prisoners
kapo	trustie
lagerkapo	head of camp
lagertischlerei	carpentry workshop
lapanka	dragnet
lauferin	runner
musselmann	weakened male on point of death; garbage
nacht und nebel	night and fog; those murdered after the selection
nebenlager	extension or subcamp
oberkapo	overseer
organizer	one who stole from the storehouses
pipel	'young assistant'; a young person with beautiful features
schmutzstuck	female on point of death; garbage
Schutzstaffel	SS; storm troopers
selekcja	selection
Sonderkommando	Prisoners; cleaned out the ashes
stammlager	Auschwitz I
'Tomorrow morning'	never
vorarbeiter	underkapo
zugange	new arrivals

Printed in the United States
91976LV00001B/1-102/A

9 781905 988167